First published in 2018 by Bloodhound Books

www.bloodhoundbooks.com

Print ISBN 978-1-912604-29-6

Also By Anita Waller

Beautiful

Angel

Winterscroft

34 Days

Strategy

Captor

Praise For Anita Waller

"This is a dark domestic chiller that gradually creeps under your skin until the very shocking and unexpected climax." **Joanne Robertson - My Chestnut Reading Tree**

"An excellent suspense filled read, and I'm looking forward to reading the sequel, Strategy." **Mark Tilbury - Author**

"Oh my goodness this book gripped me! I sat and read this book in one sitting over the weekend and honestly, I really didn't want to put it down..." **Donna Maguire - Donnas Book Blog**

"The story is well versed and the characters kept me intrigued throughout." **Louise Mullins - Author**

"Stunning, brilliant, gripping, heart breaking and touching!" **Misfits Farm - Goodreads Reviewer**

"My God ...this story is heart breaking yet such a pageturner... There are secrets...lies..betrayal ..murder... And a darkness ...so terrifying.... that lurks almost invisible." **Livia Sbarbaro - Goodreads Reviewer**

"Beware: when you pick up the book you won't be able to let it go before you have reached the final chapter." **Caroline Vincent - Bits About Books**

"A brilliant follow on book from Beautiful. Kept me guessing until the end." **Angela Lockwood - Goodreads Reviewer**

"This book scared the daylights out of me and I mean that in the best way possible." **Amy Sullivan - Novelgossip**

"The author writes well, weaving the story and sucking the reader into the lives of the characters within the book." **Rebecca Burnton - If Only I Could Read Faster**

"This is book has all the elements needed to make it creepy, read-through-your-fingers-at-times kind of read. There is spooky suspense on every page." **M.A. Comley - New York Times and USA Today best-selling author**

"The author really keeps you on the edge of your seat – the twists made me gasp and she sets the atmosphere absolutely perfectly." ***Melisa Broadbent - Broadbean's Books***

"If you are looking for a crime thriller that is somewhat unnerving as it is every mother's worst nightmare, a fast-paced page turner that keeps you guessing. Then I definitely recommend Captor!" ***Dash Fan Book Reviews***

"Captor will have you gripped from the beginning and won't let you go until you have finished. It is a suspense-filled crime thriller that will keep you guessing throughout." ***Gemma Myers - Between The Pages Book Club***

"...Waller has definitely done it again and proves herself to be one of the best storytellers in the genre of murder, necessary murder, as she likes to say." ***Rebecca Burnton - If Only I Could Read Faster***

For Mum and Dad who would have been
inordinately proud of me!

Edna May Havenhand, née Bonnington
1921-1953
Ernest Havenhand
1922-1975

It should be noted that children at play are not playing about;
their games should be seen as their most serious-minded activity.
Montaigne (Michel Eyquem de Montaigne)
1533-1592
Essais (1580, ed. M. Rat, 1958) bk.1, ch.23

Alas, regardless of their doom,
The little victims play!
No sense have they of ills to come,
Nor care beyond to-day.
Thomas Gray (1716-1771)
Ode on a Distant Prospect of Eton College (1747) 1. 51

1

The sunlight was dappled in the deepest part of the woods. It wasn't a huge wood, but their den was there; hidden from the road, hidden from the adjoining car park, hidden from everything. During the summer holidays, when school no longer gave them the interaction they enjoyed and needed, the Gang of Six, as they liked to call themselves, took full advantage of the copse's proximity to their homes.

Mark and Dominic Brownlow were the oldest; at eleven and a half, they considered themselves the leaders. However, Mark thought of himself as the sole leader, with twin brother Dom his second-in-command. Dom was quite happy to go along with that. The quieter of the two boys, he usually acceded to Mark's leadership, unless it was exceptionally crazy and likely to end with a grounding from their mother.

Physically, they were identical, with dark-blond hair, blue-grey eyes and straight noses, but the other members of the Gang of Six had no difficulty in recognising who was who. Teachers at the school they all attended insisted the two boys wore name badges. It made life easier.

Occasionally, they swapped the badges, just because they could.

The boys had a sister, two years younger, with the same dark-blonde hair and slightly bluer eyes, a much smaller nose than her siblings, and very pretty; but in the competitive stakes, she was fierce. Her parents laughingly called her feral, feral Freya. They weren't always laughing when they said it. She had to be the winner; Mark and Dom accepted this for a fact and had shown no hesitation in bringing her into the gang. They always nodded when their mum asked them to look after Freya, keep her safe. The truth was that Freya could very well look after herself. The twins simply let her get on with it.

Freya had a best friend, Ella Johnston. She had known Ella from the start of their school life, and she had invited Ella to join them. Ella had agreed, albeit a little reluctantly. She wasn't sure her mum would approve of her running free in the woods with a group of boys. Her mum always said she had to be careful around boys, and yet, here she was, blindly following Freya, as usual. Ella's skin was a lovely toffee colour, and her dark eyes and hair set off that shade to perfection. Freya didn't see it; skin tones didn't come into her world.

And at nine, Freya Brownlow was in love with skin so dark, it seemed ebonised, covering the wiry frame of Sammy Walker, another eleven-year-old from the same class as the Brownlow twins. His curly black hair and flashing dark eyes, combined with an ever-present smile, made him a cool kid at school. Sammy, in return, had found the love of his life in Freya. It was a match made in heaven, and they laughed and joked and loved without even so much as a shared kiss between them. They didn't even mind saying bye as the days headed towards evening, because they knew they would be together again the following morning. To them, their friendship was a beautiful thing.

And the sixth member of the close-knit group was Daryl Clarkson. Taller than the others, with dark brown hair and deep brown eyes, he was the sensible one. He stopped them dying from ingestion of assorted berries and fruits, by simply taking out his iPhone (they were all envious of the acquisition of this, even though it was merely a cast off after an upgrade, via his dad). He would google the berry and tell them yea or nay as to its poisonous qualities. Daryl Clarkson was probably the most important member of the Gang of Six. He kept them alive.

The woods were bursting at the seams with creatures. Squirrels, hedgehogs, tiny mice, badgers, a fox family – they had all been seen at one time or another by the children. The den had been converted into a veterinary hospital a couple of times, when they had spotted some injured animals.

It had taken them three long weeks to build the den, constructed after school during May, so that it was ready for them when summer fully arrived, and school closed for the six-week holiday. They had worked carefully, always aware that the woods were situated next to a massive police station; they didn't want to be moved along, because they knew that their parents wouldn't allow them to wander any further away from home than the current site.

The less their parents knew, the better. Likewise, the police.

The den was cosy inside. They had made seating for all six of them and had used a triangular shape formed by three thick trees to construct the erection of twigs and thicker branches. Nothing showed on the outside to give any casual onlooker the impression that it was something man-made...children-made...but inside, it sported seats around the edge covered by a couple of throws purloined from the Brownlow's and the Clarkson's homes. Tucked underneath the seats were small bottles of water, bought from a nearby Asda and paid for by Daryl; he was the only one who received any sort of pocket money. From the outside, it blended in perfectly with its surroundings. They had built in two small windows; they did not want anyone creeping up on them, so the viewing holes were at eye level when they were sitting down.

One day, they had seen Sammy's older brother Joe in the woods, with a girl from his school. He had been holding her hand, and they had seen him kiss her, not six feet away from the den.

They had remained silent; Sammy and Daryl being on lookout duty, the rest had waited for a signal from them before daring to speak.

Eventually, Sammy did. 'Bloody 'ell. That was our Joe with Kelly Marsden, an' 'e kissed 'er!'

They all giggled nervously, and then, Freya spoke. 'It shows our den's pretty good. They didn't even know it was here.'

Everyone nodded in unison. Crisis averted, their hideaway had passed the test.

One day in June, there had been an accident. They had decided to play hide and seek, and Ella had fallen headlong over a thick tree root. Wearing only shorts and a T-shirt, no protection for the skin on her legs, the resultant gash on her knee was truly spectacular.

They helped her back to the den, and Daryl, the patient, caring one, used some of the water and a leaf to clean her wound.

'Will you be able to walk okay?' he asked a tearful Ella.

She nodded. 'Just give me some of that water, I'll be okay. It hurts.'

They cancelled the rest of the day's activities and helped Ella home. Her mum was in the back garden and looked shocked when she saw the cut.

'How did you do it?'

'I fell over.'

'Let's get you inside and put a plaster on it. It needs cleaning first.'

Ella turned and smiled at the five members ranged around her. They smiled back and turned to leave. They knew Ella's day was over, but they also knew she would be back again the following day.

The next day, Daryl arrived with a first aid kit. Nobody questioned how he had got it – the supplier had struck again.

The summer of 2016 was a warm one, and once school had ended, the Gang of Six met every day in the woods. They had added supplies to the den; sparkling water instead of the ordinary stuff, because it quenched their thirst better, even if it tasted a bit iffy, biscuits that they kept in a plastic box, and some Haribo sweets because they loved them. Everything was protected from attack by animals by keeping it all in plastics of various kinds, and the days passed with nobody querying where they had been.

Tuesday 26 July was overcast. It was still warm, and Daryl was the last to arrive.

'Mum said I should stay home, because it was looking like rain.' He sounded shocked. 'Stay home? Is she daft?' He grinned at the others. 'Bet you thought I'd knocked, didn't yer?'

'As if,' Dom scoffed. 'We knew you'd turn up at some point. What we gonna do now we're all here, then?' He turned to his brother. 'Bro? What we doing?'

'Let's have a meeting.'

Mark bent and crawled inside the den, and the others followed. Daryl produced a long tube of plastic cups. 'Thought I'd get these. Then, we don't have to drink full bottles of water, we can have a small cup, if that's all we want.' He stashed them under the seats, and they all sat down.

'Right, Ella and Sammy on look-out today.'

They took the appropriate seats for looking out of the apertures they called windows, and everyone else sat around them.

Mark took charge. 'I thought we might do a bit of litter picking. There's loads of plastic bags and stuff after that gale the other night, and we don't want any nosey parkers coming in to clean up, do we? I've brought us some bags. What does everybody think?'

They nodded; they remembered the council sending some workers in to clean up before, and they had to make the decision to stay home, instead of going to the den, in case they were still in the woods.

'Okay, we work in twos. Me and Dom, Freya and Ella, and Sammy and Daryl. Any problems, blow your whistle.' They had set up the system very early on in the gang's formation. Everybody had a whistle – provided by Daryl – and each had their own distinctive call. They had practiced and practiced until they unerringly recognised all six individual sounds.

'Shh,' Ella spoke urgently. Her voice had dropped to a whisper. 'Somebody coming.'

They immediately became silent; nobody moved. They could hear twigs snapping as the footsteps drew closer, then passed by their den. Still nobody moved. The intruder progressed into Sammy's view, and the young boy continued to watch as the man drew further away. Sammy held up his hand to indicate it still wasn't safe to talk or move. He watched the man move towards the edge of the woods, then look around. He was alone, and he appeared to be checking that nobody was following him.

Sammy's eyes never left him. He watched every movement; the man knelt and took a trowel out of his backpack. He dug a hole, and then, he took a large pack of white powder out and laid it into the hole.

Sammy was no fool; he was only eleven, but he'd seen lots of television shows about white powder, along with the drug education classes they'd all sat through at school. This was drugs. He stifled the gasp that threatened to come out of his mouth and continued to watch. The man was pulling the soil back into the hole.

He stood, and Sammy froze. There was something about him… He felt sure he knew him, and then, there was recognition. The man stood perfectly still for a moment, before checking all around that nobody had seen him. He continued on his way through the woods, towards the Asda car park that adjoined the leafy, secluded area.

Sammy dropped his head. 'He's gone.'

'Did you know him?' Daryl was curious. He had been watching his friend's face and knew something was wrong.

Sammy shrugged. 'I thought so, but I'm not sure. If I do, I can't remember who he is. We need to forget about this, though.' Sammy had decided it was safer to deny he had recognised the man.

'Why?' Freya turned huge blue eyes on him. 'You're scared, aren't you?'

'What did he do?' Mark and Dom spoke almost in unison.

'He buried something…'

'Sammy, for goodness' sake, what did he bury?' Freya was demanding.

'It looked like a bag of white powder.'

Even Freya and Ella, the youngest members of the group, understood the significance of white powder.

'Shit,' Daryl said, speaking for them all. He took out his mobile phone, keyed in a few words and then showed them several pictures thrown up by the browser. 'Cocaine,' he said. 'I'm pretty sure it's cocaine. Is this what it looked like, Sammy?'

Sammy nodded. 'Yeah, I knew as soon as I saw it. It was the same as they showed us at school. It's not going to be a bag of icing sugar, is it? And if it's not cocaine, it's something just as bad.'

They sat silently, not knowing what to say.

Mark was the first to speak. 'Do we dig it up?'

'Are you mad?' His brother stared at him, horror written across his face. 'We ignore the bloody thing. We can hardly go to the police, can we, because they'd want to know how we saw it, and we'd lose this place. Let's leave them to get on with it. He'll have hidden it for somebody to pick up later.'

'We could have more people wandering around?' Ella had tears in her eyes. 'I don't like this.'

'Hey, come on, Ella.' Daryl put his arm around her shoulders and gave her a hug. 'We're safe while we're in here, as long as we're quiet, so stop worrying.'

'Can we stay in here today, then? We don't know when somebody's going to come to collect it.'

'If that's what you want to do. I know you're frightened, but there's six of us. And if the worst does happen and we're spotted, we're next to the police station. That makes it safe to be here. I know we'd probably lose this, but we can build another one. I don't see why we should lose it, though. Kids always build dens.' Daryl was ever the logical one.

'They'd tell our parents, numpty,' said Freya. 'It'd be the 'rents who stopped us. We don't want that.'

'Yeah, I know,' Daryl conceded, 'but if we're ever in trouble in these woods, we tell the coppers. Right? We don't risk getting hurt 'cos we don't want to lose our den.'

He looked around at them, and they held up their thumbs, the usual way they agreed things.

'Right,' Mark said, once again assuming command. 'What shall we do? Play cards?'

Daryl reached under the seat and produced the card box. 'Uno?'

Once again, they agreed, and Daryl took out a piece of paper and wrote their initials along the top, ready for putting scores on it. They loved Uno, and normally, the game produced gales of laughter.

That day, it didn't. They enjoyed playing it; it was better to be inside the den rather than outside it, because a fine misting of rain was falling, but they were aware of having to keep quiet. They took it in turns to watch their surroundings until it was time to head for home.

The rain was a little heavier, although inside the den, they were dry. They packed away the cards and the piece of paper because nobody had yet reached the elimination number of 500.

'We'll finish it tomorrow,' Daryl said, checking the weather on his phone. 'It's going to be like this again.'

Once more, thumbs were held up.

'We've got the dentists at ten,' Dom said. 'The three of us. We'll get here as soon as we can.'

Freya looked horrified. 'Me? I thought it was you two.'

'Sorry, sis.' Dom laughed. 'It's the three of us. Perhaps Mum gets a discount for taking us all at the same time.'

'I thought the dentist was free for kids…'

The rest of them laughed, and Freya realised they'd been winding her up. Her ponytail swished angrily, and she glared at Dom. 'I'll get you back,' she warned.

'Oh, I'm scared.' He grinned.

'You should be,' said Mark, and began the trek back to the main road. 'I wouldn't cross our Freya, not if I wanted to live.'

They exited by the small thicket at the side of the police station and crossed the road to the estate.

The Brownlows left first, then Sammy walked Ella to her door before heading home. Daryl walked the last couple of roads on his own before reaching his home.

Sally Brownlow was waiting anxiously for them. 'I expected you back before this,' she scolded. 'It's been raining for a while. Where've you been?'

'We were fine,' Mark said. 'We sat in the undercover car park in Asda and played Uno. Dry and warm, so we were fine. We're doing the same tomorrow after the dentist, 'cos we didn't finish the game.'

Sally looked at them, unsure whether to believe them or not. Eventually, she gave them the benefit of the doubt and ushered them inside.

'Fish fingers for tea. Go and have a wash, please. You've got five minutes.'

They ran upstairs, keen to get back down for fish fingers and chips.

Dom's mind was racing. That white powder, he felt sure, was going to cause problems. How could they ever feel safe there again, if the woods were going to be used for dropping off drugs? Maybe they should have dug them up and taken them to the police station? Or at least gone in and passed on the location of the stash.

He decided that the following day he would check if it was still there, and if it was, he would report it. He finished washing his hands and followed Freya and Mark downstairs. Somebody had to be the sensible one, and it had better be him.

Lying in bed later, Dom spoke to Mark about it. They shared a room and had many private discussions once they had gone to bed.

'I'm not sure about doing that,' Mark said, suddenly afraid for his brother. 'What if you're seen?'

'We can't ignore it, Mark. Don't you remember all that stuff they told us at school? People die from taking drugs. I think we've got to do something. I'll not touch it, I promise, just scrape down far enough to check it's still there. If it isn't, that solves the problem, but if it is…'

'We don't tell the police about the den, though. We'll say we were playing in the woods and saw somebody burying it. Agreed?'

'I'll agree if the others do. This isn't only down to us,' Dom conceded, 'but I don't think we can ignore it. We'll talk to everybody tomorrow, right?'

'Right.'

Agreement made, they slept.

Freya didn't. She felt a little scared and, for the first time, wasn't sure how to act. She needed to talk to her Sammy, listen to what he thought. It was no good talking to Ella, because she saw danger in everything, but Sammy was sensible, like Daryl, really.

Yes, the next day, they had to talk, but mostly, she wanted to talk to Sammy. After all, Sammy thought he knew the guy, even though he tried to deny it; she knew her Sammy, and her Sammy knew who the man was.

2

Vinnie Walmsley walked round to the back door and let himself into the kitchen. It resembled a pig sty. The sink was full of pots, clothes were everywhere, which he presumed were there for washing, and the cooker hob had several pans stacked on it.

He picked up one pile of clothes off a chair and dumped them in front of the washer. He glanced inside it and saw it was empty.

'Ma!' he roared. 'The fuckin' washin' machine's empty. Get some fuckin' washin' done.'

There was silence for a moment, and then Aileen Walmsley, her curly blonde hair like a halo around her head, appeared in the doorway, holding on to a book tightly pressed open against her not inconsiderable breasts.

Her blue eyes zeroed in on her son for a long moment, and he wished he hadn't said anything.

'If you want some washin' doin', me lad, then do it yourself. And if I ever hear you speak to me like that again, I'll cut off your balls. I'm readin' me book, not washin' clothes. Like it or lump it, I don't bloody care either way. It's a pity you didn't read more books, 'cos then you might not have ended up dealin'.'

He considered arguing back, for a moment, but then decided it wasn't worth the hassle. She knew which knife was the sharpest, and he might need his balls.

'Sorry, Ma,' he mumbled. 'I'll put a load in, shall I?'

'Aye,' she said, 'and then, I'll have a cuppa tea.'

She turned and went back into the lounge, not much better in the tidiness stakes, but it did hold a large, extremely comfortable sofa, brilliant for lying on to read her books. She settled down, satisfied that she'd sorted the little git; she'd have no more lip from him, not 'til next time.

She heard the washer start and then the hum of the kettle. As a bonus, she heard the tap gush with water, and she knew he would have to wash some pots, to get a clean cup for her. She didn't fool herself that he would do them all, but what he did tackle would be a help. She opened her book and began to read.

He brought in the cup of tea without another word being exchanged, and as he walked out of the room, she smiled. Sorted.

Vinnie was a decent-looking lad, around five-feet-eight and with an athletic build, but according to Aileen, he was more like his non-existent dad than her. His short brown hair and brown eyes gave him a look of honesty, and he used that attribute extensively. Strangers trusted him. Acquaintances were wary.

He sat at the kitchen table and took out his small black book. He would be lost without it; he needed to know who owed him what, and who he needed to lean on. That last delivery of cocaine had been more than he normally handled, and he daren't leave it in the house. The woods had been the ideal place.

He'd once watched someone on telly that spoke about hiding things, and they'd said something about the best place being to hide it in plain sight, so he'd hidden it in plain sight of the police station. He hoped that's what it meant.

It wasn't a package he needed to split; it was being sold on as a full delivery to somebody who would contact him in two days and then pay him for his part. He felt sure he'd hidden it well, far enough down in the hole to stop any animals digging it up. He had a brief flash go through his mind of a fox high on coke, and despite his worries, he laughed.

In his peripheral vision, he saw a face at the kitchen window and turned. He waved the newcomer in.

'Fuckin' 'ell, Liam, you gave me a bit of a shock. Don't do that.'

Liam laughed. 'Sorry, pal. Thought I'd call round to see what you up to. You doing your chores?'

'Nah,' Vinnie said, trying to keep his voice low. 'Ma's doing the washing.'

Aileen could hear every word. She stood and moved towards the kitchen.

'Oh, hiya, Liam. Good to see you. You've not been for a few days. Vinnie, that last load you put in, is it ready yet? Don't go out without hanging it on the line, will you? And then put a dark load in.' She turned and walked back into the lounge, a huge grin splitting her face. That'd teach the cheeky little bastard to have a go at her. His mate would never let this drop.

Liam thought it best not to say anything. Not here, anyway. Maybe when all the lads met up later, when Vinnie was bragging off about what he'd been doing, maybe then he could drop it in about the washing…

He closed the kitchen door, pulled out a chair and moved the clothes off it. Sitting down opposite Vinnie, he delved into his pockets and produced two cans of beer. They opened them and drank. It was marginally more hygienic than using a glass from the Walmsley household.

'You got it, then?' Liam asked.

Vinnie nodded. 'Don't say owt to anybody though, Liam. And keep your voice down, she's got ears like bats, has Ma. This is serious stuff now. I'll make a packet on it, but if owt goes wrong…'

'I shan't say owt, mate, don't worry. Best make sure your ma can't stumble across it, though. She wouldn't be best pleased.'

'It's well hidden,' was all Vinnie would say.

'God, Vin, I wish you'd get a proper job.'

'Like you? Stacking shelves at Asda?'

Liam could hear the mockery in his friend's voice, and he flinched. 'Yeah, but stacking shelves ain't going to get me killed.'

'And it's not going to earn you eight grand for babysitting a packet of white powder.'

Liam shrugged. They'd never agree on this. He'd never touched drugs, and he didn't think Vinnie had either, but Vinnie had touched them in a different way. He sold them.

'So, when do you meet this geezer?'

'Probably tomorrow. They'll be safe enough until he contacts me.'

'And he pays you?'

'Yeah. This is going to give me a bit more working capital. It's all happening, Liam. A couple of months and I'll be getting a new car.'

Liam nodded. He knew it was hopeless trying to make Vinnie see sense, so, as usual, it was time to simply agree with him. If it all fell apart, he'd be there to pick up any pieces that were left and try to get him a job at Asda.

'You going out tonight?' Liam asked.

'Nah, watching t'match later. I'll nip round to t'shop and get some cans in, fish 'n' chips for tea, and have an early night. Big day tomorrow.'

Liam stood. 'Right, I'll see you probably later, after its done. On nights, so I'll be in bed for seven in the morning. You take care, mate. You don't know owt about this bloke.'

Vinnie laughed. 'You're like an owd woman, Liam. I'll be fine. It's simple. I hand t'bag over, he pays me, and we don't meet up again till he wants some more.'

Liam couldn't help but think his friend was a little too blasé about the issue, but he left with a final wave through the kitchen window.

Vinnie drained the last dregs from the bottom of the can and aimed it at the overflowing waste bin. It made a clatter as it fell and rolled across the floor.

'Pick it up!' was the command from the lounge.

'Christ, she really has got bat ears,' he muttered.

'I heard that!' she called.

He did as instructed and tied the rubbish bag at the top before carrying it out to the black bin. Perhaps he should go back in and clear a few of the dishes, try to tidy things up a bit. He had a position in the area now. Things needed to smarten up around here.

Aileen smiled as she heard the gush of water once again. Maybe she'd even manage to finish this book that afternoon, then she could start a new one later, while Vinnie was watching the footie. Sometimes, life was okay.

He finished all the dishes, sorted the remaining laundry into piles and then took the black wheelie bin around to the front of the house and onto the pavement, ready for the next day's collection. He saw young Sammy Walker and waved at him; nice looking, young black kid, smart as well. Just needed to keep off the gear.

Sammy flinched, turned around and went towards the back of the houses, a circuitous way home instead of the direct route past the Walmsley house.

Vinnie watched him, a frown on his face. What was that all about? The kid had looked scared.

Vinnie shook his head. Next time he saw him, he'd damn well ask if there was a problem. He didn't like being dissed.

Liam was worried. He knew Vinnie was in too deep, but unfortunately, Vinnie didn't know it.

Liam set off for work, wondering how to make Vinnie see sense. Perhaps he should talk to Vinnie's ma; he felt sure she would do something about it. Dealing a few pills here and there was a different kettle of fish to what he had taken on, and it bothered Liam that Vinnie would only drop deeper and deeper into the drug-dealing world.

He reached Asda, not realising that his journey had taken him within six feet of the plastic bag of cocaine that Vinnie had carefully buried, scared of a repeat visit by the police. They had found nothing last time, but Liam knew Vinnie wouldn't take that risk again.

He clocked on and waited to find out what his duties for the night were to be. The next day he would go and see Vinnie, make him listen, scare him to bloody death if necessary, but he had to stop him before he took a beating, or worse.

The football match was good, Spurs beating Chelsea by two goals. Vinnie didn't particularly like either of the teams, but he did like football, and supporting Sheffield Wednesday, as he did fervently, meant you didn't always get to see quality footie. He rephrased the thought in his head. Very rarely got to see quality football.

Ma had already gone to bed, taking her damn book with her. He'd never known anybody read as much as she did; truth be told, he didn't know anybody else who read. He had commandeered the sofa in her absence and reached down to the floor to grab another can of beer. It popped with a most satisfying sound, and he drank deeply.

His phone pinged, and he scrabbled around underneath him trying to find it. When he did, he was surprised to see a text. He hoped it wasn't anybody wanting any gear at this time of night. He couldn't be arsed to go out, especially as he'd had a fair bit to drink.

The text was short:

4 pm tomorrow, Asda car park, Silver Audi ending in ECV.

He answered with a thumbs-up emoji, then put down the can of beer. Suddenly, he didn't want any more. He wanted to go to bed and sleep. The next day, if everything went well, he would be eight grand richer, and his rating would have gone up significantly.

He thought about Liam and smirked. Get him a job at Asda? Not fuckin' likely. He was going places. One day, he'd be able to text somebody that he was in a silver Audi.

He picked up the cans and took them to the newly emptied waste bin in the kitchen. Checking all the doors was second nature to him; he was usually the last in bed, anyway, and he turned off all the lights as he headed upstairs.

Aileen heard him go up. She felt troubled; she had partly heard the conversation between Liam and Vinnie and sensed Liam's concern for his best friend. She had no idea what Vinnie had got himself into, but ever since the police visit when they were looking for drugs, she had been wary, watching him carefully. She knew he didn't have the intelligence to be aware of danger. He was no Liam.

It was her mother's instinct kicking in that told her he was into something he couldn't control. It didn't take a genius to work out it was a step up in the drug dealing, but it would take somebody smarter than her to find out which local thug was employing her lad.

She doubted that Liam would know. She considered Liam to be one of the smarter lads on the estate and never really understood why he had palled up with her Vinnie. Still, he was all she had to try to get some information. So when he next called round, she'd find something out if it killed her.

She picked up her book again, her thought processes around Vinnie exhausted, and removed the bookmark. *Just two more chapters,* she promised herself, *and then, I'll go to sleep.*

She could hear that Vinnie was restless. He slept on a metal-framed bed, and every time he turned, the bed squeaked. The bed squeaked constantly, and at one point, five chapters further on into her book, she considered going into his room to see if he was okay. She didn't think he would want to talk, but she wanted him to know she could hear he was restless.

She tapped on his bedroom door. 'Vinnie?'

'What?'

'You okay?'

'Yeah.'

'Sure?'

'Yeah. Fuckin' 'ell, Ma, I'm twenty-two. You don't need to check up on me.'

'And you've been in bed over an hour, and you're still not asleep. You worrying about something?'

'Shit, Mother, leave me alone! I'm trying to drop off here, and you're mithering me from t'other side of a door. Go back to bed. I'm okay.'

'Right, g'nite, son. Sleep well.' She headed back to her own room, deeply troubled. Something was wrong, and she didn't know how to deal with it. But she still had her fallback plan.

Liam.

She took off her Harry Potter pyjamas and dressed in leggings and a top, then crept out of her room and back down the stairs. She grabbed her bag, quietly opened the door and equally quietly closed it behind her. She rummaged around in the bottom of her bag until she located the car keys, then headed towards the car. She hoped Vinnie wouldn't hear it start. She didn't want him knowing where she was going.

A twenty-four-hour supermarket is indeed a wondrous place. It's busy even at midnight, and at 12.06am, Aileen stepped onto the travellator taking her up to the shop level of the store. She grabbed a basket, deciding against a trolley. She wasn't there for shopping. She wandered around the store, looking for Liam. When she spotted him, he was stacking shelves on the stationery aisle.

She smiled. Maybe she wasn't there for the shopping, but would it be so bad if she bought a book? Only one. Or maybe two, as they were two for seven pounds. She pretended she hadn't noticed Liam and inspected the books.

She put the first one in her basket and then searched for a second one.

'Mrs Walmsley!' There was surprise in Liam's voice.

She turned around, feigning surprise. 'Oh, hello, Liam. I didn't realise you were working tonight.'

'You're shopping late.'

'I know. I couldn't sleep, and I'd finished my book, so I thought I'd nip over here and pick up another one. It wasn't so much that I can't sleep, it's more that Vinnie is keeping me awake, tossing and turning in that bloody metal bed. It creaks every time he moves, and he's certainly moving. It's like he's worrying about something. I don't suppose you know what it is, do you, Liam?'

Liam gulped. She knew. She fuckin' knew Vinnie was up to something. But he wasn't going to be the one to dob Vinnie in. It was up to Vinnie to tell his ma what he was doing.

'He's okay, I think,' Liam said nervously. 'He's not said anything to me…'

'Yes, he has, Liam. I heard him. What's happening tomorrow?'

'I don't know.' He'd never felt so miserable in all his life. Vinnie's ma was obviously upset and worried, and Liam was making things so much worse by lying to her.

'Oh, sorry, Mrs Walmsley, my supervisor's watching. I have to go. He wants me on bananas.'

She sighed. 'Okay, Liam, but if anything happens to my lad, and you haven't told me something that could have prevented it, I will find you. Is that understood?'

Liam nodded miserably. He scuttled away from her and felt immensely grateful when he saw her go through the self-service checkout and back down the travelator. He took out his phone and texted Vinnie, telling him his ma was on the warpath and to pretend to be asleep. She would be home in five minutes.

Aileen arrived home to a house still in darkness, and she knew he hadn't realised she had gone out. She crept back upstairs and into her own room, then quickly undressed to sleep once again with Harry Potter. The bed creaks had stopped, and she guessed Vinnie had fallen asleep. Climbing into bed, with the new books placed on her dressing table, she picked up the one she had abandoned to go to Asda.

She removed the bookmark and slid down the bed. 'Just two more chapters,' she muttered, 'and I'll tackle Vinnie in the morning.'

Vinnie lay silently, immobile. He couldn't face an inquisition, so he needed non-squeaking bedsprings. By two o'clock, the household was quiet, and tired brains had closed down for the night.

Time enough to think, to plan, tomorrow.

3

The Gang of Six had met by eleven o'clock. The sun beat down on them, and they decided to have a day of tree climbing. Moving further into the small woods took them to trees previously unclimbed, and this activity lasted until just before lunchtime.

Dom suddenly veered away from them and crossed to where the white powder had been buried. He had to know if it was still there. They would look stupid if they went to the police and told them about the powder, only for them to find nothing. The others looked horrified; panic set in, and they tried to persuade him not to dig, but he simply shook his head and said he had to know. It was there, and he stared at it.

'We have to talk,' he said. 'I think we should tell the police. I think we should take it, tell them we found it while we were playing, and we're guessing it's drugs. We'll be heroes for handing it in, but most of all, we'll be believed. Let's go and eat, and then, we'll have a vote.'

They returned to the den and went inside to eat the assorted items of food they had managed to bring from home. It made for quite a feast; biscuits, a few sandwiches, bottles of water, crisps. They felt satiated and decided to have a rest and finish off the game of Uno.

But Dom wouldn't let the matter drop. 'Stop ignoring it. That's drugs, and I reckon it's a lot of drugs. We've had the talk at school. We know they kill. We've got to tell somebody, and I think we have to go next door and take the packet to them. We don't mention this, though, the den. We can tell them we were playing hide and seek, and we found it while we were playing.'

They looked at each other, knowing that what Dom was saying was the sensible thing to do, but none of them wanted to go to the police station and tell them. In the end, they agreed to think about it and have a vote in ten minutes. Daryl got out the playing cards, and they once more left the grown-up world and became children.

Mark and Sammy opted to be on lookout, and whenever the laughter became too raucous, they had the job of quietening the others down a notch. But then, Dom called time, and they grew serious.

Five minutes later, after a unanimous vote, he was digging up the packet again.

'We'll hand it in as we go home,' he said. 'And don't be scared. We're doing the right thing.'

And the sun grew hotter and hotter, although in the shade of the den, things weren't so bad.

With hindsight, they agreed that was a good day. Up to a point.

Vinnie walked across to the car park via the road, instead of going through the woods. He didn't want his new white trainers to look scruffy before he met the man.

He arrived fifteen minutes early and went into Asda, waiting in the foyer that housed the bottom of the travelator. He went over to where the trolleys were lined up and acted as though he was waiting for someone – in reality, it gave him a view of the car park entrance, and he would be able to see every car driving in.

The silver Audi arrived one minute early, and the driver drove around looking for the best spot. Vinnie waited until the car drew to a stop and walked nonchalantly out of the foyer and across to the parked car. He checked the registration ended in ECV and opened the passenger door.

His contact was tall, blonde-haired and blue-eyed, and he wondered if it really was possible to fall in love at first sight. She was gorgeous, and as he sat back and closed the door, she spoke.

'And you are?' She pulled down her sunglasses slightly to look at him.

'Does it matter?'

'It does.'

'Vinnie.'

'You have the goods?'

'Nearby.'

'Nearby? I thought you understood you were to hand them over at 4pm. It's now'—she glanced at the clock in the car—'4.03, and I don't have my… shopping.'

'Do you have my money?'

'Of course. But not until I have my goods.'

He looked down at her feet. 'Can you walk in those heels?'

'Of course.'

'Then, it's stashed a minute's walk away, over there.' He nodded towards the woods. 'Buried.'

'Buried?'

'I didn't want it in the house, not that much. The police would never believe that amount was for personal use. I don't take chances.'

She sighed resignedly. 'For God's sake, man, come on, then.'

She picked up her handbag, rammed a large white sunhat on her head and opened the car door. He was stunned. He had expected to be told to go fetch it, but here was this classy bird agreeing to accompany him into the woods. He followed her across the car park, and then as they reached the woods, he took the lead. Pity, really. It had been a nice arse to follow. The striking black and white dress, cut very low both front and back, emphasised every curve, and he felt a part of his anatomy reacting to her of its own free will.

The six children went home a bit earlier than usual, knowing they had to take the packet into the station.

There were seven people already sitting around the reception area, and they looked at each other.

'We'll be hours,' Daryl whispered. 'Quick vote – shall we do it in the morning? I'll take the stuff home, if you like, as it's in my bag. It won't matter if it's busy tomorrow morning, we can wait. But if I'm late home today, I'll be in bother, 'cos we're going to my nan's house for tea.'

He looked around at the others, and they all gave a thumbs-up sign, Dom a little reluctantly.

They left the police station at around the same time as Vinnie Walmsley was arriving at the place where he had buried what he thought of as his future.

'It's over here,' he said, and turned to help her over the tree roots. 'Be careful,' he warned. 'Yer shoes aren't really suitable.'

'You don't say, Einstein,' she snapped.

He approached the distinctive tree he had deliberately chosen and saw the mound of earth, newly dug.

'Shit…'

'What? What's wrong?' She pulled alongside him and looked down. She said nothing; there was nothing to be said.

'Perhaps an animal…' Vinnie dropped to his knees, taking the trowel out of his jeans pocket. He dug frantically, but knew it was futile. The packet had gone.

'Shit,' he repeated, and dropped his head.

She reached inside her bag and took out the knife she always carried, lifted his head up by grabbing hold of his hair and slid the sharp blade across his throat. He fell forward, and she fell with him, unable to stop. She picked herself up, looked around and listened to his laboured last breaths.

He wasn't dead when she left him, but he was before she reached her car. And she had avoided spattering blood all over her designer dress, still an immaculate black and white.

The children met up at the den early next morning. Daryl brought the powder with him, still in his backpack.

'Right,' he said. 'What's the plan of action?'

Dom spoke first. He had hardly slept all night and wanted to get this over and done with.

'I suggest we act this out. We go out there and play a game of hide and seek, then stumble across the package behind a tree or something. We make a bit of a show of it, then take it to the cop shop. And whatever we've done, that's the story we tell the police. Okay?'

They gave the thumbs up.

'I'll keep hold of the packet, then,' Daryl said. 'Come on, let's get rid of it and get back to our normal lives.'

They left the den one by one and looked around. There was nobody about, and Dom breathed a sigh of relief. 'Okay, who's looking?'

'I'll do it,' volunteered Freya. 'I'll wait in the den for a hundred counts, then I'm coming. Go!'

She climbed back in the den, and they all ran. The Brownlow twins climbed upwards; the other three hid in the undergrowth.

They heard the call of *coming, hidden or not*, and Dom and Mark saw their sister barrel out of the den from their vantage points up in the trees.

Freya stopped for a moment and listened but didn't hear anything. She cautiously moved towards the densest part of the woods, looking around her all the time for any splashes of colour that would indicate somebody was hiding there.

She saw one of them laid out flat and quietly approached, thinking it strange that they hadn't attempted to move deeper into the wood once she got nearer. Her scream started when she was about ten feet away.

She pulled out her whistle from where it hung under her T-shirt and blew her own signal. There was a crashing of twigs, and she knew the others were coming.

Sammy was the first to reach her, and his huge brown eyes followed the direction of her pointed hand.

'Look,' she whispered, and then turned and vomited. He held her, then turned her so that her back was to the bloodstained ground. There was a huge spread of crimson, giving off a sickening metallic smell.

The others arrived and stared at the scene. This couldn't be happening. The corpse was laid across the hole that had once contained the packet of drugs, and it was obviously a dead body.

'It's him,' Ella said. 'It's the man we watched bury the packet.'

'Vinnie Walmsley,' Sammy said, then looked down at the ground.

'You knew him?' Daryl sounded angry.

'I wasn't sure until I went home. Then, I had to walk past him, and I recognised his clothes. I ended up going around the back of the houses, so I didn't have to pass him. He scares me. Scared me.' Sammy looked at them all. 'I would have told you...'

'So, now what do we do?'

'Should we check he's definitely dead?'

'No!' Ella's voice reflected her terror at the thought. 'No, we can't go near him.'

'We can't ignore him. We've got to tell somebody.'

'Or we walk away and pretend we've not seen him.' Mark threw in his thoughts for the first time. 'It would be better for us if some adult found him. What do you think?'

'Let's go back to the den. We need to talk about this properly.' Daryl had taken on the leadership temporarily. He was the one holding the packet, taking the risks, so they'd damn well better listen.

They nodded and walked away without going any nearer the body.

Inside the den, they grabbed bottles of water. Freya still felt sick, and Sammy sat holding her hand, trying to offer comfort, but not really knowing how to do it.

'Okay,' Daryl began. 'This is not good for any of us. The way I see it is like this. I could be wrong, but I think Vinnie came back with whoever he was selling the drugs to, to dig them up and hand them over. Unfortunately for him, we'd beat him to it and swanned off with them. I think whoever he was with killed him. They probably thought he was cheating them.' Daryl paused for a moment. 'Now, I think we could be in some danger here.'

'You don't say, Daryl,' Mark said. 'I think we're in a hell of a lot of danger, and I vote we tell our parents. It's their job to protect us, ain't it?'

'You don't think we should tell the police we found a body?' Ella spoke tremulously, and Freya nodded. 'We don't have to mention any drugs, only that there's a body. We can pour the powder into the Shire Brook. It'll wash it away.'

The others looked at Ella without speaking, digesting her words. It was so rare for her to have an opinion on anything; she was normally happy to go along with whatever the others decided to do, but suddenly, she had come up with a valid answer to their problem.

'What does everybody think about that?' Daryl looked around the group. 'Let's have a vote. Who thinks it's a good idea?'

Slowly, one by one, the thumbs went up.

Dom's thumb was a little unsteady; he wasn't convinced. He was bothered by the idea of maybe getting caught pouring away a significant amount of cocaine into a stream that was almost dry. 'I need to say something. We can't put it in the Shire Brook yet, there's not enough water flow. We went down the fields a couple of days ago with Dad, and it's too dry. We have to hold on to the packet until we get some heavy rain. Does everybody agree with that?'

Again, the thumbs were raised. 'Who's going to hide the packet?' Mark looked around at everyone. 'It needs to be somewhere safe, where our parents won't see it.'

Freya opened her mouth to speak, but then thought better of it.

Mark saw her. 'Freya?'

'Erm… there's my Wendy house in the back garden. My parents are too big to get in it, and I could hide it in the oven. It won't be for long, will it? As soon as it rains heavy, we'll get rid, won't we?' She could hear the panic in her own voice and wished she hadn't suggested it.

'That's a brilliant idea, Freya,' Daryl said, his smile lighting up his face. He had been worried he might have to take it home, and he couldn't begin to imagine where he could safely hide it.

'So, how do I do it? I can't walk in carrying a packet of cocaine, can I? I haven't got a bag with me, or anything.' Freya was nervous.

Daryl thought for a moment. 'We go to yours now. We can always say we've decided to play in your garden. We've done it before. Your mum won't think it's strange. Then, you and Ella can go in the little house and hide it. We're in the clear as soon as that's done, and we can come back down here this afternoon and find the body again, if nobody else has found it. That's when we go and tell the police.'

They checked everything was okay in the den and set off for the Brownlows' house.

The traffic was heavy, and it took them some time to cross the road, to get back onto the estate.

They trekked up the road leading to Sunnyside Close; a young man was walking down on the opposite side of the road.

He waved when he saw them. 'Sammy!'

Sammy gulped. 'Liam…'

'Don't suppose you've seen Vinnie, have you? He didn't make it home last night, and his mother's going mental. She's got me out of bed to go and look for him.'

Sammy's face showed fear. Daryl hoped Liam couldn't tell from that distance. 'No,' Sammy squeaked. 'I've not seen him. I'll look out for him, though.'

Liam acknowledged Sammy's words by lifting his hand again and continued down the road.

'Liam's his best mate,' Sammy said. 'He's okay, though. Likes a kick-around with us kids at night on the field. Works at Asda stacking shelves. Nowt like drug-dealer Vinnie, not at all.'

'Well done,' Daryl said. 'You handled that good.'

They continued on their journey and eventually arrived in the back garden.

The sun was still relentlessly hot, and Sally Brownlow looked at the six children, surprise etched on her face. 'To what do I owe this honour?'

Mark grinned at his mother's words. 'We thought we'd do something a bit different today. We're going to set the croquet up. Is that okay?'

'Of course it is. Orange juice, everyone?'

They all thanked her politely, anxious not to cause any concern for her. She brought out their drinks and then said she was nipping down to Asda.

'Can I trust you all to behave while I'm gone?' she asked.

Their nodding heads made them appear like angels, and Sally Brownlow smiled. She grabbed her car keys and left them to play, hoping against hope they wouldn't have burnt the house down or anything in the time she was away.

They heard the car leave, and Freya and Ella ran down the garden and into the Wendy house. Inside the oven was a plastic casserole.

Daryl, easily the tallest in the group, had no chance of getting in, so he carefully took the packet out of his backpack and handed it through the window.

Freya placed it in the casserole, then asked the boys to gather some grass. She sprinkled the grass on top of the packet until it was completely covered, put on the lid and slid it back into the oven.

'Done,' she announced, and both girls backed carefully out of the Wendy house. 'Now, let's get this croquet set up, or Mum will know we were lying. She's good at knowing that.'

Mark nodded. 'Okay. And after we've had a sandwich, we'll pack this away and go back down to the woods. Then, we'll find Vinnie.'

It didn't take long to set up the croquet, and, despite their worries, they enjoyed the game.

Sally Brownlow came back with breadcakes and ham and made them sandwiches, then they packed away the croquet, said polite thank yous and headed back down the road. Daryl's backpack felt much lighter, and he was almost convinced that they were doing the right thing.

They didn't see Liam, so presumed he was out, still looking for his mate. Reaching the den, they gathered inside. They could see Vinnie Walmsley through the window; they knew it was there, it was all too clearly a body.

'Right. Five minutes to get our story straight. We came down to the woods to play hide and seek and found the body. I think four of us should stay with Vinnie, and two go to the cop station.' Mark was well into his leadership role. 'What do you think?'

'Who's going to the police?' Ella prayed it wasn't her.

'Daryl and Sammy? You up for that?'

They nodded, and so the plan was born.

4

Sammy and Daryl were nervous. The others were standing around the body; it looked gruesome after a night of foxes and other animals having a nibble on it.

'Can I help you?'

Daryl leaned into the window and spoke to a PC. 'I hope so. We've… erm… found a body.'

'You've found a body? Where?'

'In the woods.'

'What woods?'

'Next door. Can I speak to somebody who understands me, please?' Daryl was nothing if not polite.

'Hang on a minute.' The PC disappeared, and a couple of minutes later, another policeman came through the door connecting the offices with the reception.

'Now then, young man, what's PC Lacey telling me? You've found a body?'

'Yes. It's Vinnie Walmsley.'

'You know him?'

'I do.' Sammy finally spoke, having felt it was less terrifying if Daryl did all the talking.

'Er… sir…' PC Lacey interrupted. 'His mother rang this morning to see if we'd arrested him for anything.'

'Who? This young man?' He smiled at Sammy.

'No, sir, Vinnie Walmsley's mother. She said he hadn't come home last night, and she was trying to find him. I confirmed we hadn't arrested him, and that was the end of the conversation.'

DI Roberts immediately stopped patronising Daryl and Sammy. 'Right, lads, come through here and tell me what you know.'

He led them through the door, and they looked around nervously. This wasn't good. They'd imagined they would tell their news, a group of policemen would go and look, and that would be the end of it as far as they were concerned.

That wasn't the way it was going to happen. Roberts told them to sit down, and he moved behind his desk. 'Talk to me,' he said.

'We can show you where it is,' Daryl said. 'But we need to go now, because our friends have stayed with it, and it's not very nice.'

'Where is it?'

'It's in the little wood next door.'

'Next door to here?'

'Yes. We've already told him out there.'

'Right. Names.'

'Daryl Clarkson.'

'Samuel Walker.'

'He's called Sammy,' Daryl said helpfully.

'Addresses?'

They told him their addresses, and Daryl said, 'Why do you want to know that? The body's in the wood, not at our addresses.'

'We need to get your parents in.'

'What?'

'Now, show me where this body is. I'll get a couple of our lads to go with us.'

He was praying the kids left on guard, allegedly, hadn't contaminated the site too much. He was also praying it was some sort of shop dummy, even though the young black lad had said he knew him.

Roberts stood. He looked around the main office. 'Brian, Dan, I need you to come with me. We seem to have a dead body.'

They picked up their jackets and followed their boss and the two young lads out of the door.

'Shall we get a pool car, sir?' DC Brian Balding asked.

'No, we're walking.'

They followed him around the building and across the small service road.

'Right, lads, take the lead. We'll follow you. Show us this body.'

Daryl and Sammy looked at each other, then walked the short journey through the woods that led them to where the others were waiting. Daryl and Sammy joined them and then pointed to the body, lying some twelve feet away from them.

'Bloody 'ell,' Roberts said. 'I thought they were mistaken.'

'Right, Balding, take these children back to the station, give them a drink and get their parents in. They must have had a hell of a shock.'

Balding nodded, and the children, thoroughly scared because of the change in Roberts, followed him back the same way Daryl and Sammy had walked.

Roberts took out his phone, and within five minutes, the area was sealed, blue and white police tape fluttering in the soft summer breeze.

Balding took the six children through the door at the back of reception and to a room that boasted a couple of settees and some comfy chairs. He told them to sit down, and he would have some drinks sent in.

'Cokes okay?' he asked, and they nodded mutely. They had heard the instruction to bring their parents in, and nobody much fancied that.

Balding, along with a female police officer who told them to call her Angela, brought in the drinks and then sat down with them.

'Right,' he said. 'I need all your names and addresses, and don't worry, your parents will be here shortly. There's nothing to be frightened about.'

He wrote quickly as each one in turn admitted to having an address, and the dreaded parents that went with those addresses.

'What were you doing in the woods?'

'Climbing trees, playing hide and seek… we play there a lot 'cos it's a safe place to play. Our parents know we go there,' Daryl said, not hiding his irritation. He was starting to feel like a criminal with the threat of his mum hanging over him. 'We've done nothing wrong, you know.'

The others followed his lead of non-cooperation and sat and drank their cokes, waiting to see what would happen next.

And what did happen next was that assorted parents descended on the police station, demanding to see their children. Mark, Dom and Freya all stood as John and Sally Brownlow entered the room. Freya ran to them and hugged her mother. Dom and Mark were a little warier. They weren't sure yet if they were in any trouble.

Sally enfolded all three of them in her arms. 'Hey, don't look so scared. You're not in trouble. I'm so pleased you had the common sense to tell the police and not run away.'

They breathed a collective sigh of relief. Was it possible they'd got away with everything?

Cissie Johnston and Janey Walker had arrived in reception at the same time, and Cissie was in tears as she pulled Ella tightly to her.

Janey Walker looked at Sammy and smiled, and his world was okay again. It was only when Carl and Megan Clarkson arrived to be with Daryl that things turned a little sour.

'Daryl,' his father demanded, 'what the fuck have you been doing? I told you no police on my doorstep and—'

'That's enough, Carl,' John Brownlow interrupted. 'The kids have had a shock. They found a body, and they're always going to remember that. Don't make it worse for any of them, not only Daryl. They were good kids to report it.'

Megan Clarkson walked across to her son and hugged him. 'Take no notice of your dickhead father. I'm proud of what you've done.' She turned to her husband. 'And it's our house, not your house.'

Angela stepped forward. 'No arguing, please. These children don't need that. Can I ask you, now that you all have a responsible adult,' she looked pointedly at Carl Clarkson, 'to tell me what happened today?'

Daryl looked at the others. 'Shall I tell, and if I miss anything out, you jump in?'

They nodded.

'Okay. We played croquet this morning at the twins' house, and their mum did us some lunch. We cleared everything away, then we went down to have a muck-about in the woods, you know, climbing trees, hide and seek and stuff. We climbed trees first and then played hide and seek. That was when Freya blew her whistle. She was doing the seeking, and she came across the body. We heard her scream and then her whistle.'

'Do you all have a whistle?'

Daryl nodded. 'They're always round our necks, and we all have our own call on it.'

'Really?' Angela looked impressed. 'Show me.'

They all looked to Mark, and he nodded and pulled up his whistle from beneath his T-shirt. He played his call sign, and one by one, the others followed.

Their parents were clearly astounded. These kids had each other's backs, to a major extent. And they hadn't known.

'And then what happened?' Angela prompted.

'We came out from our hiding places and ran to where we could hear the whistle. Freya was being sick. Sammy went to help her, and we looked at the body. Sammy knew who he was, he lives near Vinnie Walmsley.'

'Vinnie Walmsley?' Janey Walker looked shocked. 'Aileen Walmsley's lad? Oh my God, she'll be devastated.'

'Sammy?'

'Yeah,' Sammy mumbled. 'He's a bad 'un. I seen him selling his drugs. He didn't deserve to die, though.'

'Anyway,' Daryl continued, 'we decided to leave Mark, Dom, Freya and Ella with the body, but not too near it, and me and Sammy came here. And that's it.'

'You didn't touch the body?' Angela pushed them again.

Mark jumped in with the answer. 'Not bloody likely. We di'n't even stand near it. It looked like his fingers had been eaten.'

Angela looked at the parents. 'We can arrange counselling for the children, if you feel it's necessary.'

'I think I need bloody counselling,' Carl Clarkson muttered, 'never mind the kids.'

'Do all of you know Vinnie Walmsley?'

The children looked at each other.

'We know about him,' Mark eventually admitted. 'He has drugs. Everybody knows that.'

'He scared me,' Sammy blurted out. 'Threatened to kill me if I said owt, 'cos I saw him handing drugs over and taking money.'

'When was this, Sammy?' Angela spoke gently to the scared child.

'About four weeks ago. I was on my own. I live a bit higher up the estate than the others, so I'm always on me own, after we go home.'

'I see,' she said. 'And did you know who was buying his drugs?'

Sammy shook his head. 'No, miss. I di'n't.'

'Okay. Now, I'm going to organise cups of tea for the adults – are you kids all okay, or do you need another drink?'

They all said they were fine, so Angela took orders for what the parents wanted and left the room to organise it.

With Angela's departure, the parents spoke at once, until Mark shouted, 'Will you lot listen to yerselves? It's about us, you know, not you. In fact, it's nowt to do wi' you. We found the body, and you're only here 'cos we're still young. So, give us a break, will yer?'

There was a shocked silence.

'Cocky little kid, aren't you?' Carl Clarkson said. He turned to his wife. 'Did you know our Daryl was mixing with the likes of these?'

'Oh, shut up, Carl,' Megan said. 'These kids have obviously got something special. Didn't you see that with the whistles? If I whistled, would you come running? No, I thought not. So, leave them alone. They did exactly the right thing. They haven't done anything wrong, and I bet it's going to be weeks before they get a decent night's sleep. You, on the other hand, won't get any sleep at all if you suddenly find yourself homeless and out walking the streets every night.'

Carl's mouth closed with an audible snap, and Daryl grinned. One nil to his mum.

Sammy, however, burst into tears, and the other five looked at him in horror. Was he going to tell the real story?

He hiccoughed and turned to his mum. 'Can we go home? I don't like him,' and he pointed at Carl.

Megan knelt and spoke to Sammy. 'Don't worry about him, sweetheart. Nobody else likes him, either. I won't let him bully you. You answer their questions, be honest, and we can all be going home in half an hour.'

Sammy looked up at his mum. Janey Walker smiled at him. 'You listen to Daryl's mum, Sammy. She's right. And I won't let anybody get to you, either. Now drink your cokes, and let's sit down and calm down. Carl, any more of that behaviour, and I'll punch you.'

Janey Walker: one, Carl Clarkson: nil. He wasn't having a good day.

Angela returned and detected a strained atmosphere. She handed out the teas and coffees, and then sat down and asked the children to come and sit by her.

'I want to double-check everything you've told me, and when we've all calmed down, your parents can take you home.'

She read through her notes, and the children nodded. 'You've nothing to add to this?'

Daryl looked around at them. 'I don't think so. We were together, so nobody saw anything the others didn't. And really, there was nothing there. It was a body. We didn't see anybody kill him, we found him dead.'

'And you play in the woods every day?'

They nodded.

'You were there yesterday?'

Again, they nodded.

'You see, that's the strange bit. I've spoken to DI Roberts, and the forensic people seem to think he's been there some time. Certainly since the day before. You didn't see anything suspicious?'

'No,' Dom said. 'We would have done the same yesterday that we've done today, if we'd spotted a body. You're talking daft.'

'Dom,' his mother warned. 'No back-chatting, please. I can fill in on a little bit of what they've done today. They went out to play this morning and then, mid-morning, came back to ours. They set up the croquet, I went to Asda and bought food for them, then came back and did some lunch. It was after that they went down to the woods again, and here we are. If these kids had seen that body at any other time, there's no way they would have been laughing and giggling, playing croquet.'

Angela looked at them. 'Right, I'm going to let you go home now, but I'm sure the DI will want to talk to you. We've got your addresses, so we'll be in touch. And, kids, I'm so sorry you had to go through this. Try not to dwell on it too much and stay together. You're a good crowd; you've got each other's backs. Stay away from those woods for a bit. It's a crime scene, anyway, but do as I ask. Stay away even when the tape's been taken down. Understood?'

They nodded or said yes and, ten minutes later, were on their travels back to their various homes, under strict instructions not to speak to anyone for at least two hours about what had happened. Aileen Walmsley still had to be told her son was dead.

With the removal of the body, it was clear that the indentation that had cradled Vinnie Walmsley's head was, in fact, a hole. A hole that had been excavated. It could have held drugs, it could have held money, but the bottom line was, it had probably held something illegal.

Roberts pursed his lips and emitted a low whistle. This wasn't good, a possible drugs murder on his patch. The body had now been taken away for the pathologist to do his job, and the DI knew he now had to go see the lad's mother.

Aileen wasn't reading. She couldn't concentrate; until Vinnie came home, her mind wouldn't settle. She heard the knock on the door and didn't want to answer it.

Sometimes, you just knew things were going wrong.

'Mrs Walmsley? DI Roberts, and this is DC Shaw.' They showed their warrant cards. 'May we come in, please?'

She stared at them. 'It's Vinnie, isn't it? They said he wasn't under arrest…'

'He's not under arrest, Mrs Walmsley. Can we come in, please? We need to speak with you.'

She opened the door wider, and they passed by her. 'To the right,' she said, her voice dulled by fear.

They sat, and Roberts spoke. 'I'm sorry, Mrs Walmsley, but I have to tell you a body has been found in the woods at the side of the police station, and we believe it to be your son. Although we're not sure of time of death yet, we believe he died yesterday, but was only found today, by some children. Do you know why he would be in those woods, Mrs Walmsley?'

She stared around her wildly, as if looking for a means of escape. 'No-o-o,' she moaned. 'Not my Vinnie.'

There was silence for a few seconds, and Heather Shaw spoke. Her soft voice was exactly what was needed. 'Tell me where the kitchen is, Mrs Walmsley. I think we all could use a cup of tea.'

Aileen Walmsley pointed with her hand, and Heather left the room. She could hear the sobs coming from Aileen and knew they would get nothing helpful from her today. She poured the hot water into the teapot and glanced up at the kitchen window.

A young man was peering through, his hands shielding his eyes as he tried to see if anyone was in the kitchen. She moved to open the door, and he jumped, startled to see her.

'Can I help?'

'Oh, sorry,' Liam said. 'I've been out looking for Vinnie, and I thought I'd call and see if he's turned up yet. It's not like him to miss his meals, so I've had a good scout around for him. Not found him, though.'

'And your name is?'

'Liam, Liam Blake. Aileen asked me to go out and look for him…'

The significance of a police presence at Aileen's slowly dawned on him.

'What's wrong? What's he done?'

'Mr Blake, I think you'd better come into the lounge. I'll bring you a cup of tea through. We have something to tell you, and I think Mrs Walmsley might need a friend.'

5

Nicolas Grausohn was angry. He had a small-time drug dealer dead, a knife-wielding tramp who had gone beyond the call of duty by killing the small-time drug dealer before he could question him, and a missing haul of drugs.

The fact that Johanna Fleischer was good in bed was irrelevant now; the way he was feeling, he could kill her rather than fuck her. He removed his glasses and ran his fingers through his hair, now so grey, it showed no evidence of the black it had been in his early years. His huge bulk filled his chair, and it creaked loudly as he leaned forward to stare at her.

'Look,' she said, attempting to placate him, 'he knew nothing. He was shocked – and frightened – to see that empty hiding place.'

'Then, who has got my goods? I suggest, Johanna, you find out, and find out quickly. *Sehr schnell.*'

She stared at him. He never reverted to their native German, insisting that they must be as English as the English, if they were to take over the supply of drugs to South Yorkshire and, in time, beyond that.

She turned and walked out of the room, closing the door with a slam. 'Fuck you,' she muttered, 'and that's in English.'

The slam of the door, combined with an exit when he hadn't dismissed her, was the final straw. Grausohn looked at Tommy Raines and simply nodded.

Tommy left the penthouse only seconds behind Johanna and reached the private lift as the doors were closing; his extended arm stopped the closure.

'Tommy,' she acknowledged, as he stepped in with her. He pressed the button for the minus one level and, in the same fluid movement, swung his arm around, connecting with her chin with a loud crack. She dropped to the floor instantly, and he bent over her, pressing his thumbs against her throat. By the time the lift arrived in the basement, she was dead.

She felt like a feather in comparison to others he had terminated, and he wedged the lift door in the open position with her body. The basement contained a row of large wheeled containers for waste disposal, and he found an empty one. He returned to her and quickly lifted her top, exposing her breasts. He fondled them and kissed them before dropping his hands lower, removing her panties. This part of the job he enjoyed.

He dropped his trousers, and twenty seconds later, it was over. He'd waited months to screw her.

Common sense finally prevailed; he was in a garbage disposal room used by tenants. Tommy picked her up, had one last touch and dropped her, and her panties, into the empty container.

He activated his walkie-talkie, speaking first to Grausohn. 'It's done. I need Kenny down in the basement.'

'I'll send him now.'

A minute later, the two men moved across to a half full refuse container. They wheeled it across to the one containing Johanna's body, and Kenny took out his phone and took a photo of her in the bottom of the bin. He knew Grausohn would want confirmation of her death.

Their huge muscles strained, and they picked up the half full bin, transferring the contents into the one containing Johanna. They repeated it with a second one and then closed the lid.

'Let's stick it near the outside door, furthest away from the lifts,' Tommy said.

They wheeled it across and put the two empty ones back in line. Tommy rubbed his hands together. 'Job done,' he said.

'Yeah,' Kenny agreed. 'Let's hope he's not changed his mind.'

They ambled across to the lift as the bell pinged, signalling the general lift that serviced the other flats arriving in the basement.

Moving quickly, they entered the penthouse lift, rising rapidly back for the next lot of instructions.

Grausohn lifted his bushy eyebrows in query as they walked back in.

'All done, boss,' Tommy said.

'*Gut*,' he said. He'd miss her, Johanna, but she'd caused him hassle. Now back to the problem of the missing drugs. He'd have some of his people out on the streets, tracking down anybody selling in copious quantities, because the fucking package had been a large deal. He'd sort out another woman as soon as he'd sorted the delivery non-arrival.

'Okay. I need some of the local boys out there. Grunt, Carl, Mikey, Dicko – they'll do for starters. If we don't find anything from this, we'll bring more in, but I want that package found before it all disappears. Kenny, you sort it. Tommy, you stay with me.'

The two men nodded, and Kenny left the room. He sent the photo he had taken to Grausohn's phone, followed by a text to the four men, and within an hour, they had joined him in the back room of the local Chinese takeaway. A hefty pay-out each week ensured the room was kept free for Grausohn's use, the hefty pay-out then disappearing into the local betting office.

Kenny was precise in the way he spoke. He was muscle, that was undisputed, but he was educated muscle, a dangerous combination. The four men waited patiently while he checked the door that led from the shop was locked, then he bolted the back door.

'Don't want anybody knowing our business, do we, lads?'

They muttered no and sat down around the round table in the centre of the room.

He outlined what had happened, although they all knew of the discovery of Vinnie's body. 'So,' he continued, 'the drugs were acquired by Mr Grausohn, and he wants them back before some estate low-life sells them all. It's a fair-sized package, and I understand it's worth close on quarter of a million.'

He looked around at their reactions. They sat, their faces inscrutable. This was serious stuff. 'There's a bonus in it. The boss wants whoever's got them, alive. If they're dead, the bonus for finding him will be ten grand, if alive, twenty grand.'

Carl Clarkson sucked in his breath. Twenty grand. With twenty grand, he could go, leave that prissy Megan and their smart-arse Daryl. He could start a new life, hopefully still working for the big boss, but away from Sheffield. And he had an advantage; the others had been shipped in, he was local. He'd get out on the streets and find out what the gossip was, who was spending money they didn't normally have, or even who was looking a bit more glassy-eyed than usual.

They left quietly, one at a time, not drawing attention to the meeting place. Kenny was the last to go, and he knocked on the door leading into the shop telling them the room was now empty. He fancied the idea of a twenty-grand bonus, and stood for a while, leaning on his car.

He looked around; it was just after five o'clock, and people were pulling up in cars collecting orders from the takeaway – he thought he might enjoy a chicken in black bean sauce himself, later.

He got in the car and drove down to where Vinnie Walmsley's body had been found. It was a shame the silly bitch had killed him; he'd seemed a willing enough lad, one Kenny had had his eye on to bring into the fold for Grausohn.

This must have been a massive transaction. Grausohn's supplier had sourced Vinnie Walmsley to be the middleman, but unfortunately, the delivery had gone to an inexperienced Vinnie, who probably hadn't wanted it in his house. It hadn't taken Kenny long to figure out what had happened. Vinnie had hidden it, Johanna had turned up to give Vinnie his cut for collecting it, then gone with him to get it. That's where it had all fallen apart because it wasn't there.

Kenny hadn't understood at first; normally, the boss would send him and Tommy to dispose of any bodies, but this one was right at the side of the police station, and Grausohn had been forced into giving some thought to what to do next. And then, it seemed some bloody estate kids had found Vinnie and run straight round to the station.

So, no Vinnie, no Johanna, no drugs, and worst of all, no money. Grausohn had paid up front for the delivery, as a show of faith to a new supplier.

Kenny parked in the Asda car park, as close to the woods as he could get. He stared across and saw the crime scene tape was still strung between the trees; no chance of having a nosey yet. He wanted a walk around the place. Johanna had said, before her unfortunate demise, that Vinnie had buried it in a pretty big hole under a tree. What if it was still there? What if Vinnie had got the wrong tree?

He'd stop by his sister's in the morning, he decided, and borrow the dog. He'd have a genuine reason for being in the woods if he happened to bump into a policeman.

Knowing there was nothing he could do, he put the car into gear and drove back to the takeaway. He picked up his meal and drove home to an empty house; Billy was away overnight. Kenny didn't start eating until after he'd rung the boss and told him about the meeting.

Grausohn didn't waste words. 'See you in the morning,' he said, and put down the phone.

Kenny decided it made sense to try bringing the dog the next day, see what the crack was. See if he could get anywhere near the crime scene.

Aileen Walmsley couldn't sleep. Her Vinnie, gone. And for what? She knew he was dealing, but only on a small scale, not enough to have his throat cut.

She switched on the bedside light and, once more, picked up her book. She read two pages before putting it down; she couldn't concentrate on the story.

She got out of bed and crossed to the open window; a hot night, and she leaned out to try to inhale some fresh air.

Liam had been an absolute brick. He had stayed with her, even after the police had left. They had searched Vinnie's room and found nothing, but she knew Vinnie had learnt his lesson. There would be nothing left lying around to incriminate him. What had gone so wrong that he had died?

And who had killed him?

It was clear Liam knew nothing. She had questioned him, while trying to pretend it wasn't an interrogation, but she had soon come to realise that other than knowing Vinnie was collecting some drugs, that was it.

He had no idea who the person was who had arranged to meet Vinnie, no idea where, no idea about anything. She had initially thought he was keeping quiet because it was the police asking the questions, but his answers didn't change, even when she asked through tears.

Carl Clarkson saw her standing at the window and wondered if she would answer his knock on the door. He had to be careful. He decided to give it a miss, but tomorrow, he would find some way of accidentally bumping into her. Or maybe take her some flowers from him and Megan, to say how sorry they were.

Nobody had any idea that he was in with Grausohn; not many really knew the man, anyway. It wasn't Grausohn's name out on the streets; it was the likes of Vinnie Walmsley who did the actual dealing. Grausohn supplied the schmucks, laughing at them, knowing they probably sampled and would keep coming back for more.

Carl didn't touch the stuff; he preferred being in control of his actions. He had got used to the money, though. Money that he earned from collecting debts, delivering packages, doing a little roughing up. Money that Megan knew nothing about, that he was saving to escape from a marriage that bored him, her and the bloody kid. It used to bother him that Daryl didn't want any contact with him, preferred the company of his mother, but now, he switched off from the pair of them.

And, of course, it had to be bloody Daryl who was the hero of the hour, finding Vinnie before Grausohn's men could dispose of him. He found it incomprehensible that the silly bitch, Johanna, had killed him anyway. Anybody with half a brain would have left him crying into the hole he had dug and walked away to go tell Grausohn what had happened. But, no, she had to kill him. Psychopathic birdbrain, or what? Tasty, of course, but way out of his league. For now.

Carl stood a few minutes longer, watching Aileen until she went back into her bedroom. He left the security of the tree he had leaned against and walked home. With a bit of luck, they'd be in bed, and he could have a very large whisky, without being nagged about it.

None of the children slept well. They had all suffered ministrations from their parents, and bedtime was a welcome escape from the "don't worry about anything" that was being thrown at them by any adults they encountered.

Mark and Dom were scared, and they knew Freya, despite her couldn't-care-less attitude, was equally as frightened.

'Did we get away with it?' Mark whispered.

'Dunno,' his brother replied. 'I wish they'd stop talking about it. God knows what they'd do if they found out about that package in the Wendy house.'

'I'll be glad when it rains. We need to get rid. Shh… footsteps.'

The footsteps stopped outside the bedroom door, and slowly, it opened. Both boys feigned sleep, and they heard their mother whisper, 'They're both asleep', before closing the door. They heard their parents continue along to Freya's room and then disappear back down stairs. They guessed Freya was pretending as well.

'Didn't rate Daryl's dad, did you?' Mark kept his voice low.

'Nah, proper thug. His mum's nice, though. Never talks about his dad, does he?'

Mark thought for a moment. 'Gave him a phone, though.'

'A cast off. Didn't buy it for him.'

They lay quietly for a couple of minutes.

'I don't ever want to see another dead body,' Dom said.

'Me neither. Gruesome. Can't get it out o' mi 'ead.'

'Must have been worse for Sammy, he knew him.'

They mulled this over.

'He was scared of him. Wonder why.' Dom was the thinker.

'We'll ask him.'

They finally drifted off to sleep, but all three children didn't make it through the night without waking.

Daryl was still awake when he heard his father creep in. So was his mother. The sounds of movement from downstairs carried on for a while, then he heard footsteps climbing the stairs.

The argument began as soon as he heard his dad go into the bedroom. He heard his own name mentioned, then his mum telling his dad he'd have to find somewhere else to live, and quick. It went on for some time, and then he caught the sound of footsteps retreating down the stairs, although he wasn't aware of the bang of a door, so assumed his dad was, once again, sleeping on the sofa.

Daryl sighed. Sometimes, he wished his dad would go. The atmosphere was much nicer when it was his mum and him, but he guessed it was never going to happen. His dad would never cope on his own.

He rolled over and pulled the pillow tighter around his head. *Sleep*, his head moaned, *sleep*.

Every time he closed his eyes, he saw Vinnie. If there was anything better designed to put kids off drugs for life, the sight of Vinnie Walmsley's body, chewed by the animals they loved and cared for in their den, certainly did the trick. It had been horrific. When the others had voted for him and Sammy to go to the police station, he had breathed a sigh of relief. It wasn't him and Sammy who had showed bravery by facing the law; it was them for staying with the body.

His eyes finally closed as daylight crept into his room, and he fell asleep wondering if the others had suffered a sleepless night as well.

Sammy hadn't closed his eyes at all. He had lived with the threat of being killed for so long, that now it was finally at an end, it sent his mind into free fall. The day he had seen Vinnie Walmsley swapping money for small packets outside the big school had proved to be the scariest day of his life. Until the day they'd found his body, of course.

On that day outside the school gates, Vinnie had seen him. Later that night, he had come looking for him, and the threat had been life changing.

'Don't tell nobody, or else.'

'Or else what?' he had bravely squeaked.

There had been a pause long enough for Sammy to recognise he was in deep shit.

'Or else I'll kill yer.' Vinnie had drawn his finger across his own throat, somewhat prophetically as it turned out, and then pointed at Sammy. 'Now, fuck off, kid, and keep that big mouth shut.'

He had never told the other five, taking heed of the stark warning that had come from Vinnie. He had avoided him ever since, taking the long way home in preference to passing the Walmsley house.

The relief, to him, was enormous; it occurred to him that he could lead a normal life now, instead of being scared of his own shadow. He would tell the others; they didn't keep secrets, and he didn't want this to be only his any longer.

He got up before six and watched the sun slowly rise in the sky. They had arranged to meet at the Brownlows', recognising they wouldn't be able to go to their den; he liked it there, and it would be even better when they managed to get rid of that stuff in the plastic oven.

Life would be normal again, once that happened.

Ella slept, thanks to a double dose of six plus Calpol, a hot chocolate, and a bed full of teddies. Her mum stroking her head had helped as well. She stayed with her daughter until she knew for certain sleep had claimed Ella.

Ella did wake briefly around three, thanks to an overfull bladder. She drifted back to sleep as soon as her head touched the pillow, after her stagger to the bathroom.

Cissie Johnston didn't sleep too well. There was something not quite right about all of this, and she couldn't for the life of her work out what it was. Ella knew, of that she was convinced, but she wasn't saying anything.

Cissie would bide her time. One day, Ella would break; she wasn't the type of child to be keeping secrets.

And then, she suspected, the police would really have to be called in.

6

DC Heather Shaw watched the CCTV pictures for the third time. The cameras in the Asda car park had picked up Vinnie Walmsley exiting the shelter of the undercover car park and walking across the open-air one to a car, a silver Audi. The number plate had proved to be false; it was registered to a retired teacher, a Mrs Lorna Cuthbert, living in Brighton, who was currently enjoying the summer in her holiday home in France.

Heather watched as Vinnie had got into the passenger seat, then saw both front doors open and a stunning woman climb out of the driver's seat, dressed in an eye-catching black and white dress that emphasised her curves. Vinnie had followed her across the car park, and there, the cameras lost the picture.

Fourteen minutes later, at 4.19pm, the camera registered the woman returning, still looking immaculately dressed from that distance. It was only when the zoom feature was engaged that the dirt on her knees showed up.

Her sun hat hid her face, and although they suspected this was the murderer of Vinnie Walmsley, the CCTV gave them no clues as to who she was.

The forensics had revealed he had been killed by someone standing behind him, right-handed, drawing the blade from left to right. It would have been a quick death.

Heather sighed. How effective was the programme they were running, and had been for a few years, of going into schools and talking about drugs? Vinnie Walmsley had still been so young and must have heard the talk about the dangers, and yet, here he was, walking to his drug-related death.

She logged out of the CCTV file and pulled the folder of the initial interviews with the children towards her. They would have to be seen again, interviewed a little more in depth, but she knew of the difficulties they faced when talking to kids. These days of *CSI* and *NCIS* on television made them wise to police procedure beyond their years, and they tended to only say what they could get away with.

She checked the Brownlow's number and picked up the phone. Sally Brownlow arranged to take the three children down to the station for 2pm.

Sally called them in from the garden and explained what was to happen and watched as the three of them immediately returned to the garden and went into a huddle.

What did they know? Had they seen something? Apart from a dead body, of course…

'Stick to our story,' Mark said to his brother and sister. 'Forget the bit about the drugs. We're expecting rain at the weekend, according to Daryl, so we can get rid of them then.'

'It scares me,' Freya said, biting her bottom lip. Both boys looked at her. She'd never been scared of anything. 'It scares me that they'll come and find it, the police. I've seen it on telly. They wave a piece of paper at the front door, barge in and search the place.'

Dom smiled. 'They're not going to wave a piece of paper at the front door of your Wendy house, are they? You're only nine.'

'And they're not really going to suspect Mum and Dad of stealing some drugs, are they?' Mark added.

'Who knows,' Freya countered, stubborn as always. 'Why can't we flush it down the toilet?'

'Because it's a big bag of the stuff. What if it blocked the drains? What would we do, then?' Dom pulled her close. 'Come on, little 'un, think about it. We've done nothing wrong. We've got all these drugs off the street, and I bet they're worth a good… oh, I don't know, perhaps a thousand pounds, so the police aren't going to shout at us, are they?'

Her eyes widened. 'A thousand pounds? Who do they belong to, then? I bet they're good an' mad.'

The boys looked at each other and grinned. The real Freya was coming back.

'We know what we're saying, don't we?' Dom pushed the point. 'When the others get here, we'll talk a bit more about it, make sure we're all saying the same thing, exactly as it happened yesterday afternoon, forgetting yesterday morning. Yesterday morning, we played croquet here. Yesterday afternoon, we went to the woods for a game of hide and seek and found the body.'

They nodded, their faces serious.

The garden gate banged, and Ella ran across the lawn towards them. 'Sammy and Daryl are walking down the road,' she said breathlessly. 'They'll be here in a minute. I've got to go to the police station this afternoon with Mum.'

'We have to also. All three of us. We'll talk about it when the other two get here.'

The gate banged again, and Daryl and Sammy joined them. The six of them sat around in a circle on the grass, and Daryl produced a packet of biscuits. Sally watched from the kitchen window and smiled. She liked Daryl and had always got on with Megan from the first day of taking their boys to school, but Carl she couldn't tolerate. Megan never had a good word to say about him, and Sally felt there was something strangely untrustworthy about him.

She opened the window and listened for a moment. She couldn't tell what the discussion was about, but they looked serious.

'Drinks?' she called.

Mark stuck up his thumb. 'Thanks, Mum.'

She filled two jugs with orange cordial and carried a tray out to them.

Daryl stood to help her, and she left them to pour it out for themselves. Strange how they stopped talking as she approached them…

Katie Wild wasn't particularly keen on lending Fluffy to her brother.

'What do you want her for? You've never taken her for a walk before. You don't even like her.'

'She's a lovely dog,' he said, 'and it's such a lovely day, I thought I might go for a walk.'

'You've come in the car.'

'I know, but I'm going to park it up and walk. Perhaps round Rother Valley.'

She stared at him, knowing he was lying. So, why did he want Fluffy? To impress somebody? And if he was going to walk round Rother Valley, she suspected it would be a step too far for the little Bichon Frise.

'Is there a woman involved?' she asked, the suspicion evident in her voice.

He jumped at the opportunity. 'Might be.'

'And she walks her dog?'

'Might do.'

'At Rother Valley?'

'Might do. Katie Wild, you're a nosey cow.'

She threw a tea towel at him. 'You big oaf. Why didn't you say that in the first place? Of course you can borrow Fluffy, but don't let her off the lead. She won't come back for your shout; she doesn't know you.'

He wanted to punch the air and shout "yes." It seemed strange that his own sister hadn't realised he was gay, but in retrospect, that was a good thing. He'd lived with her for some time back in 2006, and she'd never suspected – or at least never mentioned any suspicions. Katie had handed him the perfect reason for borrowing Fluffy.

She wandered into the hallway and got the pink lead. She attached it the pink collar around Fluffy's neck, then handed the lead to Kenny.

'Lose her, and you're dead. Let her eat berries, and you're dead. Bring her back pregnant, and you're dead. Bring her back scruffy, and you will live, but your balls will hurt.'

'Stop worrying,' he said. 'I'll take care of her.' He hooked the lead over his hand and edged towards the front door. 'See you in a couple of hours.'

He put the dog on the backseat; she promptly climbed over to the front seat, then dropped down into the footwell. She stared at him expectantly.

'Okay, Fluffy,' Kenny said. 'Let's go see what we can find.'

He drove carefully, covering the five or six miles without any mishap, and pulled up in the Asda car park. Fluffy waited patiently for release, and he hooked her lead over his wrist once again.

'Right, Fluffy, we're going for a walk in the woods. You've got to do what I tell you to do, don't go running off, stay with me.'

The dog was clearly listening, and he smiled to himself. What did Katie know – don't let her off the lead, she'll not come back to you? The mutt obviously liked him and wouldn't run off.

He led her around the car park, cut through the petrol station and entered the edge of the woods. He could see the crime scene tape fluttering in the breeze and headed over towards it.

Fluffy was pulling on the lead, and he viciously yanked her back to his side. She yelped.

'Stay with me,' he growled, and the dog growled back at him. For such a little dog, it was certainly noisy. He strolled casually over towards the last resting place of Vinnie Walmsley, then stopped. Two police officers, leaning against trees until they spotted him, stood up and moved as one in his direction.

'Can we help you, sir?'

'What's going on?'

'As you can see, sir, this is a crime scene.'

'What sort of crime?'

'A young man died here.'

'Shit.' Kenny thought he put the right amount of shock into the word. 'I had no idea. We'll get out of your way. I volunteered to bring the dog for a walk, thought this was a good place to bring her…'

'Not today, it isn't, sir. Can we have your name, please?' He took out a small notebook.

Kenny considered giving a false name, but then thought they might ask for his driving licence as proof of ID.

'Kenneth Lancaster.' He pre-empted the request and handed them his driving licence. The officer made a note of his address, and Kenny dragged Fluffy away with him. Damn dog, he'd have to borrow her again. Thank God for the woman he was supposedly seeing.

He bundled Fluffy back into the car and set off to drive back the same way he had only recently driven. He'd have to have a convincing story for Katie, no way would she believe he'd walked Fluffy round Rother Valley in that short space of time.

He delivered the dog, undamaged and clean, back to Katie, explaining his "friend" had texted to say she couldn't make it.

'Anytime you want to borrow her for chaperoning duties, she's available.'

'Thanks, sis,' he said, with a grin. 'In a couple of days?'

'Ring first. Don't just turn up. I might not be in.'

He nodded and left her to fuss over the dog. Bloody animal.

He drove back to Grausohn's penthouse and headed up in the lift.

Grausohn glanced up as Kenny walked through the door. 'Anything new?'

Kenny shook his head. 'Went to have a look where the kid died, but there's still a police presence. Acted dumb and came away. I'll go back in a couple of days. Do we know who these kids are, the ones who found him?'

Grausohn shook his head. 'Not yet. What you thinking?'

'Not sure. Maybe they saw more than they're letting on. Carl Clarkson's local to that area. We'll tell him to keep his ear to the ground, ask around. Somebody will know who they are. Need to cover all bases, boss, with this one.'

'Get Carl in.'

Kenny took out his phone and spoke briefly. 'Boss wants you.'

Within ten minutes, there was a knock on the door. Kenny went to open it and admitted Carl.

'Special job, Carl,' Grausohn said. 'These kids, the ones who found the lad. Word has it that they're from your neck of the woods. Find out who they are. Ask around. I need to speak to them.'

Carl hoped nobody noticed his face had turned white. He knew it must be; he had felt the colour drain away. Damn and blast that bloody kid of his.

Grausohn looked up. 'Now, Carl. Report back tomorrow with their names.'

'Okay, boss.' Carl heard the stammer in his voice and coughed to hide it. He left the room, and Kenny followed his exit with a questioning expression on his face. *What was wrong with the man? It was a simple instruction. Find the kids.*

'Anything else you need doing today, boss?'

Grausohn checked his watch. 'No, Kenny, get off home. I'll ring if anything crops up.'

'Thanks. Where's Tommy?'

'He's meeting somebody. He's okay. Doesn't need back-up.'

Kenny gave a brief nod, then said bye as he exited the luxury penthouse. He didn't know whether to follow Carl Clarkson or go straight home.

In the end, he decided to head for home and have a quiet night in with Billy. Quiet nights in were a rarity, but Billy understood. He knew who Kenny's boss was.

Dom, Mark and Freya were the first ones to be interviewed properly. All of them stuck to their story, nobody wavered, and DI Roberts almost believed them. After speaking at length to Daryl, Sammy and Ella, with their ever-watchful parents present, Roberts had to admit defeat. If they did know anything else, it was staying within the close-knit circle. Every story was the same, almost word for word, and every child appeared to be open and honest.

He thanked them all for their time and told them he didn't think they would be needed again. He also asked them not to return to playing in the woods; until the murderer was caught, it had to be regarded as a dangerous place. Whatever had been in the hole where Vinnie's head had lain was most probably still missing, and people would be wanting it back.

'We're having a couple of officers stationed in the woods for the next few days, but we can't do that indefinitely. So, be careful, eh, kids?'

They nodded solemnly, privately thinking that they would be glad when they could return to their den.

'So,' Roberts said, as they stood to leave the room. 'You got a leader?' They looked questioningly at each other, and then, Dom spoke. 'I suppose Mark. He's the oldest. Why?' He sounded defensive.

'Here, Mark.' He handed him a twenty-pound note. 'Get yourselves some ice creams. And thank you for what you did, all of you.'

They shouted their thanks as they left the interview room, and Roberts smiled. They didn't have many interviewees they treated to ice creams.

'What did you think?' he asked Heather Shaw.

'I don't know. Their stories haven't changed at all – they're smart kids.'

'Exactly. I'm still not sure…'

'But they've not killed Vinnie Walmsley. They're not big enough or strong enough for a start. And I'm not convinced they saw who killed him either. They'd be a lot more… oh, I don't know… mentally upset. And they're not.' Heather frowned as she spoke.

'I'm not saying they did see the murder, but I'm wondering if they saw Vinnie Walmsley burying whatever he buried in that hole. The law says I can't torture it out of them, so we'll have to bide our time on that one.'

Heather laughed. 'Don't forget they've got their whistles. You wouldn't get away with torture; the other five would be there straight away. One toot of a whistle and you'd be done for.'

'You know, young Mark might be the leader because he's the oldest in the group, but I think the clever one is Daryl Clarkson.

We got anything on his father? He doesn't seem to like his family all that much.'

'I'll have him checked out. Bad-tempered bloke, isn't he? Obviously didn't want to be here.'

'Let's hope they've listened to me. I don't want them in that wood from now on. It's not safe.' Roberts had a worried frown on his face. 'Forensics found nothing, did they?'

'Not a thing. We've CCTV showing the woman who probably killed him, but no clear picture of her, a car with false reg plates and a dead body that's telling us nothing. Oh, and a hole. To be honest, we don't know if anything was in that hole. Animals could have scraped around his head. His face was chewed, and he had dirt under his nails, so he could have scrabbled at the earth as he was dying.'

He shook his head. 'Something was there, I'm sure of it. Could have been a drugs haul, could have been cash. Whatever it was, she killed him because it wasn't there. Come on, let's have a walk across, see that those two buggers on duty aren't having a crafty fag, and take in the scene now there's nothing there.'

Heather nodded, and they left the building. It took just over a minute to reach the tape, and the two officers jumped to attention. Fortunately, they had put out their cigarettes.

'All quiet, lads?' he asked.

'Yes, sir,' PC Craig Smythe responded. 'No problems.'

The second officer turned his head to look at his mate. 'We had a visitor, sir, with a dog.'

'What? Who the hell didn't know this was a crime scene?'

PC George Marks took out his notebook. 'A Kenneth Lancaster, sir. A dog walker, who hadn't realised it was these woods. He went as soon as we told him.'

Roberts held out his hand for the notebook. 'He lives here?'

'Yes, sir. I copied his address from his driving licence.'

Roberts took out his phone and took a photo of the address. 'We'll have a look at this, DC Shaw,' he said. 'This address is about six miles or so from here, across in the north of the city.

Why would somebody walk a dog in this particular very small wood? Doesn't make sense, does it?'

They stayed for a few minutes longer, looking around and generally making the two officers increasingly nervous. George Marks was pissed off with himself – it hadn't occurred to him that the address was distant from where they were.

And that, he realised, was why he was a PC and Heather Shaw was a DC, to say nothing of her boss being a DI. He felt a complete idiot.

7

It was raining, not torrential, but heavy nonetheless. The six children had taken themselves off to the twins' bedroom and were undecided what to do. Ella and Freya were staring somewhat morosely out of the window, watching the raindrops race down the windowpane, and the boys were sprawled across the two beds, talking.

'If this keeps up, the stream will start to flow a bit better. We can dump the stuff as soon as it's running,' Mark said. 'Everybody agree?'

Ella was half listening. She turned to look at them. 'This is that little stream that runs at the side of the new road?' The new road was now over twenty years old, but in the absence of any sort of name it was known locally as the new road.

Dom nodded. 'It's nearly dried up, but it soon gets going again when it rains. Another day of this, and it'll be flowing.'

'But doesn't it run into the pond, then out of it again at the far side?' Ella was speaking slowly, checking the facts in her head. Always aware of the two-year age gap she and Freya endured with the boys, she liked to think before she spoke.

Daryl nodded. 'Yeah, goes under the road then.'

Freya was ahead of her friend. 'What I think Ella is saying, is there are at least eight swans on the pond, and lots of ducks.'

The four boys looked at Freya. 'Shit,' Mark said.

'We need a new plan,' Dom added.

'Now,' Daryl followed on.

Sammy rolled around on the bed, laughing. 'Your faces...' he said, spluttering. 'Two nine-year-old girls have seen what we didn't.'

The girls turned to each other and grinned, then high-fived. One nil to them.

'Sammy, you're not helping,' Mark said, disgruntled. He knew he hadn't thought things through properly. They couldn't have swans waddling around, high on cocaine. Or laid by the side of the pond, dead.

Sammy stopped laughing and sat up. 'We need a meeting. Suggestions for what to do with it.'

'No idea. Maybe we're back to the idea of flushing it down the bog, a bit at a time. Or splitting it into six, and us all taking some to flush.' Dom was thinking aloud.

'But that makes three lots for us to get rid of,' Mark pointed out. 'More chance of summat going wrong.'

'We could give it to the police.' Ella, ever the timid one, spoke carefully. She didn't think for one minute the others would agree with her, but she had to try. 'I know we'd have to confess to not telling them before, but we're kids, we were scared about telling them. I'm sure they'll understand.'

Daryl shook his head. 'Let's think this through. If we take it to DI Roberts, I'm sure he'd be dead chuffed. He'd send for our parents… and they'll ground us. Probably 'til we're eighteen,' he added glumly. 'Or even longer. You all saw what my dad was like.'

'Has it occurred to anybody that this stuff is worth a lot of money? It means it belongs to somebody who must be good and mad he's not got it, and when they find out…' Dom shivered. 'We should have left it alone. I bet if we hadn't touched it, Vinnie wouldn't have been killed. And none of this would be happening. We've got to be careful what happens next. We seem to make things worse, whatever we do.'

Aileen Walmsley stood under the shower and let the cool water run over her. Despite the rain, it was still hot and muggy, and she needed to feel a little bit more alive.

Tomorrow, she had to identify her only son, a son she loved deeply, despite all his faults. It hurt her that she had known about the drug dealing, and he had ignored her efforts to make him leave it alone, but according to DI Roberts, it seemed he had stepped up to playing with the bigger boys and had paid for it with his life.

She heard the doorbell and grabbed a towel. Wrapping it around her, she moved downstairs; placing her eye against the spyhole Vinnie had insisted she install, she recognised Carl Clarkson.

Aileen hesitated, then opened the door with the chain still on. 'Carl?'

'Hiya, Aileen.' He produced a bunch of flowers from behind his back. 'These are from Megan and me, to say how sorry we are to hear about Vinnie.'

'Oh.' She felt a little nonplussed. 'Er… I've just got out of t'shower…'

'I can wait. I'll stand here until you're dressed, don't worry.'

'No, don't be daft. It's raining.' She closed the door, took off the chain and re-opened the door. 'Come in, I'll put the kettle on, then go and get dressed while it's boiling.'

Carl followed her down the hallway to the kitchen and sat at the kitchen table. 'We feel awful, me and Megan, especially as it was our Daryl who was one of the kids…'

'I'm glad they found him when they did. He could have been out there even longer if they hadn't. He's a good lad, your Daryl.'

'And have the police said anything? Owt helpful?'

Aileen shook her head and wiped away a tear. 'Sorry, can't seem to stop crying. No, they came last night and went through the house, had a good scout round in his bedroom, but they only took his laptop, nowt else. They wouldn't have found any drugs, or owt like that. It scared our Vinnie shitless when they turned up last time.'

She leaned against the counter with her back to him and dropped her head. He stood and went towards her.

'Come here,' he said, and turned her round to face him. 'Let me give you a hug.'

She leaned against him, and her breasts pressed into his chest. She enjoyed it for a few moments as he held her. She felt him kiss the top of her head; her wet hair smelled of coconut.

Aileen wrapped her arms around him and pulled him closer. His erection pressed into her, and she lifted her head. Pulling him to her, she kissed him. He knew she was using him, needing the comfort of somebody caring, even if only for a few minutes. A tug on the towel, and it dropped away from her.

He stared at her curves. 'You're beautiful,' he whispered. 'Absolutely beautiful.' And then, he stepped back. 'I'm so sorry, Aileen, I shouldn't have done that…'

She took him by the hand and led him into the lounge. 'Tell me that in a bit.'

My God, he thought. *That was easy*.

Aileen let him out of the back door; he didn't want anybody running straight round to Megan telling her he'd been seen coming out of Aileen Walmsley's. Somewhat to his surprise, it had been an awesome couple of hours.

She certainly knew what she was doing and had taught him a thing or two. He might have to go back and comfort her again. What she hadn't done was tell him about any stash of cocaine that her darling boy had left hidden somewhere. That had been the idea behind going around there in the first place; the towel wrapped loosely around that very tidy body had definitely been a bonus.

Now, he had to decide what to do about the instructions from Grausohn – find out who the kids were.

The second he told them his own son was involved, they would realise he had known all along, and where would that leave him? Dead. He knew they had killed Johanna, and he knew they wouldn't hesitate to "off" him. So, what to do?

He couldn't even leave Daryl out of the equation, because the second they went to work on any one of the kids, they would tell them everything they wanted to know, including the fact that Daryl was there when they were.

Should he give Daryl up to them? Act as if it was the first he'd heard of it? Bloody Daryl would probably tell them his dad had had to be there when they gave their statements.

Why did life have to be so fucking confusing? All because one daft bint had killed Vinnie Walmsley without stopping to think about the consequences.

He reached his own home and went in via the back door. All seemed quiet, and he went through to the lounge and lay down on the sofa. He'd had an energetic afternoon and needed a little kip before going out later. He didn't wipe the smile off his face quick enough.

'She made you smile, then, did she?'

'What?'

'Whoever you've been with. Don't deny it, Carl, I can smell sex on you. Go and pack, and don't come back. I don't want you anywhere near us.'

He stared at her. 'Don't speak to me like that, tart. I'm going nowhere.'

'You are.' She slipped her mobile phone from her jeans pocket and rang her brother. 'Owen? He won't go.'

She disconnected the call, and Carl knew he was beaten. Or he would be, if he didn't get his arse in gear in the next ten minutes and leg it out of there. He'd taken a beating from Owen Davies once before, after Carl had blacked Megan's eye, and he didn't want another one. This time, he might not survive.

'Fuck you,' he snarled. 'She was better than you in bed, anyway.'

'Get out, Carl. Just get out. And don't try to contact either of us again. We don't need you. Never did, really.'

He walked upstairs slowly, hurling insults at her every step of the way.

Once inside their bedroom, he packed a bag fast. He wanted to be well on his way by the time Owen Davies arrived to comfort his sister and batter his brother-in-law.

He didn't say goodbye, simply slammed the door and left.

Aileen Walmsley was surprised to hear the doorbell. She was even more surprised to see Carl Clarkson once again as she peered through the spyhole.

It was hardly any time at all since they'd both agreed their frantic bout of sex had been a mistake brought on my grief and loneliness, and they wouldn't be seeing each other again. In the current climate, it wasn't a sensible thing to do. So, she wondered why he was on her doorstep for the second time that day.

'Carl?'

'Can I come in?'

She stepped back without speaking, and he walked past her. He headed towards the kitchen.

He dumped his bag on the floor and turned to her. 'Megan's thrown me out. I've nowhere to go tonight, and I wondered if I could sleep on your sofa. Honestly, Aileen, it's only for the one night. I wouldn't ask if there was anybody else I could turn to, but there isn't.'

She paused for a moment. 'I guess it's okay. But I'm being collected tomorrow morning to go and identify Vinnie. You'll need to be out of the way early.'

He nodded. 'That's no problem. I need to find somewhere to stay anyway. I'll be gone by nine. Okay?'

She nodded. 'That's fine, DC Shaw is coming about nine-thirty for me.'

Carl carried his bag through to the lounge and dropped it by the side of the sofa. He took out his wallet and extracted a twenty-pound note.

'Pizza?' He handed Aileen the money.

She laughed. 'Doesn't get much more romantic than that. Pizza it is.'

Daryl arrived home to find his Uncle Owen there. Daryl's mum had obviously been crying, and he went to give her a hug. 'What's wrong?'

'It's your dad. I've told him to leave.'

Daryl looked first at Owen and then at his mum. 'Why?'

'I can't really explain… You know we've not been getting on for a while, and I'd had enough. Anyway, he's gone. And he won't be back.'

'Promise?'

Of all the responses Owen and Megan had expected, that was nowhere near what they had pre-supposed.

'I promise,' she said softly. 'You're not upset?'

Daryl looked at her with a grin on his face. 'Couldn't stand him. Do me a favour, Mum, if you get me another dad, let me have a say in it as well, will you?'

Owen and Megan were left open-mouthed as Daryl disappeared upstairs to his bedroom.

Daryl lay on his back and stared at his bedroom ceiling. They still hadn't come up with any decent answers as to what to do with the hefty package of cocaine, and he could tell Freya was getting quite upset about it – Freya, the feral Freya, who couldn't care less about rules, who did everything she was forbidden to do; suddenly, she was acquiring a conscience. Or she was concerned that if it were found in her Wendy house, she would get the blame.

He didn't know what to do. And neither did Sammy, Freya's champion. They had left the Brownlow house to walk home and had discussed everything as they climbed the hill. He had left Sammy to carry on alone once he reached his own path and had made him promise to give it a lot of thought overnight. Those drugs had to disappear.

Sammy had responded with a high five, and 'Yo, man!', but it didn't mean either of them would have an answer by the morning.

And now, Daryl had got the additional news of his dad. He wondered for a moment where he had gone, but it was only for a moment. He didn't really care. He had felt humiliated by him at the police station; the other parents had been fully supportive of their kids. Carl had been stroppy, thuggish and a pain in the backside.

Daryl heard the front door open and close and guessed his Uncle Owen had gone. He hoped his dad hadn't hit his mum; was that why Uncle Owen was there? He had sorted Carl out last time that had happened. Daryl's mum didn't look injured, no black eye or anything… Maybe he'd better check on her.

He climbed off his bed and headed back downstairs. 'You okay, Mum? Has Uncle Owen left?'

She turned to face him. 'I'm absolutely fine, Daryl. A big weight's gone. I brought Uncle Owen here to stop any bother, but I think your dad remembered last time and disappeared pretty damn fast after I made the call. You sure you're okay? It's a massive thing for a son to lose his dad.'

Daryl stared at her. 'It would have been better if he'd died. Now we'll always wonder if we'll see him again. But I'm getting bigger now, Mum, and he'll not hit you again.'

She pulled Daryl towards her and kissed the top of his head. 'Where did I find one like you?' she whispered softly, hugging him. 'I'm going to treat you, to celebrate him going and to say thank you for being you.'

Daryl pulled away from her and grinned. 'McDonalds it is, then!'

Carl turned in his sleep and the feel of Aileen's soft breasts against him woke him. He leaned his head down to kiss them, and she moaned. She reached her hand down the bed and touched him.

'Ready again?' she murmured sleepily.

He pushed her onto her back, and she opened her eyes.

'Eager, aren't we?' She felt him enter her and immediately responded.

Five minutes later, they were once again lying side by side, satiated, spent.

'You're gorgeous,' he said.

'Yeah, you're okay too,' she answered, smiling into the darkness. 'Glad you didn't sleep on the sofa. It feels good to have a man in bed, again.'

'Never known you to have a feller.'

'Just the odd one or two one-night stands, nothing serious. Vinnie's dad left before Vinnie was born, and I chose to bring him up on my own.'

'I didn't know.' Carl raised himself up onto one elbow and looked at her. 'I'm sorry. That must have been rough.'

'It was. I've missed out on having the help from a father figure, and I've wondered a lot of times if that's why Vinnie turned to dealing.'

'You knew he was?'

'Yeah, but small time. I'd no idea he was handling bigger stuff. DI Roberts seems to think that's why he was killed. He was supposed to hand some drugs over, but they disappeared. I've checked his hiding place, where he used to put stuff, but it's not there.'

'Shit. He was crazy enough to hide stuff in the house?' Carl tried to sound shocked.

'Nah, there's an overgrown patch of garden down at the bottom end. He used to dig a hole there and put stuff in it. He could have found a different area for this latest delivery, but I've had a good look round and can't see any newly dug earth.'

Carl touched her breasts again, almost absent-mindedly. The garden. He'd watch for her to go with this policewoman tomorrow and then head back.

Aileen turned on her side, her back to him. 'I need to sleep, babe. Got a big day tomorrow.'

'Sorry, sweetheart.' He kissed her back. 'Sweet dreams, see you in the morning.'

She smiled. The sex had been good, and she didn't regret for one minute inviting him to sleep in her bed. And the biggest bonus was that tomorrow, she might get the back garden dug over, without having to employ a gardener.

8

Aileen left the house around nine-fifteen and went to sit on the front garden wall, waiting for the arrival of the police car. Carl had left fifteen minutes earlier, but she guessed he was around somewhere, watching for her to disappear.

He really was stupid, thinking he could fool her. She was looking forward to confronting him later and thanking him for turning the heavy soil over in the back garden. She could even ignore the digging in the back garden and suggest Vinnie had also buried stuff in the front garden.

She knew he had believed he was using her in the afternoon, for the sex, but the reality was, she had needed to be held, to have someone inside her, wiping out her grief, comforting her with sex how she liked it. So, who had used whom?

She saw the police car coming up the road, and she stood. Let the digging commence.

Within a minute of Aileen leaving, Carl was walking around the house and into the back garden. These drugs had to be somewhere, and if he could find them and produce them for Grausohn, he would be well in. And certainly quids in.

Carl slipped into the shed and found a spade. Would Aileen believe he'd tried to say thank you for giving him a bed, and some awesome sex, by trying to tidy her garden? He thought so. He began with the overgrown weed area that she had mentioned. Luckily, the rain of the previous day had softened the baked soil, and he could dig deep, but there was nothing.

He checked his watch. Half an hour. He was guessing she'd be away about an hour, so he moved on to another area where it seemed as if they'd attempted to grow vegetables at some point. He dug. He heard his spade clang, and the impact jarred his shoulder.

Dropping to his knees, he scrabbled feverishly in the soil and pulled out a canister, round, muddy and old. Whatever was in it, it wasn't half a million pounds worth of cocaine. Come to think of it, he didn't know if the particular package he was trying to find was worth that much, or if the entire deal was for that amount.

He leaned back on his heels, feeling frustrated. Picking up the canister, he bashed it against a brick until it cracked. There were papers inside, and a couple of toys that looked as if they had come from McDonald's. He picked up one of the papers. It was headed "Time Capsule by Vinnie Walmsley."

He threw it against the shed side and stood. Maybe he was tackling this all wrong. He walked carefully around the garden, looking intently towards the ground, searching for any small areas that might have been newly dug.

And that's what he was doing when Aileen walked out of the back door.

'Sometimes, he buried things in the front garden!' she called. 'Want to go and turn that over as well?'

He jumped, guilt all over his face. 'I… er… I thought I'd try to tidy the garden up for you.'

'Really?' Her tone was scathing. 'Want to have a shower now, and we'll slip back into bed? Get out, Carl, before I ring the police. I'm sure they'll be interested in hearing what you have to say.'

He had no words, or at least no words that would get him out of this. He stumbled as he headed for the garden gate, picked up his bag and began to walk down the path that ran around the house.

'Wait!' she called.

He stopped.

'You're looking for the package that seems to have gone missing, that my Vinnie died for?'

He nodded, still not trusting himself to speak.

She looked at him, holding him there with her eyes, thinking. 'Come into the kitchen. We need to talk. The truth, not your bullshit.'

He turned to follow her, not sure if he was more scared of her, or Grausohn. She clicked on the kettle and told him to sit down. He still hadn't spoken. He was beginning to realise that she had had the upper hand from the beginning, from the second he delivered the flowers, that now stood in a pint pot in the middle of the kitchen table, to the moment she had caught him in the back garden.

She made two cups of tea, still without letting him off the hook in any way, and he remained equally silent.

He still couldn't speak, even when she put the cup down in front of him, sat across from him and used the immortal words, 'Start talking.'

He opened his mouth a couple of times, but had no idea what to say, or even what she wanted to know.

She suddenly seemed to relent. 'You're in trouble, aren't you?'

Finally, his brain engaged. 'A bit,' he admitted.

'That's a start. Let me tell you what I've worked out, and then, you can fill in the bits I don't know.'

He nodded, acknowledging he'd better not hide anything, she seemed to be five steps in front of him anyway.

'I think you're looking for the drugs my Vinnie was killed for. When I told you he buried stuff in the garden, he did, but that was the little stuff. He thought the police wouldn't bother bringing in a sniffer dog, or even digging up the bloody garden. I turned a blind eye, because I thought he was too naïve to progress to the bigger boys. He was a little dealer, that's all.'

She paused, took a screwed-up tissue from her sleeve and dabbed at her eyes. 'It now seems, according to Roberts, that he took delivery of the package, like a middle-man, and he was to be contacted by the final recipient of it, then hand it over. He would have thought it was easy money, because he didn't have to sell anything, simply hold them. But that visit by the police, months ago, had scared him. He must have decided to bury it, like he did here, only he used the woods. Roberts thinks he was seen burying it, because it wasn't there when he went to get it. He was with a woman, apparently, but the drugs squad here aren't aware of any women they're watching, not ones that look like her, anyway.'

She paused again. 'It seems she killed him, immediately. Didn't give him a chance to explain anything, so now, the bloody drugs are missing, no clues as to who they really belong to, nothing. But I think you know something. Who are you working for, Carl?'

He hesitated, but when she repeated 'Carl,' he spoke.

'You're right, of course you're right. It doesn't take a genius to work out what happened with Vinnie, and I can tell you now you'll never see proper justice for him, 'cos I think she's already dead, the woman who killed him. I know names, but I can't tell you if you're going to go straight to the police. I'd be dead within the hour if you did that. These are big boys we're talking about here, Aileen. They're not the kids Vinnie was learning his trade with.'

'Why do you think she's dead?'

'I heard the bloke who killed her talking about it, laughing, saying he'd copped a feel as he tipped her body into a bin. Everybody wanted to cop a feel of her but couldn't. She belonged to the boss. He would have ordered her to be done.'

'Nice bloke. Nice outfit you work for.'

'Yeah, but now, 'cos I live local to where Vinnie died, I've been sent out to find who the kids are who came across his body. The boss wants to… talk to them.'

'But—'

'I know! One of them is Daryl. So now do you see why I'm panicking to find these bleedin' drugs?'

'Shit.'

There was silence between them. A long silence, while they digested what they knew.

'How big, how powerful, are they?'

'Think of the Krays… I would say, the main difference is, they stay in the background. Don't brag it off, like the Krays did.'

'So, why you?'

'Got talking in the pub one night to a bloke. No idea he was the top man's right-hand man. Ended up doing a couple of jobs for them, debt collections, and I was in. Introduced to the boss, welcomed aboard, here's ten grand to get you started sort of thing, but now, I'm fucking scared, Aileen. So scared, I actually thought about telling him Daryl's name.'

She gasped. 'He's your son!'

He covered his face with his hands. 'I know. We don't get on, but he's still my lad.'

'You're not going to dob him in, are you?'

'Course not. But I don't know what to do. Do you?'

'Doing nowt isn't an option.' She picked up her cup and sipped at it thoughtfully. 'Does Megan know?'

'Nah. It must be best part of three years since I had any sort of conversation with her. We don't like each other. And Daryl's all for her. We don't get on. I'm well out of it.' He stood and carried his cup over to the sink. 'Thanks for listening, but I've got to go and find somewhere to sleep tonight. You have my number, if you want to ring.'

'Sit down, Carl,' she said tiredly. 'Sit down and stop being a prat. You can stay here. We need to work things out, and we can't do that over a phone.'

'But why? Why would you want to help me?'

'It's not all about helping you. If I can't have proper justice for my Vinnie, then I'll take what I can get. I want to see this big boss dead. So, I need his name. Are you in or out?'

Carl came back to the table, sat down once again, and took her hand. 'In. He's a German called Nicolas Grausohn, and he's a proper shit. He's the one who ordered Johanna Fleischer to be killed.'

'More,' Aileen demanded.

'What?'

She crossed to the fridge to a magnetic shopping list. She tore off the top sheet, picked up a pen and sat down again. 'Right. Nicolas… what did you say?'

Carl spelt it out for her and then repeated Johanna's name.

'Who else?'

'Tommy Raines – he actually killed her, and there's another one, assists Tommy in everything, Kenny Lancaster.'

'Kenny Lancaster? I think I know him. He's gay?'

Carl laughed. 'I wouldn't have thought so. He's never said anything that would make me think he was.'

'Was he the one who recruited you in the pub that night?'

'Oh my God, he was!'

'I rest my case.'

She wanted to laugh at his face, but she was still feeling a bit at odds with him. 'So, you're staying, then?'

'If it's okay with you. I feel safe here, 'cos nobody knows we're connected.'

She nodded. 'Then get upstairs, superstud. I fancy a good seeing to, calm me down after seeing my lad this morning.'

Carl didn't argue.

Daryl had been quiet most of the day, and the others noticed it, but didn't comment. They assumed he was worrying about disposing of the drugs where they wouldn't hurt wild life or humans, and as the clever one in the group, he was the one who usually came up with solutions.

It was only as home time arrived that he apologised and said he'd a lot on his mind. 'My dad's left. Really, it's more my mum's chucked him out, but either way, he's gone. It's a bit strange at home, it's quiet. I'm worrying about her, I don't want him coming back and giving her a beating.'

The others looked at him. 'Why didn't you say earlier?'

The ever-practical Sammy said, 'We could have gone to yours for the day. We'd have been there if he did show up. He wouldn't touch her if he knew he had witnesses.'

'And I'm sorry you're sad,' Freya said. 'I would hate my dad to go.'

Mark nodded.

'Oh, don't get me wrong,' Daryl continued. 'I'm kinda glad he's gone. It's more of a worry that he might come back. I've told Mum to ring me if he does, and I'll go straight home.'

'Right,' Mark said. 'We still can't go back to the den, so tomorrow, check with your mum that it's okay, and we'll all come up to yours. Don't let on why we're doing it. She's an adult, and she'll not want to feel like we're baby-sitting her, but we are. Everybody agreed?'

They all gave the thumbs-up sign, and got ready to go to their homes, gathering together the assortment of things they had arrived with earlier.

Before they left the bedroom, Daryl spoke. 'Thanks, you lot. Thanks for understanding. You're the best. And now, we've got to find the answer to getting rid of the packet. We can't take it to the police, we've had it too long.'

'No, but we can do what we did when we kind of found Vinnie's body. We can pretend to find the packet.' Dom looked thoughtful as he spoke. 'We can't say we found it in the woods, that's been searched, but we could find it near the recycling point. There's loads of packages around the area, when people can't get them into the bins.'

'We could, but I don't believe they've searched the woods properly. No mention's been made of our den. And they would have asked us about it, if they'd found it. They've assumed somebody's had it away with whatever was in the hole, and I think it's made the search a bit sloppy. If we find it down the bottom end, we might get away with it. It's a fair way from the crime scene, and a fair way from our den. We don't want them doing a second search and finding our place. We'll not have a vote on this yet, have a think about it. We'll talk more tomorrow at Daryl's.'

They trooped downstairs, and Sally waved as they passed her kitchen door. Freya went into the kitchen and gave her mum a hug, then stepped back. 'Love you, Mum,' she whispered. 'Dad wouldn't leave us, would he?'

Sally laughed. 'Of course he wouldn't. What's brought that on?'

'Daryl's dad's left him and his mum.'

'Really? Oh my. I need to give Megan a ring, let her know we're here for her. No, your dad won't be going anywhere.'

The front door closed, and Mark and Dom came into the kitchen. 'Is Daryl okay?'

'A bit quiet. He'll be fine.'

'You're good kids. Don't let him be sad. Make him talk about it. Now go upstairs and wash your hands, tea won't be long. Chicken dippers and rice?'

The three children groaned. 'Can't we have chips?'

'You had chips yesterday.'

'We like chips. We like vinegar. We like tomato ketchup. Just do us chips, Mum, please.' With Freya in this mood, she was hard to resist.

Sally sighed. 'Chicken dippers and chips, it is, then. Fifteen minutes and I want you sitting at that table with clean hands. Think you can do it?'

They nodded, and she grinned. She hoped Daryl would one day be able to laugh and joke again, when he'd got over the initial shock of his dad leaving.

Daryl was feeling fine, now he'd told the others why he was a bit down. He walked up the main road with Sammy and Ella, dropping Ella off first at her front door. Sammy then split off to pass by Vinnie's house, leaving Daryl to finish off the journey alone.

Daryl walked quickly, eager to check that his mum was doing okay. He had received no phone call, but if his dad had returned and hurt her, she maybe wouldn't be able to ring. His imagination was causing chaos in his brain, and, in the end, he was running towards his front door. He burst through, and she turned to smile at him.

'Hello, sweetheart. Chips and egg for tea?'

'Brilliant.' He stared at her, searching for any signs of injury, but there were none. Maybe he had really gone then. There were no sounds from upstairs, no music playing – his dad liked Billy Joel, and it seemed to be on all the time. He had noticed that morning that his dad's coat had disappeared from the hall; it was still missing, and Daryl could only assume it meant his dad hadn't come back.

'Mum, will it be okay if the others come up here tomorrow? We feel a bit guilty about being down at the Brownlow's every day. She always feeds us, must be costing her a fortune.'

Megan laughed. 'Of course you can all come here. Tell you what, we'll nip down to Asda later, get some snacks and stuff in for lunch tomorrow. How does that sound?'

'Sounds brilliant. I'll phone the others in a bit and tell them it's on.'

Sammy split from Daryl, whistling quietly to himself. He no longer felt afraid of passing the Walmsley house; it was an unexpected bonus to finding the body. No longer could Vinnie hold the threat of a good hiding over him. Sammy looked at the front of the house as he passed it and saw someone at the bedroom window, about to close the curtains. A naked man. His first irrational reaction was that it was Vinnie, but then he saw quite clearly who it really was.

Carl Clarkson.

9

Sammy didn't know what to do. Should he ring Daryl? Should he wait until tomorrow? How should he tell him*? I saw your dad at the bedroom window of Aileen Walmsley's house, and he had no clothes on.*

Or shouldn't he say anything at all? Carl Clarkson was a bad man, he had been horrible at the police station, and maybe Daryl wanted to forget all about him. He'd leave it 'til the morning and then make the decision whether to tell or not.

The phone rang, and his mum answered it. He was heading upstairs when she called his name.

'Sammy! It's Daryl for you.'

Decision time. Was this meant as a sign? He had ten seconds to decide.

'Yo, dude. Mum says fine for tomorrow. We're going to Asda to get some stuff for lunch. She wants to get some flowers or something, to take to Mrs Walmsley. She's okay, Dad hasn't been back.'

Sammy could hear the relief in Daryl's voice. He was about to kill that relief with his next few words.

'Daryl, you can't let her go to the Walmsley house.' He looked around to make sure his mum had gone into the kitchen. He didn't want anybody hearing what he had to say.

'What? Why not? Has summat else happened?'

Sammy hunted for the right way to say it. 'Daryl, your dad's there.'

Daryl sat down on the floor with a thud. He could feel his hands shaking, and he clung tightly to the receiver. 'What d'you mean, Dad's there?'

'I saw him, no clothes on, at the bedroom window. He was closing the curtains. Ten seconds later and I wouldn't have seen him.'

There was a long silence as if Daryl were thinking through what Sammy was telling him.

'I can't tell my mum that!' Sammy could hear the difference as the relief turned to anguish in Daryl's voice.

'There's not much you can do about it. Unless you text your dad as you leave Asda and warn him to stay out of the way. That might work.'

'You're sure it was him?'

'Certain. Saw that tattoo on his arm clear as anything. He's definitely there, Daryl.'

'Shit, dude. This is bad news. Perhaps I should tell her...'

'Tell me what?' Megan Clarkson leaned against the kitchen doorjamb.

'Sammy, I'll see you in the morning, bye.' Daryl ended the call abruptly and looked at his mum. He was still on the floor, feeling at a disadvantage.

'What's your father done now?' Megan had obviously heard part, if not all, of the conversation.

'Nothing.' Daryl stood and faced her.

'Daryl... what's your father done that you feel you can't tell me? And don't bullshit me.'

'He's down at the Walmsley house. With no clothes on,' Daryl blurted out the words. He'd never been on the winning side against his mother – she knew when he was lying.

She took in the words then spoke. 'That didn't take him long, did it?'

She turned and walked back into the kitchen, leaving Daryl with an open mouth, and a new respect for his mother.

Once away from her son, Megan gave rein to her thoughts. She wondered if he was with Aileen Walmsley for the sex, or if he was there to pick up the business in which Vinnie Walmsley had been involved. Or both.

Megan felt nothing. The man was a born loser, and she had put up with him for too long; his behaviour towards his son at the police station had been the final straw, and she was glad to be rid. Good luck to Aileen Walmsley, she'd need it.

The sun was already baking the earth when the six of them met at Daryl's house the next day. It put paid to any thoughts of the Shire Brook filling up, with or without the added problem of the swans and ducks, and they sat to talk through the issue once again.

Daryl handed around a packet of biscuits. 'Okay, has anybody come up with a good idea, instead of all the bad ones we've had so far?'

Ella smiled. 'I have.'

Even Freya looked shocked. Ella was their quiet member, although the noisiest when playing Uno.

'What? Is it a good one?'

'I think so,' she said. 'The police will have gone soon, and we can start going back to the den. Why can't we put the stuff back where it came from? Nobody will look there again, 'cos it's not there. Except it will be. We need to clean our fingerprints off the plastic bag that it's in, then wear gloves when we bury it.'

None of them could remember such a long speech from her before.

'Wow!' Mark said.

Ella looked around at the others. 'Well? What do you think?'

Slowly, one by one, they gave the thumbs up sign.

'What if a fox, or a dog, digs it up?'

'It won't matter. It can't be traced back to us if our fingerprints aren't on it, and they'll have to assume they missed it first time around.' Ella had obviously given a lot of thought to it.

Daryl looked pensive. 'I like it; it's a brilliant idea. Well done, Ella. I suggest we go down the beginning of next week and have a scout around. There's a possibility they've found our den, you know. To them, it would just be that, a den. Something kids have always done. It's only to us it's special, so they wouldn't bother telling us if they'd come across it, or even knocked it down.'

'Knocked it down?' Freya looked aghast. 'Don't say that.'

'Freya, if they have, we can build it again. So, don't worry. It's agreed, then? We'll go across to the woods, first thing Monday morning.'

Six thumbs went up. Business was finished.

'I'm not hearing anything much, boss. I've put out the word that I want to know who the kids are, but so far, nothing. I've told people I want a result by tonight.'

Nicolas Grausohn looked at the man recruited into his organisation by Kenny and wondered why Kenny had settled on him. He didn't seem to be the brightest button, although he was easy on the eye. Could that have been the attraction for Kenny?

'I want results, Carl.'

'I know, boss. You'll get them. Somebody must know who they are. Unless, they're not from our area…'

Kenny interrupted. 'Why would they be from a different area? It's a bloody tiny wooded bit. Nobody would travel to go to it.'

'Yeah, you're right,' Carl conceded. 'Leave it with me, boss. I'll lean on a couple of people. See what they know.'

'That should have been done already,' Grausohn said drily. 'Results, Carl, results.'

Carl was shaking when he reached the ground floor. There had been something stronger than merely an implied threat. He had no idea how to get out of it; even Aileen hadn't been able to come up with an answer.

A taxi pulled into the turning circle outside the impressive apartment building, and he flagged it down. He needed a car; he didn't think for a minute that Megan would let him have the car they had shared, and did he really want a bright yellow Astra? It was now a priority, even if it was to make his escape when he couldn't come up with the goods. And that was a definite possibility.

An hour later, he was the owner of a Renault Megane, a conservatively coloured silver, that he hoped would last him longer than the price suggested it might. He drove back to Aileen's, parking on the road that ran around the back of her rear garden. He slipped through the opening in her broken-down fence and up to her back door.

'Well?'

He shook his head. 'He wants results. The thing is, he'll find some way of getting what he wants, and then, he'll see Daryl's name. And if he doesn't click it's my lad, Kenny will. Kenny's seen Daryl with me.'

'You're stuffed.' Aileen said it very simply, and very succinctly.

'Thanks,' he said. 'That's a comfort to know. I've bought a car, in case I have to leg it a bit sharpish. It's parked on that road round the back.'

'You think it'll come to that?'

'Deffo. I've got to take him the answers by tomorrow, or else I've got to go.' He grinned. 'Come with me?'

She snorted. 'I hope you're joking, Carl. You work for the man who shagged the woman who killed my Vinnie. We were never gonna work in the long term. No, I'm going nowhere. I'll be sorry you're gone, though.'

'I'm not gone yet.' He glanced upstairs, and her eyes followed his.

'Half an hour. I've an appointment with the hairdresser later.' She took his hand and led him upstairs.

The hairdresser understood that Aileen couldn't make it. The circumstances were tragic. 'I'll book you in for next week, Aileen. You take care now.'

Aileen grinned at Carl. 'Sorted.'

Kenny drove down to the Asda car park and parked as close to the crime scene as he could get. He lit a cigarette and strolled across the short strip of tarmac to the woods. The tape had been taken down, and there was no longer a police presence.

He didn't want to be seen. After showing them his address the previous week, he'd had a visit from some young copper wanting to know why he was in those woods, miles away from his home address. He'd had to tell the same stupid story about a woman he fancied, who had cancelled their date in Rother Valley when he was en route, so rather than not take the dog for a walk, he'd pulled by those woods and taken her in there. He was shocked to find the police, and its elevation from woods to crime scene.

He didn't want his address showing up in PC Craig Smythe's notebook again, but he likewise didn't want to risk going in those woods without a valid reason. He pulled out his phone and rang Katie.

'I need Fluffy.'

'Okay, no problem. But you know the rules.'

He laughed. 'I do. I promise she'll be fine. What on earth can happen to her in Rother Valley?'

'You want a list?'

'I'll be there in quarter of an hour,' he said, and disconnected.

It took him twelve minutes to cross the city, and Katie opened the door to him, holding Fluffy in her arms, with the lead already attached.

'Have a good time,' Katie said. 'She was at the groomers this morning, so don't let her get mucky.'

He put the dog in the car and drove away. Katie's eyes followed him all the way to the end of the road. He knew she had no idea what he was playing at, but no doubt, one day, he would tell her.

Fluffy was the perfect lady. She sat in the footwell all the way and didn't move. He took hold of her lead before opening the car door, ever mindful of the threat to castrate him if Fluffy didn't return in pristine condition. Once again, he parked near the woods.

They walked across the tarmac strip and into the leafy greenness of the woods. It felt quite cool, a welcome relief from the heat of the afternoon. Kenny initially manoeuvred the dog towards the site where Vinnie had met his end, but Fluffy was having none of it. The hole had been filled in, but it was obvious it was disturbed soil.

'Come on, Fluffy, there's not much to be seen here. We'll have a walk round, see if anything looks off.' He tugged on the pink lead, and the dog followed him.

They trudged through thick undergrowth, with the tiny Bichon Frise eager to enjoy her walk. She wanted to inspect every tree, every random bit of paper or plastic and enjoy the freedom, albeit on the end of a lead.

Kenny stood for a moment and took in the atmosphere. Although the wood was bordered by a busy road on one side, the Asda car park on another, with the additional issue of the police station at the top end, it was quiet. He couldn't hear bees, animals, crickets chirruping… nothing.

'We'll head back, Fluffy,' he said, and turned. His arms flailed, and he landed face first, his foot caught in a tree root. Fluffy ran. Her freedom was now total.

'Shit,' Kenny groaned. 'That hurt. Fluffy! Come back here. Now!'

Fluffy continued to investigate the wood but on her terms. She ran, ignoring the pink lead trailing behind her. She stopped a couple of times to dig in the undergrowth, getting a little grubbier every time she did so. And then, she stopped.

She could see an opening. She could also hear the man coming up behind her, fast. She slipped into the opening and hunted around. She used her nose to bring out some plastic boxes from under the seats and tried to prise off the lids, without success. Frustration led to growling, and Kenny followed the sound. He could hear the damn dog, but he couldn't see her. He stood still and called her name.

The growl seemed to be almost by his side, and he turned to inspect the shrub. He pulled apart the branches, and they actually moved to one side. The little dog was crouching, trying to gnaw its way into a plastic box.

Kenny pulled some branches out of the way and saw the seats.

'Fuck me,' he said. 'It's a fucking kids' den!' He climbed over the mound of branches he had created and grabbed hold of the dog's lead. He lifted her out of the jumble of greenery and tied her to a tree, before going back to investigate.

The box Fluffy had been gnawing clearly contained biscuits, but there were bottles of water, about half a dozen, under what appeared to be a seat. He couldn't help but think what a brilliant little place it was, especially when he sat down on one of the seats and found his eye level was just above a window aperture. For a child, it would have been a perfect observation point. An observation point that looked directly at Vinnie Walmsley's crime scene.

Kenny continued to sit there for a few minutes, working out what had happened here. He knew that this den belonged to the six kids who had found Vinnie's body, but what had they seen?

Did they see Vinnie bury the drugs? Did they see Johanna cut his throat? Did they see somebody dig up the drugs? Or did they dig them up?

Kenny found the tin box almost by accident. He'd heard Fluffy bark and decided it was time to go. His foot caught underneath the seat – he really was a bit big to be sitting in a den for kids – and heard the clang of metal. He reached beneath his legs and pulled out the tin box.

Inside it was a couple of pencils, a biro, a pack of Uno cards and a little notebook. He opened the notebook. Written across the top of two pages were five initials and one name; Daryl, M, D, F, S, and E. He presumed Daryl was written in full because there was another D in the group of kids.

'Bingo, fucking bingo,' he breathed.

He put everything but the notebook back in the box and slipped it into its original hiding place. The book went into his pocket. He pushed some branches to one side and climbed back out of the den. The police had obviously not come across it, because it hadn't been disturbed in any way, but he had to admire the kids; he had walked past it and not seen it. It looked like a shrub growing out of the undergrowth.

He stopped in shock when he saw Fluffy. She had been digging around the base of the sapling; he might have tied her up, but it didn't mean she couldn't try to escape. The white Bichon Frise was now a grey Bichon Frise and definitely didn't look as though she had been to the groomers.

He freed her from the sapling and looked at her. He had no idea what he was going to say to Katie, but whatever it was, her response wasn't going to be pleasant.

He put the dog back in the car and attempted to brush off the dirt. She didn't look any better, and he started the car with a sigh. The music would have to be faced.

The music wasn't pleasant; Katie was livid with him. She banned him from borrowing Fluffy again, charged him fifty pounds for a return visit to the groomers and threw him out of the house. He rubbed his groin and considered he'd got away lightly.

His drive to the penthouse was short, and as he travelled up in the lift, he realised he felt slightly nervous. He was, after all, about to give the names of six kids to a man known for being ruthless; Kenny realised that his interpretation of 'kids' had been 'teenagers', but he now realised they were little kids, kids who played Uno.

How would Nicolas Grausohn react? And how would Kenny react if Grausohn gave the nod to Tommy, as he had done with Johanna Fleischer?

The elevator, spectacular in its lavish interior, drew to a gentle stop, and he stepped out. Standing outside the door, Tommy nodded as he saw him.

'He's expecting you,' he said, and opened the door.

Grausohn was sitting at his desk. 'You have good news?'

'I have the initials of the six children. I only got them half an hour ago, so haven't had time to find full names. That's my next job, but I wanted you to know we have solved a big part of the mystery.'

He reached into his drawer and pulled out an envelope. 'There's ten grand. Another ten grand when I get the surnames. And another twenty when I get one of the kids.'

10

Monday morning started at 5.10 in the Brownlow household. Freya was sick. Her mum sorted everything out, popped her back into the clean sheets and said stay in bed.

When the boys got up, oblivious to the traumas happening with Freya, they clattered downstairs to Sally telling them to be quieter, their sister was sleeping and wouldn't be playing. She needed to rest.

They looked at each other. That meant they were down to four, because they knew Ella wouldn't want to be there without Freya. Maybe that would be better; two less to get caught if things went wrong.

Daryl and Sammy arrived just after nine, nervous and yet happy at finally getting rid of the drugs. Mark had already put the large package into his backpack, aware that they wouldn't really be able to go down to the Wendy house if Freya wasn't with them. He had also rung Ella, and she said she wouldn't go, not without Freya, so the four boys set off armed with gloves borrowed from underneath Megan Clarkson's sink and a pack of baby wipes for cleansing the package.

The shock when they reached the den was evident on all four faces. The immediate reaction was that the police must have found it, but then common sense prevailed. If the police had found it, it would have made their involvement much more suspicious, and DI Roberts would have been straight round with further questions. So, who had found their haven?

'I think we should change the plan,' Mark said slowly. 'Think about this. What if somebody who's looking for the drugs found the den? I'm not sure we should leave them anywhere near here.

And I think we should stay away, like that policewoman said. We're in danger, aren't we?'

He looked around at the others, and their thumbs crept up.

'Let's take everything we have here back home and flatten this. We're not going to be able to use it again, are we?' Daryl was his usual ever-practical self. He and Mark had brought backpacks, so they stuffed as much as they could into them and carried the fleece blankets.

They stamped on the den and scattered the branches around. Nobody spoke. It was too heart breaking.

An hour later, they were back at Daryl's house, feeling no better. Megan had been driving down the road as they walked up, and she handed them a key to get in.

'I'm going to get some food,' she said. 'Make yourselves at home, boys.'

So, they did. Slowly, they came around and tried to decide what to do with the drugs now the original plan wasn't feasible. The only conclusion they drew was that they preferred cheese and onion crisps to salt and vinegar.

'Okay,' Mark said. 'I'll take it to ours and put it back in the oven in the Wendy house.'

'What if we dump it in a waste bin? There's loads of them. Two of them at the shops.' Dom was desperately looking for answers.

'CCTV,' Daryl reminded them. 'We don't want the police to catch us dumping them. I think this is gonna take a lot more thinking about.'

Grausohn looked at the list of names. Bloody kids. Should all be strangled at birth. 'Kenny!'

Kenny popped his head around the door. 'Boss?'

'These kids. Do we know anything?'

'Not yet, boss. I've called Carl in. He's likely to know them.' And then, it hit him with the force of a wrecking ball. Daryl.

He'd met him, Daryl. With Carl. Carl's son. No wonder Carl had been acting stupid. He'd known from the start who the kids were. But now what? He'd bet anything on Carl already having done a runner; he couldn't hand his own son on a platter to Grausohn.

'Kenny? You've thought of something? You know them?'

Kenny lied, to give himself time to think. 'No, it took my mind back to that young kid we had to… dispose of. He was called Darrell, wasn't he?'

'I remember him. Darren, not Darrell. Helped himself to some of our funds. Him and his brother.'

'Yeah, he's the one. They didn't die easy and seeing the name brought it back. Sorry, boss.'

'Is Carl coming in? You've rung him?' Grausohn's German accent was getting stronger by the second, and Kenny knew he was feeling the frustration. Six kids seemed to be getting the better of him, and that couldn't carry on.

'He's on his way, had to go to the dentists first thing. Coming straight here after that.'

'*Gut*. I want to see him as soon as he gets here. Understood?'

'Sure thing, boss. I'll text him and make sure he knows it's urgent.'

Grausohn nodded and waved him out of the door.

Kenny took out his mobile phone and clicked on Messenger. He typed. **I know who Daryl is. Tell me one of the others, and I'll keep your lad out of it. You've been dentist, lied for you. Don't let me down. Get in here ASAP. Send me the name or address NOW.** He attached the photograph he had taken of the Uno score sheet and hit send.

The reply was immediate. **Ella Johnston. 8 Darwin Close. Thanks pal.**

He hesitated momentarily before heading back to Grausohn. 'Clarkson's come up trumps with an address.'

Without further thought, Grausohn growled, 'Get me that child. I'll speak to it.'

'She's a girl, boss.'

'Even better. I'll give her to one of the lads when I've got what I want from her. Take an untraceable car, just in case, and take Tommy with you. So much bloody CCTV these days.'

Kenny felt sick. It was one thing to kill a woman, but a little girl? He headed down to his own car, collecting Tommy on the way. They drove to the car repair shop Grausohn kept for specific activities and swapped cars, driving away in a nondescript Citroen Picasso, big enough to throw a child in the back and subdue her. And Kenny still felt sick.

They found Darwin Close easily and pulled up by the side of the road. Tommy was driving, and Kenny knew this meant he would have to grab the kid. They sat for quarter of an hour, watching the house and trying to formulate a plan for getting her anywhere near them. They couldn't snatch anybody who was probably lain on her bed playing computer games.

And then, the front door opened. The kid wasn't laid on her bed.

Cissie Johnston wasn't convinced she should be letting Ella go down the road to visit Freya, but she'd been miserable all day because of her enforced captivity. But still, a sickness bug…

'Look, little miss miserable, don't stay too long. I want you back here by…' Cissie checked her watch, 'five at the very latest. Are you listening, Ella?'

Ella grinned. 'I'm listening, and I promise. See you later, Mum.'

She walked sedately down the path, picked up her scooter, then turned and waved as her mum closed the door.

Once through the gate, she increased her pace until the scooter was flying down the road. Her ponytail bobbed up and down and gradually the little scooter reached its maximum speed. It had been such a boring day, and now, she felt alive again. There was a possibility that all her friends would be at the Brownlow house, and maybe they would be telling her the drugs were no longer a problem.

She had no idea there was a car containing two men bearing down on her. Equally, the two men had no idea how to orchestrate the snatch, but not to do it was unthinkable. Grausohn wanted the kid, and the kid would be "questioned."

She increased her speed, her white trainer on her left foot beating down on the hot pavement, her thoughts flying ahead of her to seeing Freya and the boys.

She didn't hear the quiet purr of the engine, simply glanced behind her and, without losing speed, pointed the scooter to cross the road.

Tommy hit the brakes, yelling 'shit' as he realised the inevitability of the collision. The tyres screamed as they sought traction on the hot road surface, and both men felt the thud as the sloping bonnet of the Picasso hit Ella, tossing her small body upwards and onto the windscreen. The momentum carried her some yards, before she slid, an inert figure, down the bonnet and onto the road in front of the now stationary vehicle. The scooter came to a rest on the pavement, mangled out of shape.

'Reverse, reverse!' Kenny yelled at the immobile figure in the driving seat. 'Come on, man, we've gotta get out of here. Shit! Come on!' He pulled out his phone and took a picture of Ella, legs at an impossible angle, her hair splayed out around her and covered in blood. The boss would want proof.

Tommy looked blankly at Kenny for a moment and then the look of absolute horror on Kenny's face ignited him.

'Fuckin' 'ell, Kenny, we're in trouble now.' He dropped the car into reverse and sped around the lifeless form lying on the road. The white trainers were stained red, as was the tarmac underneath her. People were running towards her.

The souped-up Picasso was touching seventy miles an hour by the time it was flying past the Brownlow house.

And Freya slept, unaware of the activity outside on the road.

'She's dead.'

'I know she's fucking dead.' Kenny spat out the words, trying desperately to come up with some answers to an impossible question.

He'd seen the kid's face splatter on the windscreen before she'd been catapulted off as the brakes finally brought the car to a screaming halt. He'd seen the blood that seemed to spurt from every part of her… He had no doubt she was dead.

Thank God they'd brought some random car and not one of their own.

Tommy's hands were shaking. 'What do we tell the boss?'

'The truth. The kid ran into us, we didn't run into her.'

'He'll not be pleased.' Now, his voice was shaking as well.

'Well, I'm not fucking jumping for joy,' Kenny growled. 'Get a grip, Tommy. We need another name. That one didn't work out.'

'You're all bleedin' 'eart, you, Kenny.' Tommy was still shaking. 'You'd better drive.'

Kenny laughed. 'Not bloody likely. My fingerprints aren't going anywhere near that steering wheel while we've got blood smeared all over the windscreen. Let's get this back to t'garage, needs a full valet and might need some repairs to that bumper.'

Tommy sighed, pulled at a lever to spray liquid over the windscreen, then jabbed at the wipers, the little girl's blood running down the sides of the glass before disappearing from sight. He then put the car into gear and left the relative security of their parking place, slipping into the mainstream traffic.

DI Roberts looked at the covered body lying on the tarmac road surface and shook his head. The mother was understandably distraught, but they couldn't move the little lass, not yet. Forensics hadn't finished doing their jobs.

He moved across to the group of three women – Sally Brownlow, Cissie Johnston and Megan Clarkson – supporting each other by crying together. Cissie was softly moaning, unable to comprehend that she'd lost her only child.

'Ms Johnston, I'm so sorry for your loss. We have officers going up and down this road checking for CCTV cameras on the houses. We'll find this bloody car, I promise you.'

Cissie couldn't speak. Half an hour earlier, she'd had a daughter. Now, she had nothing. No future, nothing.

Sally pulled her close and held her. 'Cry all you want,' she whispered. 'All you want.'

There was a flurry of movement as the ambulance men were given permission to move the little girl, and Cissie found her voice. She screamed, and Megan and Sally pulled her close and held her tightly.

They loaded Ella into the vehicle, and the three women, horror etched on their faces, watched it go. Everyone stood, jobs forgotten for a moment as they paid their respects to the young victim of the hit and run murder.

'Come home with me,' Sally said.

'I can't.' Cissie's voice came out as a long, low moan. 'My front door isn't locked.'

Megan squeezed Cissie's shoulder. 'Go with Sally. I'll make sure your house is secure. Is the key in the back of the door?'

Cissie nodded and allowed Sally to lead her away, both studiously avoiding the blood congealing on the tarmac.

Freya was waiting in the kitchen, wide-eyed and with bright red cheeks. Her brothers were by her side.

'Mum?' Mark said.

'Let me get Cissie in,' Sally said. 'Mark, can you put the kettle on please?'

She led Cissie through to the lounge, and Freya followed.

'Freya, you look dreadful. Please go back to bed.' Her mum touched her forehead. 'You're burning up.'

'No.' Freya was at her stubborn best. 'Is Ella okay?'

Cissie looked frantically at Sally, as if not wanting to say the words, not really believing them.

Sally hesitated and then knew she had no choice. 'I'm sorry, sweetheart. She was hit by a car that didn't stop.'

'N-o-o-o…' The exhaled word was full of grief. 'Ella's my best friend.'

Cissie sobbed. Sally, unable to decide who to help first, delegated. 'Dom, Mark, take your sister back to bed, please, get her some water which she must drink, and stay with her. I'll be up in a bit.'

'Cissie, here.' Sally handed her a box of tissues. 'I'm going to make us a cup of tea. Or do you want something stronger?'

'Tea will be fine, Sally,' Cissie sobbed, clutching the tissue to her mouth. 'Is this really happening?'

'It is, my love,' Sally said gently. 'I can't begin to imagine how you're feeling, but you can be sure we're all here for you. Will you stay here, tonight? We've a spare bedroom.'

Cissie looked horrified. 'I… I can't go home, I don't want to be there alone.'

'Then stay. It's no trouble. I'll make sure the kids give you some peace.'

She heard the kettle click off and headed for the kitchen. DI Roberts peered through the kitchen window, and she waved him in.

'I understand Mrs Johnston is with you?'

'She is. She's staying here tonight. You want a cup of tea?'

'Thank you, I will. It's hard when…'

'I know,' Sally said, and touched his hand. 'Go through to the lounge. Cissie's in there. I'll bring in the drinks.'

She could hear sobs from upstairs and felt torn. Sobs in the lounge, sobs upstairs; who needed her the most? She went through to the lounge and handed out the drinks before sitting in the armchair.

'Do you know anything further, DI Roberts?'

'We have two independent witnesses who both confirm Ella suddenly veered across the road and didn't see the car until it was too late. However, both also seemed to think the car was tracking her. It kept up with her, travelling much slower than cars normally do going down this road. One of them got the registration.'

'And?'

'False number plates. Again.'

'What do you mean, "again"?' Sally stared at him.

'It's the second case of false number plates in a few days in this area. I'm not saying they're connected, but it seems mighty strange to me.'

'Both hit and runs?'

'No, the first one was connected to the murder of Vinnie Walmsley.'

Sally held her hand to her mouth. Her eyes flitted between Cissie and Roberts. She was scared. 'Pardon me for pointing out the obvious, but I can see the bloody connection.'

Roberts hung his head for a moment, then looked at the two women. 'So can I, Mrs Brownlow, so can I. What we don't have is a proven connection. I'm going to find one.'

Cissie's hands were shaking as she picked up her cup. 'If the connection is that our children found Vinnie's body, you'd better prove it pretty damn quick, Detective Inspector, because there are still five children we have to protect.'

She looked haunted. Her pretty face was blank, and Roberts knew this was only the beginning for her. She would have many bad days in the next few weeks. He had to find these killers before anybody else came up against them.

His phone rang, and he quickly took it from his pocket. 'Excuse me, ladies, I have to take this,' he said, and moved towards the kitchen. They could hear his muttered tones, and then, he returned to the lounge.

'I'm sorry, I'll have to leave my tea. We've managed to find two CCTV systems that worked, so I'm heading in to see if they're of any help. I promise I'll keep you informed, Mrs Johnston, and I really am sorry for your loss.'

Cissie nodded in acknowledgement of his words, and he left. He stopped by the crime scene and had a brief word with the forensics team, telling them to keep the road closed for as long as they needed it like that and to ignore complaints from the locals. There had already been a few.

He arrived at the police station a couple of minutes later and headed for his office. They were setting up the CCTV taken from the two houses, and he stood by the window and allowed them to get on with it. He knew he was going to see the actual collision, and his stomach churned at the thought. That pretty little lass, the quiet one of the group of kids, dead. Hard to come to terms with, but he'd find her killer if it was the last thing he did.

11

Grausohn was angry. The ineptitude of his two senior men was astounding. All they had to do was bring him a little girl. A little girl, for fuck's sake. How difficult could that be? Clearly too difficult for these brain-dead planks.

He watched as they entered his room, the expressions on their faces telling him the whole story.

'Who was driving?' he barked.

'Me, boss,' Tommy admitted. 'But she drove into us.'

'A little girl on a scooter drove into you two clowns, and you're blaming her?' The bark had turned into a growl.

'We couldn't stop the car quick enough,' Tommy tried to explain.

'Get out,' Grausohn said. 'Get out of my sight.'

Tommy turned and headed towards the door. Grausohn nodded at Kenny and silently drew his finger across his throat. Kenny nodded back and followed Tommy out of the door.

The lift arrived, and Kenny placed a finger across Tommy's lips. They got out on the ground floor and left the building.

Heading for Kenny's car, Tommy tried to speak.

'Not yet, mate,' Kenny said.

Silently, they climbed into the car, and Kenny drove away.

He drove for a couple of miles and then pulled into the car park of a McDonald's.

Still without speaking, they left the claustrophobia of the car behind them and hit the noise engendered by numerous children in the fast food outlet.

'Big Mac?' Kenny asked.

Tommy nodded and went to find a table.

When Kenny carried the tray to the table, Tommy finally spoke. 'Is this my last supper, then?'

'According to the boss, yeah.'

'All these bleedin' years I've done his dirty work…'

'The difference is, this could finish him. He's into this one with big money. Bigger than he's ever been before. It seems that package that Vinnie had was the first of several, and that one was big enough.'

'And did Vinnie have it all stashed away?'

'Doubt it. I imagine they did a trial run with him, before letting him loose with the rest. I do know Grausohn paid up front, though. Now it seems whoever was supplying the stuff to Grausohn has shut up shop, doesn't like publicity like this. They've dropped below the radar, with the money, whether temporarily or not. Somebody's got to pay, and it's you. You killed the kid.'

'She killed herself.' The stubbornness showed in Tommy's voice.

'I know. It's why we're here and not driving into some woods where I make you dig your own grave then slit your throat. I am going to have to hurt you, pour some blood on you, and you will have to dig the grave, but it's for a photo shoot. Then, you'll have to go, somewhere where he'll never hear of, or see you, again.'

There was a long silence.

'Sh…i…i…t…' The expletive was long and drawn out, as Tommy sucked in his breath.

'Go, after I've *killed* you. Send for the family a few weeks later. Give Grausohn enough time to go around and see them to say how sorry he is that some lowlife from another gang offed you, and he'll hand over a hefty pay-packet and never think about you again. You're well out of it, mate. But don't go to Spain. Too many people know you and him. Try a little place in France, or somewhere. And go legit.'

Tommy dropped his head. 'Will you look out for the family, 'til I can get them to me?'

'I will. Don't tell them the plan until you're ready to get them to move. They've all got to believe you're dead, so they don't make mistakes with Grausohn. If the boss suspects you're not dead, I will be.'

'How you gonna explain not having a body to be buried? My Fran will want a proper send-off.'

'I imagine he'll come up with the usual – shot or stabbed on the ferry and dumped overboard. Whoever did it contacted him to tell him, and he's now going after them. It's his usual line when he gets rid of somebody. The photo I take of you in the grave will be for his eyes and personal files only.'

The Big Mac sat untouched on the table, and Kenny understood why Tommy had no appetite. Kenny picked up his own burger and bit into it. Speaking with his mouth full, he said, 'Of course, I could always do it for real.'

Tommy looked shocked. 'Bastard. That been the plan all along, then? Feed me bullshit so I go along quietly, then shoot me?'

Kenny laughed. 'You'd be dead already if I intended killing you. I wouldn't have wasted money buying you a Big Mac, would I? Eat up. We've some fake killing to do. You've been my mate for too long for me to be the one to kill you, so it's not going to happen, whatever he thinks.'

Tommy reluctantly picked up the burger, and ten minutes later, they were back on the road.

Kenny pulled up at a butcher's in Rotherham and returned a minute later with a carrier bag in his hand. He placed it in the boot, and they drove a couple more miles before turning off the main road and driving down a track leading deep into a large wooded area of mainly coniferous trees.

Kenny stopped the car, and they climbed out. He opened the boot and handed a spade to his friend. 'Pick your last resting place and start digging,' he said with a laugh. 'I'll bring the blood.'

Tommy gave a salute in acknowledgment and walked a few yards deeper into the woods, looking for softer soil. He dug, and the two men chatted, mainly about football and the upcoming new season. It took some time to dig the grave, taking it in turns to wield the spade, until it was deep enough for the fake burial. They both knew it had to be convincing.

Finally, Tommy leaned on the spade. He was sweating and feeling a little disgruntled that Kenny hadn't offered to help more with the strenuous backbreaking work of the final few inches where the soil was more compacted. He hadn't said anything; he knew Kenny was putting his own life on the line if the plan backfired, and he was grateful for his friend's help in getting him away from Grausohn's revenge.

'Think that'll do?'

Kenny inspected the pit. 'Lie down and let's make sure. It's got to be convincing. Got to be deep enough. Pass me the spade and get comfy,' he laughed. 'Sorry I didn't think to bring a pillow.'

Tommy shook his head and smiled before handing up the spade. 'Always the clown,' he said, and lowered himself into the grave. He wriggled his hips. 'Comfy enough.'

'Good,' Kenny said, and fired one shot into Tommy's chest. His eyes looked momentarily shocked, and then, the light faded.

Kenny pulled out his phone and took the obligatory picture, quickly covered the body with the excavated earth and dragged some twigs across it. He walked over the area to flatten the raised mound, then climbed back into the car.

He'd miss Tommy.

Kenny handed the phone across to Grausohn, who smirked.

'Well done,' he said, before passing it back. 'We'll wait a couple of days, then go see his woman. Tell her I sent him to France on business, and somebody in the Dover gang didn't like him. Chucked him overboard. Send me the picture.'

'Sounds like a plan, boss,' Kenny agreed. He kept the smile from his face.

'Right, back to business. I want the stuff back, and I need one of those kids. Get Clarkson in here. Let's see what he knows. He must know who that girl's mates are.'

He reached into the desk drawer, and Kenny stiffened. The man was unpredictable. Taking out an envelope, he threw it across the table. 'A little bonus. You've done well. Now, get me a kid.'

'Thanks, boss,' Kenny said.

He left the room and went down to the ground floor in the lift, feeling relieved it had been an envelope and not a gun that came out of Grausohn's desk drawer.

Sitting in the car gave Kenny thinking time. For the first time since meeting up and joining up with Grausohn, he felt at a loss. He'd killed before; killing Tommy had been the hardest. They'd been through some bad times together and had shared life almost as brothers. But killing kids was another matter altogether. Would he have been able to stop in time to save the Johnston kid? He doubted it. And on that simple fact alone, he was alive, and Tommy was dead. Also, he was several thousand pounds richer. It was time to take the kids out of the equation by removing the one person who had knowledge of their names.

Kenny took out his phone and rang Carl Clarkson. He heard the hesitant 'Hello, pal' and knew that Carl was in deep shit, in a place he wouldn't want to be sharing.

'If you can't give me another kid's name, I know Daryl's your lad.'

There was a short bout of coughing, and then, the call was disconnected.

Kenny put himself inside Carl's head and knew he was about to run. Possibly with his missus, and Daryl. He slipped the car into drive, reflecting that he wouldn't really want his own manual car back. He could get used to lazy driving. He headed in the direction of Carl Clarkson's house, hoping he would be in time.

He stopped a hundred yards away from his destination. He could see the rear end of the yellow car from where he was parked.

He waited patiently; it briefly occurred to him that the biggest part of his job involved patience – waiting for people to arrive who owed Grausohn money, waiting for information that could be passed on to the boss, waiting.

Quarter of an hour later, he saw the tail lights of the car glow red, then switch off. He started up his own car and prepared to move. The Astra reversed off the hardstanding and paused briefly before swinging out onto the road.

He followed it, knowing that sooner or later he would have an opportunity to stop it.

The Astra left the estate behind and headed towards the M1; Kenny kept three cars behind it. He saw the indicator come on, so activated his own. The yellow car pulled onto the garage forecourt, to the petrol pumps. He drove through and pulled up, ten yards back from the exit.

He wasn't surprised to see a woman get out. He could see a child in the front seat and guessed Carl was laid on the backseat, keeping out of sight. That was good – if he were lain on the backseat, he wouldn't have a seatbelt on. Kenny smiled.

Petrol paid for, the woman returned to the car, clutching a bottle of water. She started the engine and drove towards the exit.

Kenny let her pull out, and then, he moved. The traffic was light, and he waited until there were three cars between them before moving again.

Megan drove carefully, aware that things had changed. She didn't normally have her eleven-year-old son in the front, that had always been either her or Carl, and Daryl had been safely strapped in the rear seat.

Their decision to go get Daryl his new school shoes, ready for the next term starting, had been a spur of the minute thing; he was deeply upset by Ella's death, and Megan thought it might take his mind off the horror of it.

Daryl was quiet. He knew their parents were worried; they didn't want the remaining five children to move outside without them. This compounded the issue of the bag of cocaine, because now, they couldn't even discuss its removal.

He glanced in the wing mirror and saw the dark grey car that had been with them since leaving home. Why hadn't it disappeared when they pulled in for petrol? He was sure it was the same car.

'We're being followed.' He smiled at his mother.

'Really?' She returned his smile.

'Think so. Dark grey car, think it's a Mondeo but not sure, about three cars back. Been with us since we left home.'

'It can't have, numpty, we stopped for petrol.'

'Huh-uh.'

She glanced in her wing mirror, to locate the car. 'Let's see then.' She laughed. 'There's a road off to the left in a minute called Pocket Handkerchief Lane. Nice road, bit bumpy. Let's see if it follows us down there.'

'This is good,' Daryl grinned. 'It's like James Bond. Floor it, Mum. Let's see what he does.'

'Is it a he?'

'There was a man in it when it waited in the petrol station for us to go out first.'

Suddenly, it wasn't a game. Daryl's words made Megan shiver. She decided not to indicate the left turn onto the quaintly named road; she simply accelerated around the corner into it, negotiated two large potholes and then put her foot down. The two cars that had been immediately behind her continued on the main road, the driver of the first one having used the horn to indicate his annoyance.

The Mondeo didn't indicate, either, but it did follow her. She couldn't increase her speed; the road was badly surfaced, and the last thing she needed was something to happen to the car. She knew there were houses further along, once she had passed the wind farm, and she saw that as safety.

Megan's mind was racing. This was something to do with Carl, she knew it. He was into something really bad, and It seemed that his family were about to pay for it.

'Mum?' Daryl looked scared.

'Daryl, there's a bend coming up. Take off your seatbelt, and slightly open your door. Be careful. Hold on to something, I don't want you falling out. I'll slow down, and you get out and run. Make your way to a house, they'll help you. Get my mobile. DI Roberts' number is in it. Ring it as soon as you're moving.'

Daryl reached down for the phone, thinking how useless his own was without that number in it. He put his phone into Megan's bag.

'You've got my phone, Mum,' he said, his voice trembling. 'Take care.' He slipped Megan's mobile into his pocket and pulled the zip top closed. He didn't want it falling out.

He clicked his seatbelt and opened the door a fraction. The car slowed, and he waited until the right moment. He tumbled out onto the grass verge and felt instant pain in his shoulder. He heard the car door slam, and his mother sped away. He rolled down into the ditch and waited, unzipping the pocket and removing the phone. The dark grey car shot past him, picking up speed.

Kenny's face was grim. She'd obviously spotted him, and Carl was probably giving instructions from the backseat, but Kenny had reckoned without her having to slow down for that last sharp bend. Now, she would be easy to catch. Three of them, all at one go. Shame about the kid, he didn't deserve this. With Carl gone, it lessened their chances of finding the surnames of the kids, and no more would have to die. He didn't agree with killing kids.

He could see the houses in the distance and knew he had to finish it now. He put his foot down hard and slammed his left wing into the right bumper of the Astra. The yellow car took off, rose into the air, and flipped, three or four times. He only saw three, he was gone by the fourth turn that crushed the one occupant left in the car.

Kenny smiled. Job done.

Daryl was crying on the phone as he tried to tell DI Roberts what had happened, and then, he screamed as he heard the heart-breaking sound of the car overturning.

'Daryl! Daryl!' Roberts was shouting down the phone at the child. He had heard the sound of metal against road, down the phone. 'Stay where you are. We're coming to get you. Don't go to anyone who isn't a policeman. Promise me. Hang on.'

Daryl heard Roberts tell somebody to get on to the fucking Dinnington police and get them out to Pocket Handkerchief Lane, and then, he spoke once again into the phone.

'Listen to me. Are you hidden from the road?'

'I'm in a ditch,' Daryl sobbed.

'Then, I need you to stay there. Police will be with you in two minutes, I promise. Stay in that ditch. I'll come and get you myself when I get there. Listen out for me shouting your name. I'll call you Charlie. Only answer to Charlie, not Daryl. Understand?'

'Okay,' he sniffled. 'Find my mum.'

'I will,' Roberts said, hoping he wasn't lying. 'Five minutes, Daryl, five minutes, and I'll be with you. But you must stay in that ditch.'

'Okay,' Daryl said, and disconnected. He curled down even lower into the ditch, and then, he heard the first sirens and saw the blue lights. He remained still. DI Roberts would get him. DI Roberts would find his mum, get her off to hospital, if she needed it. He guessed he wasn't going to be getting his new shoes today. He brushed the tears away from his face and began to shake. Every limb felt like jelly, and his shoulder was hurting so much. He hoped his mum wasn't hurting.

Charlie, that was what he had to listen out for, Charlie, not Daryl. When he heard Charlie, the nightmare would be over.

12

Cissie Johnston and Sally Brownlow walked back up the main road toward Cissie's home. Sally had offered to go and feed the cat, but Cissie insisted she needed to go to her own home. She had to get it over with, that first footfall knowing Ella wasn't going to be there waiting for her.

Cissie retrieved the key that Megan had brought to her after securing the house and inserted it into the front door. She hesitated, and Sally put her arm around her, giving her the support she needed.

'I'm here for you,' Sally said gently. 'Do you want me to go in first?'

Cissie shook her head and turned the key. She pushed open the door and let out a small cry.

Ella's night-time teddy was on the stairs, where it lived during the day until it was time to take it back to bed. Cissie turned and buried her head into Sally's shoulder, sobs exploding from her, her slight frame shaking as if it couldn't hold up any longer.

Cissie lifted her head, spent and drained. 'I'm sorry.' She was broken.

'Hey, come on. Let's go in. We're all here for you. You don't need to be on your own until you're ready.'

Cissie moved towards the stairs and picked up the teddy. 'Mr Grumps can go with me.'

'And so he should.' Sally smiled at the still-distraught woman. She had no idea if she was handling things properly. She'd never had to deal with a woman who had lost the only person in her life who mattered to her.

They went into the kitchen, and Cissie poured away water that had been left on the kitchen table, then immediately re-filled the glass. She took a long drink, then asked if Sally wanted anything.

'Water, please,' Sally responded. 'I'll get it.'

Glasses were in the first cupboard she checked, and they both sat at the table cradling their drinks.

'What do I do next?'

'I'm not sure. I think you have to wait until they tell you Ella's body has been released, and then, you can organise the funeral.' Sally reached across and clasped her friend's hand. 'I'm here for you, and I'll help,' she said gently. 'Is Ella's dad in the picture?'

Cissie shook her head. 'Not really. He didn't want to know when I told him I was pregnant, so I moved to a different part of the city, and I don't think he even knows what I had. I've no idea where he is now, but I do know where he used to live. Surely I don't have to tell him?'

'That's up to you, Cissie. I wouldn't, but you're not as hard as me. You have time to think about it.'

Cissie sat deep in thought, occasionally wiping a tear from her cheek. She stood and took the glass to the sink, rinsed it out and stood it on the drainer.

The cat flap clattered as Misty heard her mistress rattle the cat food, and Cissie placed the dish carefully on the floor before refilling the water dish.

'I'll go and get a few things,' she said with a sigh, 'and we'll head back to yours, if that's okay. There's more food than usual in the cat dish, so she will be okay now. I thought I might be able to stay here, but I can't. It's too soon. Is that okay?'

'Cissie, you stay with us as long as you need to.'

Sally watched as her friend left the kitchen and went upstairs. She couldn't do anything to help her, other than be there, and she could damn well do that.

'Charlie? Charlie?' At the sound of Dave Roberts' voice, Daryl stood.

'I'm here,' he called, and waved with his right arm. His left shoulder was too painful to move.

Roberts scrambled down the bank, landing in the ditch with a thud. 'You okay, Daryl?'

Daryl shook his head. 'I've hurt my shoulder. Have you got my mum?'

'I can see two ambulances, but I came straight for you. Let's get you back up to the road, and then, I'll see what I can find out. We'll get the paramedics to take a look at that shoulder.'

Roberts half carried Daryl up the incline and back onto the closed-off road, waving a paramedic over.

The woman led Daryl away, limping, to the ambulance and sat him inside while she checked him out. His knee was badly swollen and causing him discomfort. She laid him on the stretcher bed and placed an oxygen mask over his face.

'Breathe this in, Daryl, it will help with the pain.'

'But my mum…'

'Somebody will be here soon to tell you whatever you want to know.' Her voice was soothing, and he felt the pain lessening. She stayed with him, monitoring him, talking in a gentle way until he felt relaxed. He wanted to see his mum.

Roberts was at the other scene, the one with the upturned car. The car with Megan Clarkson's body still in it, and a lot of blood.

She had saved her son's life, there was no doubt about that, but at the expense of her own. And now, Roberts had the challenging task of breaking the news to Daryl. Ideally, the lad's father should be the one doing that, but he had seen the intelligence in Daryl, and Roberts knew he would have to be honest with him.

He stayed a few minutes longer and then walked back to the ambulance containing a much more comfortable Daryl. He climbed the step into the body of the vehicle and sat across from the young boy. Looking at the paramedic, he saw her nod. He took hold of Daryl's hand.

'How's Mum?'

Roberts paused for a heartbeat and then spoke. 'I'm sorry, Daryl, your mum didn't make it.'

Daryl's eyes widened. 'What do you mean? She's dead?'

Roberts couldn't simply say yes, he couldn't. 'The car overturned...'

Daryl's eyes filled with tears. First, Ella, now, his mum.

'Daryl, I need you to think. The car that was chasing you, did you get the registration? Something about it?'

Daryl didn't want to think about anything but his mum, but he sensed the urgency in Roberts' words.

Daryl pulled away the oxygen mask and closed his eyes. 'It was a dark grey, quite posh-looking car, I think a Mondeo, but I'm not sure.' He hesitated. 'The registration I'm seeing is JWW 51KA.'

Roberts wrote it down and stared at it. 'This isn't a reg number. Did the plate look odd?'

'No, that's in the wing mirror. You need to read it the other way 'round. I thought it best to tell you how I saw it, so I didn't get it wrong. I did see the man, though. I got a good look at him when he waited to let us pull out of the petrol station.'

'Daryl Clarkson, you're a genius. I'm so, so sorry about your mum. I have to go now to find your dad and tell him. Let him know where you are. Is he at home?'

'No, Mum threw him out. I think he's living with Vinnie Walmsley's mum.'

Dave Roberts hoped his face didn't show the shock he was feeling. When Aileen Walmsley had been interviewed, she had laughed aloud at the idea of a partner in her life.

'How long has he been with her?' He was trying to be careful with the questioning. The boy had enough to cope with.

'Two days, I think. Have you got to tell him?' He sobbed, great heaving sobs that made Roberts lean forward and hold him as gently as he could, aware of the shoulder injury.

'I have to tell him,' he explained. 'He's your parent. He has to know. He'll want to know.'

His brain was racing. Three deaths, clearly all linked, and it seemed that Carl Clarkson was tied closely to all of them.

'I have to go, Daryl, now that I know you're safe, but I'm going to send Heather Shaw with you in the ambulance. She'll stay with you, she won't leave you alone. And I'll get your dad to you as soon as I find him. You're a brave lad, Daryl, and I promise we'll find whoever did this to you and your mum.'

He climbed down from the ambulance and immediately patched the now-reversed registration into the station. He received the answer he expected. False number plates. Three different vehicles, three false number plates. This wasn't a small operation. This was someone with enough backing to hold a fleet of vehicles that couldn't be traced. And he'd stake his reputation on it being drugs and not cash that had been buried in that hole underneath Vinnie Walmsley's head.

Aileen Walmsley saw the police car pull up outside. Carl had decided to wait 'til after dark before leaving, and they were cuddled up on the sofa, him watching the television, her reading her newest book. The slam of the car door caused her to look up.

She sighed. 'It's the police again, Carl. You'd better go upstairs. They'll be wanting to tell me something else about Vinnie.'

Carl stood and headed for the hallway. He was at the top of the stairs when Roberts spoke. 'I need you to get Carl Clarkson, Ms Walmsley.'

'He's not—'

'Yes, he is. Stop pratting about, Aileen. Is he upstairs?'

She didn't answer but opened the door wider to allow him access.

'Mr Clarkson? Get down here please. I need to speak with you urgently.'

There was silence, no sound of movement.

'Carl!' Aileen shouted. 'Get the fuck down here pronto, or I'll send the DI up there.'

There was the sound of a door opening, then a curse as Carl hurt himself on something. He limped to the top of the stairs. 'What?'

'Can you come downstairs, please, Mr Clarkson?' Roberts remained polite.

Carl continued to limp as he came down the stairs. 'Fucking door, stubbed my fucking toe,' he grumbled.

'Into the lounge, please, sir,' Roberts insisted, secretly hoping the toe was broken.

Carl lounged on the sofa and waited. He didn't like this one, this Roberts bloke. He guessed he was pretty smart.

Dave Roberts sat down in the chair opposite Daryl's dad and waited for the smart alec comments he suspected were about to come out of Carl Clarkson's mouth.

When they didn't, he spoke. 'Mr Clarkson, I'm sorry to have to inform you that your wife, Megan Clarkson, died in a car accident earlier today.'

Shock was all over his face, and Roberts knew Carl Clarkson had known nothing of the events.

'Megan? Dead?' He was spluttering. 'And Daryl? Was he with her?'

'Yes, he was. He has an injury to his shoulder. His mother slowed down and made him get out of the car before she was rammed. Her car overturned. She saved his life.'

'Where is he now?' Carl stood, casting his eyes round wildly, as if looking for clothing or shoes to get him on his way to his son.

'He's been taken to the Children's Hospital. Do you have transport?'

'No, my wife had the car.'

Roberts noticed the look of surprise on Aileen's face, and he filed the information away in his brain for later.

'I can take him, DI Roberts,' she said.

'I want to know more.' Carl's attitude was changing. The bullying that Roberts had witnessed when the children had been in the station was re-surfacing.

'What do you want to know, sir?'

'Who fucking rammed the car, for a start.'

'We don't know. Your son remembered the registration, but they were false plates. We know it was a man behind the wheel, and that your son saw him, so maybe we'll know more when he's looked at some photographs.'

'I'll go see him. Aileen, get ready. I'll make him fucking remember who's done this.'

'No, you won't, Mr Clarkson. Daryl doesn't actually want to see you, but my DC is with him, and she won't be leaving his side. She has instructions to arrest you if you upset Daryl in any way. I can assure you, we'll find some charge that will stick.'

'He won't upset Daryl, DI Roberts. I'll see to that.' Aileen's voice was unyielding, and Carl slumped backwards.

Roberts stood. 'I'll be in touch, Mr Clarkson. Don't leave the area, will you? I may have some questions.'

They stood together at the window and watched as the driver held open the rear door for Roberts. The car pulled silently away, and still, they hadn't spoken.

Carl turned, and then, Aileen spoke. 'Shithead.'

'What?'

'I said shithead. That kid of yours found my lad, took the police to him, and you couldn't bloody care less about him. You only want to go see him to find out what he knows, not how he is, and I tell you what, shithead, Roberts knows that. That's why he's put a DC with Daryl, to protect him from you. And you seriously need to think about why your Megan's died. She's nothing like you. I reckon that feller who rammed her thought it was you in that car. Now, your lad is an orphan, 'cos you don't want him, do you?'

'Of course I want him,' Carl blustered. 'He's my boy.'

'No, he's not. He's Megan's boy. He'll never be yours. And it's irrelevant whether you want him or not, 'cos he don't want you. Now, get dressed, and I'll take you to see him. I'm warning you, though. One word wrong to that little lad, and you're on your own.'

Kenny felt good. That was the second time he'd used that manoeuvre to tip over a car, and this effort was more spectacular than the previous one. Clarkson couldn't have escaped death with this one; shame about the rest of his family, but now the kids' names could die alongside him. Grausohn would write that avenue off. He'd try to find some another way of getting his money back.

He drove the car into the car repair shop, and the mechanic strolled over to him. 'Kenny.'

'Ross.'

'What you done this time, then?' The mechanic bent down to inspect the front wing.

'Hit a lamp post.'

'Two lamp posts in two days, then,' Ross observed drily.

'I could do with a replacement. What we got in?' Kenny looked around, hoping for another automatic.

'Depends,' Ross drawled. 'You going for a hat trick of lamp posts? If you are, you can have that little Fiesta in the corner.'

Kenny wasn't sure if he was joking. He hoped he was. 'What about the Jag? Is that good to go?' He knew Tommy had been in some sort of trouble with it, but that had been a couple of weeks earlier.

'It is, but you're not taking it.' Ross fished some keys out of his pocket and threw them towards Kenny. 'Take the Audi, and I don't want a scratch on it when you bring it back. Understood?'

Kenny flinched. 'As if. Thanks, Ross.'

Kenny walked over to the Audi and climbed into the driver's seat. It was while he was adjusting the seat and the mirrors that he heard his phone ping. It was a message from Katie, saying that a woman he'd dated some years earlier was trying to find him and had contacted her via Facebook. She'd passed his email address on to her. Was that okay?

'For fuck's sake,' he growled. What now? Katie was obviously determined to find him a woman, and a few years earlier, when he wasn't sure himself, that might have worked, but not now, not now he'd got Billy.

Who is she?
Messenger thing said Cecily Ann.
Thanks very much, Katie. Can't remember her.
Wait for email, dickhead. Then you might.

He switched off his phone, glaring at it. He threw it onto the seat at the side of him and edged out of the garage. Ross held up a finger as if to remind him of no damage to the car, and Kenny pulled out, heading for home. He had no intentions of telling Grausohn what he'd done, just be there to commiserate that he'd lost a valuable resource in Carl Clarkson. He was the only one who knew who the kids were.

He pulled the Audi onto the drive, and Billy came out to greet him. He kissed him and then looked at the car.

'Wasn't that a Mondeo earlier?'

'It was, slight mishap with a lamp post, so now, it's an Audi.'

'Just like magic,' Billy mused. 'You must have a very understanding boss, is all I can say.'

'Fancy eating out? Or have you cooked?'

'We can go out if you want,' Billy said. It occurred to him that his love looked a little frazzled, and a nice meal at the Chequers or somewhere might sort him out. Maybe the lamp post had been a bigger obstacle than Kenny was letting on.

'I'll have a shower first.' Kenny entered the hall, dropped his phone onto the antique console table after re-activating it, and climbed the stairs.

'Want your back washing?' Billy called after him.

'Thought you'd never ask.' Kenny grinned. 'That'll do me a power of good.'

Billy followed him upstairs, and a few seconds later, the shower was running.

Neither of them heard the ping as the phone received an email from cecilyann2008@inbox.co.uk.

13

Daryl had broken his clavicle. He didn't know if he was lucky to have got away with only that injury, or unlucky that he had any injuries at all. It didn't hurt so much now that his arm was in a sling and they'd given him some medication, but it was uncomfortable. He couldn't rest properly, because it triggered the pain.

And then, to make matters worse, his father arrived. He felt Heather stiffen, and then, she leaned across to him. 'Your dad's here, sweetheart, I can see him at the nurses' station. I'll control him, don't worry.'

Daryl gave a slight nod and then instantly regretted it. It sent a shooting pain down his arm.

Carl walked through the door and looked around. 'Private room, eh?'

Heather remained in her seat; she wasn't going to stand for this thug. 'Mr Clarkson, the chairs are down the corridor.'

He mumbled something under his breath and went out the door in search of two chairs.

Aileen smiled at Daryl. 'Hi. Is there anything you need, Daryl? Drinks, sweets, magazines?'

He shook his head. 'No thanks, Mrs Walmsley. I'm fine. Have you heard about my mum?'

'I have, Daryl, and I'm so sorry. Your dad will be looking after you from now on.'

'What?' Daryl looked horror-stricken, and Heather stood.

'That's enough, Mrs Walmsley. Nothing has been decided about Daryl's future, and I'm sure that when the time comes, the judge will consider Daryl's feelings on the matter.'

'Sorry.' Aileen looked shocked at Daryl's reaction. 'I didn't realise…'

Carl arrived back with two stacking chairs, and the atmosphere lightened a little. He seemed genuinely interested in how his son was feeling, but Daryl responded with very few words. He clearly didn't want this man anywhere near him, and after half an hour of strained conversation, Aileen suggested that they leave Daryl to get some sleep.

Carl jumped up immediately, gathered the two chairs into one bundle and departed at speed down the corridor.

Aileen leaned forward and kissed Daryl on the cheek. 'I'm so sorry about your mum, love, she was a lovely lady. If you need anything, this is my number.' She slipped a tiny piece of paper into his hand. 'Anything at all.'

'I'm sorry about Vinnie,' Daryl whispered. 'We're the same now, aren't we? Both lost important people.'

'We are.' She smiled. 'But we'll get through it. Together, if you want.'

He smiled back at her, but by the time Aileen and his father had walked the length of the ward, his smile had turned to tears.

Heather held him best she could, but all she could do was wait for the tears to stop. This little kid was broken, and she was damned if that father of his was going to make it worse.

Billy and Kenny arrived at the pub and ordered a lemonade and a pint. The waiter handed them menus and went away to get their drinks. The atmosphere was peaceful, and Kenny thought how much he appreciated that, after the day he'd had. It had been strange working without Tommy, for a start.

He wondered if the boss would promote somebody from the ranks or bring somebody new in. He hoped it would be someone from the ranks – Kenny had recruited most of them. He should start tomorrow drip-feeding a couple of names to Grausohn, see what the reaction was.

The waiter handed the lemonade to Billy and the beer to Kenny, then stood patiently while they chose their meals, only to change both choices before making their final decisions.

'Queers,' he muttered as he walked away.

'He won't get a tip at the end.' Billy grinned. The comment hadn't been far under his breath, so he knew the waiter would hear.

Billy leaned towards Kenny. 'You want to talk about what's wound you up?'

'Nah, not really. Not yet, anyway. Maybe in a couple of days.'

'That's fine,' Billy said. 'I'm here when you're ready. You doing anything next Monday evening?'

'I'll check.' He took his phone out of his pocket. 'Have you got something planned for us?'

'The cinema, so it's nothing we have to do on Monday. I thought I'd try to pin you down.'

Kenny looked at his screen and saw the email icon with a small 1 on it. He checked his appointments first; he was free Monday evening.

'Then put it in your diary,' Billy said. 'But as I said, it's moveable if something crops up.'

Kenny loved the way Billy understood the complexities of his life. He could tell him anything without him being judgmental; he knew he would tell him about the little girl, and about the Clarkson family. He wasn't ready to talk yet.

He typed in *cinema,* then pressed the email icon.

In retrospect, he should have waited. Possibly until the year 2026. Possibly until after his death.

Cecily Ann was Cissie.

Cissie, the girl he'd used as he'd tried to make decisions about his own sexuality. The girl who had made the decision for him by telling him she was pregnant. The girl who had shown him that he couldn't spend the rest of his life married to a woman; it was unthinkable. And he had run. He had left Katie's house, had found a small flat and hidden away for nearly a year, scared he would bump into the ever-expanding waistline that was Cissie Johnston.

It seemed she, too, had left the area, because he had never heard from her again. He had always assumed she aborted the kid, but the email gave the lie to that supposition.

The kid had grown up into one smart cookie, a little girl called Ella, now nine years old and dead.

He read most of the email, then leaned over and retched.

'Toilets,' Billy whispered. 'Now.'

Kenny pushed his chair back and almost ran for the gents' toilets. He thrust the phone at Billy as he passed him, and Billy picked it up.

He stared at the email, read it through once, then re-read it.

Dear Kenny,
I have some sad news to tell you. Our daughter, Ella, has died in a road accident. A car hit the scooter she was riding, and she died instantly. The car didn't stop. It is now in the hands of the police, of course, but I wanted you to know because she was your child too. I know you didn't want to know her, but the truth is, I didn't abort her as you suggested, I continued with the pregnancy, and I have brought her up single-handedly. She was my life. I am bereft now she has gone, she was a beautiful star.

I can't do anything about a funeral until I get permission from the police, but I will let you know, in case you want to pay final respects to her. If you had met her, you would have loved her. Everybody did. I am attaching her latest school photograph so that you can see for yourself this beautiful child we made together.

Cissie x

Billy clicked on the attachment and stared at the face smiling up at him. He didn't think Kenny had got as far as looking at it, and the writer of the email was certainly right – she was a beautiful child.

Now, he understood the retching – Kenny hadn't known of this child, and suddenly, it had been thrust upon him in the most brutal fashion; this is your awesomely stunning child, but she's dead.

Billy turned around in his seat, searching for the man he loved utterly and completely. He had to support him.

The waiter meandered through the tables, bearing two plates, but Billy didn't think they would be eating. He thanked the homophobic employee, noted his name was Paul for the Trip Advisor rating and review and stared once again at the picture.

It had seemed like an extreme reaction; perhaps Billy should check Kenny was okay. Billy pushed back his chair and then saw Kenny staggering out of the gents.

He stood as Kenny drew near. 'What do you want to do?' he whispered.

'Eat. Our meals are here, aren't they?' He sounded strung out. 'Let's have our bloody meal and go home. You read it?'

Billy nodded. 'And saw the picture.'

'What?' Kenny grabbed for the phone. 'Oh my God. No...'

The last time he'd seen that face it had been smashed against the windscreen of the car being driven by Tommy.

He switched off the phone and put it back into his pocket. He needed thinking time; an adjustment period to come to terms with being a dad. With losing his daughter. With Cissie's email.

They ate without speaking, declined a dessert and paid the bill with no gratuities added.

The journey home, with Billy driving, was also in silence. Billy knew his man; he needed to process things before discussing anything. He couldn't help but feel there was more to this than he knew, but he also knew Kenny would eventually talk. It was a massive part of their relationship, their honesty with each other.

Billy pulled onto the drive, and Kenny jumped out, leaving Billy to follow him. He went straight upstairs, and Billy sighed and went through to the kitchen. This issue was obviously going to be a hard one to sort; he hadn't seen Kenny like this for a long time.

He switched on the kettle, then switched it off again, opting for a whisky instead. He drank it slowly, then followed Kenny upstairs.

He was sitting on the edge of the bed, deep in thought.

'Want to talk?'

'Not yet.' Kenny's voice was hollow.

'Okay. Want anything? Whisky? Tea?'

Kenny simply shook his head.

'Right. I'm going to watch a bit of telly. If you need anything, come and find me.' Billy bent down and kissed Kenny's head.

There was no reaction.

Billy left the bedroom knowing he was going to have to ride this one out until Kenny couldn't bottle it up any longer.

'You need to leave here tomorrow. Have you still got your key for Megan's house?'

Carl nodded. 'It's my damned house as well, you know.'

'Then, I suggest you go back to it. That little lad will need a home to go to, when they let him out of hospital. He'll need to grieve for his mum, and he doesn't need you being a dickhead. I saw the way he cringed away from you. Don't let me see that again. We'll talk about our relationship when I've seen how your relationship with your son pans out. Get it?' Aileen's face was set. She was angry, angry with his unfeeling attitude towards Daryl, and also his lack of care for the death of his wife. He was the most selfish man she'd ever met.

She continued in the same flat tone of voice, the one her Vinnie had dreaded hearing. 'And you're on the settee tonight.'

Carl nodded, almost afraid to say anything. She was magnificent when she was mad, and boy, was she mad.

She went upstairs and returned carrying a blanket and a pillow. She handed them to him without speaking, picked up a book, climbed the stairs once more and went to bed.

Carl lay on the sofa, deep in thought. It was okay Aileen saying he had to take care of Daryl, but she didn't know his problems with Grausohn. He would have to come up with another name from the list to pacify him. One of the Brownlow kids? Janey Walker's little lad? If he said the Brownlow three kids were involved, it would take the pressure off him, and Kenny and Tommy could grab any one of them.

Tomorrow, he needed to speak to Kenny.

The sky was overcast, with a promise of rain for later. Kenny stared out of the window; after an almost sleepless night, he still had no idea how to respond to Cissie's email.

The child Tommy had killed was the only child he would ever father, and he knew deep down he would have to go to the funeral.

He moved across to the kitchen table, taking a notepad with him. He sat for several minutes, pen in hand, before he wrote.

Dear Cissie,

I am so sorry to hear of your daughter's death. I had always assumed you had taken abortion as your option; if I had known you were keeping the baby, I would have supported you financially. I hope you realise that.

If you send me your address,

'Eight Darwin Close,' he muttered.

I'll send you a cheque that will cover all funeral costs. Please let me know the details of the funeral, as I would like to pay my respects, if I am in Sheffield.

'I'll be in Timbuktu.' There was no way he could face the funeral. Maybe.

If you need anything in the meantime, please email me.

With best wishes,

Kenny

He read it through one more time, pulled the laptop towards him and typed it in. He stood to make a cup of coffee and went back to staring out of the window. A fine drizzle had arrived, matching exactly his mood.

He sipped at the coffee, then switched on the kettle again as he heard Billy moving around upstairs. To function as a normal person for the rest of the day, Kenny had to start off with two mugs of coffee.

Kenny heard him thud downstairs, the clatter of the letterbox as he removed the newspaper, and then, he felt his presence behind him. Billy calmed him simply by being there.

Would Katie understand this relationship, this love? He doubted it, and he knew, one day, he would tell her. He could possibly lose his sister, but he wouldn't give up Billy.

He turned around, and Billy hugged him. 'Have you replied?'

'I've written it.'

'You haven't sent it?'

'Not yet. I wanted you to see it first.'

Kenny handed Billy his coffee and watched as he moved across to the laptop. He read through it quickly, then re-read it.

'It's good. Be prepared for rejection, though. She'll probably tell you to stuff your cheque up your arse.'

Kenny shrugged. 'I know, but I had to offer, didn't I?'

'You did, and I admire you for that. I'm not convinced about going to the funeral, though. You want me to go with you?'

Kenny shook his head. 'No, you're okay, I won't be going. I thought it would make her feel better if I put that.'

Billy smiled. 'You're all heart, Kenny, all heart.'

'Should I send it, then?'

'Yes, and do it now, before you change your mind. It must have taken guts on her part to contact you, and I bet she's in a mess emotionally, so send it and get it over with.'

Kenny thought for a moment. 'Okay, click it.'

Cissie heard the ping but chose to ignore it. She was half asleep on Sally's spare bed, cuddling Mr Grumps, thinking about Ella. Cissie was in a temporarily good place and didn't want the outside world of mobile phone pings to intrude.

She could see Ella's light brown skin, glowing in the sunlight; her voice was soft and gentle, her manner the same. How could she live without her? She pulled Mr Grumps closer and wiped away yet more tears from her cheeks.

She knew she had to smarten up – the appointment with the undertaker was for three o'clock, and she couldn't go looking like this, although she guessed most people who had to visit an undertaker looked like she did.

She felt truly grateful for the way Sally had looked after her and knew she couldn't have done the afternoon's traumatic activities without her. But sooner or later, she would have to return to the awful empty house. No more giggles, no more pleadings to be allowed to go down to Freya's house, no more nights at the kitchen table, doing homework. Was a broken heart a genuine illness? She felt she had it.

There was a gentle knock on the door, and Sally popped her head around. 'Cup of tea, sweetie?'

Cissie nodded and pulled herself up so that she was leaning against the bedhead. 'I'm sorry,' she said. 'You shouldn't be waiting on me. Can you put up with me for one more night? I don't think I'll be up to going home after the undertakers, but tomorrow, I must make the effort.'

'Cissie, you stay as long as you need to. This is our spare room, you're not putting anybody out of their bed. Don't rush home because you think you're intruding, you're not.'

'It's not that. You'll think I'm crazy, but Ella isn't here. I'll be able to connect with her back at home. I know it will be quiet, but maybe that's what I need. I'll go home tomorrow. If I can't handle it, I'll come back to you. Does that sound sensible?' She gave a huge sigh and pulled Mr Grumps towards her.

'You do whatever you think is for the best. Our home will always be open to you. I'll go and get that cup of tea.'

Sally went downstairs, deeply troubled. She had no idea how Cissie was keeping going; children were so precious, and now, Cissie had none.

She made a cup of tea for herself and Cissie, then carried them both upstairs. Cissie was still resting against the bedhead but, this time, staring at her phone.

'I told him, Ella's father. He's emailed me.' She handed the phone to Sally and waited.

Sally read it, slowly and carefully. She lifted her head and stared at Cissie. 'Do you need his money?'

'No, not at all. It's more him attending the funeral that's bothering me. I thought he would say no. But he has the right, doesn't he? Ella was his daughter. I'm not telling him my address, so he can forget the cheque. I've asked him for nothing for nine years, I don't intend starting now.'

'Then, forget about it. Send him a very brief email saying you don't need help with the funeral costs, and you'll see him on the day. We'll have the date in a couple of hours. Email him after that, and you won't need to be in contact again.'

14

DI Roberts hated his job at times. He visited the Brownlow home first, where he explained about Megan Clarkson's death and Daryl's injuries. Fortunately for him, Cissie Johnston had also been there; it meant he only had two explanations to give, instead of three. The children, however, had been distraught.

He couldn't have chosen a worse time to go; the two mothers were getting ready to head off to the undertakers, and John Brownlow was left to deal with three very unhappy children.

Roberts heard the little girl, Freya, speak in a whisper to her brothers. 'Are we going to be next? They've got two of us now.'

Mark placed a finger on his lips, and Freya stopped speaking. Roberts knew that these kids were hiding something. Perhaps through fear? Tomorrow, this would have to be sorted.

He moved from the Brownlow's to Janey Walker's home, higher up the estate. He drove past Aileen Walmsley's house and wondered if Carl Clarkson was still there, or if she had recognised him for the loser he really was.

Janey Walker opened the door and ushered him through to the kitchen. She was baking buns with Sammy, his shiny black face covered with bits of flour.

'I have some unwelcome news for both of you,' he began.

Sammy instinctively reached out for his mother's hand. She pulled him towards her.

'Mrs Clarkson, Megan, was killed in a traffic accident yesterday. Daryl was in the car with her, but he escaped with a broken collarbone. He's in the Children's Hospital.'

Sammy's lips quivered, and Janey hugged him tightly. 'We'll go see him tomorrow, okay?' She turned to Roberts. 'A traffic accident?'

'Yes, hit and run.'

'Like Ella? Was it the same car?'

'No, it wasn't the same car. It did have false number plates, though, like the car that hit Ella Johnston.'

The questions were the same as the ones put to him at the Brownlow's. Roberts stayed a few minutes longer, then left them to come to terms with what had happened.

His next stop was at Aileen Walmsley's house, but she was quick to tell him that Carl Clarkson had moved back to the home he had shared with Megan and Daryl, in preparation for Daryl coming home.

The funeral arrangements were made with sympathy and care. The death of a child was never going to be easy to deal with, and they finally agreed that Wednesday of the following week would be the best time.

Cissie felt as though her legs wouldn't support her as she staggered through Sally's front door.

'Go and have a lie down,' Sally insisted. 'I'll bring you a drink, but if you're asleep, it doesn't matter. You need to switch off for a time.'

Cissie nodded and climbed the stairs, feeling as though the ascent was comparable to scaling Mount Everest.

She collapsed onto the bed and closed her eyes. A couple of minutes, she told herself…

Sally looked down at her and placed the fruit juice on the bedside table. She left her without disturbing her and went back to join the children, sitting at the garden table. They were subdued; two of their gang were out of the picture, and Sally sensed Freya was falling apart.

They stopped talking as she approached. 'Where's Dad?'

'Think he's in his shed,' Mark said. 'He's putting a new lock on that gate down the side of the house.'

Sally hurried to the shed and stood watching him.

'I'm fitting a new lock. We need to make sure it's locked every night before we go to bed.'

She nodded. 'That's good.'

He turned and fixed his blue eyes on her, eyes that looked troubled. 'You understand?'

'Of course. And when the kids go back to school, one of us will take them and pick them up every day. We'll sort out a rota with Carl and Janey. We can't let these kids be alone at all until Roberts has caught whoever is targeting us.'

'Have you thought this through?' John spoke slowly, showing his worries.

'I have. I don't understand why our kids are being hounded simply because they found Vinnie Walmsley's body. It doesn't make sense. I'm going to have a walk up to Aileen's later and talk to her. See if she can come up with anything.'

'No, you're not. Megan's death shows it's not only the kids who are being targeted, so none of us go out alone. Is that clear, Sally?'

She blinked. She had never seen John put his foot down about anything before. 'It's clear. I'll call her instead.' She leaned into the shed and kissed him. 'Thank you. Love you, boss.'

He didn't smile. 'Love you too. Now let me try to make us a bit safer.'

She walked back to the children, who once again stopped talking as she approached. 'Time to talk, kids,' she said, and they groaned.

'Have we done something wrong?' Dom asked.

'Have you?' his mother countered. Her eyes were on Freya. She would be the one to break first, she sensed.

She reckoned without the iron will of her daughter. 'I think we've been good,' Freya said. 'Ask Dad, he'll tell you.'

'Okay, let's go back to the day you found Vinnie.'

'No,' Mark said, sounding so like John, it almost made Sally cry.

'What do you mean no?'

'Mum, we're struggling with it. You didn't see him, we did, and it wasn't a nice sight. Please don't ask us to talk about it, because we can't. It's scary.'

Four sentences, and he'd knocked everything from under her. Now, she had to back-pedal.

'I'm sorry, it's just that in view of this last episode, with Megan and Daryl, I reckon DI Roberts might want to talk to you again. Think about it, see if there's anything you've forgotten to tell him, that's all I ask. Now, does anybody want some ice cream?'

They said no, and then she really knew something was troubling them. She hoped Roberts could get it out of them, because she was drawing a blank.

Kenny had spent most of the day with Grausohn; Kenny had popped in hoping it would be a quick half hour of instructions, then he could disappear. That didn't happen; he was introduced to the new Tommy – a tall, hefty guy called Fraser.

Fraser Blake was only thirty-one but looked fifty. He had been working in London, but things had gone wrong, and he had been forced to disappear for a while. He didn't go into details, and Kenny had enough on his plate without having the new guy's woes piled on it as well.

They went to the pub, and although Kenny tried to get him to try Yorkshire beer, he refused, explaining if he drank, he killed people.

Kenny knew he wasn't joking, so bought him Diet Coke.

'You got rid of Tommy, then?'

Kenny shrugged. He wasn't admitting to anything to a stranger.

They moved on to football, then Fraser steered the conversation back to the organisation. 'What do you think to Grausohn? Bit unstable?'

Again, Kenny shrugged. If you wanted to live, in his line of work, you didn't slag off the boss. 'He's okay. Pays well. I don't socialise, keep work and family separate.'

'I'm looking to make this move long-term. Truth is, can't really head back down to London, not for some time, anyway.'

Kenny's phone notified him he had an email, and he looked at the screen.

Cissie.

'Got to go,' he said to a surprised Fraser, as if he had anticipated killing more time with Kenny, finding out anything he could about Grausohn.

Kenny stood and shook Fraser's hand. 'See you tomorrow.'

Kenny walked casually out to the car, then drove a little way before pulling up. He took out his phone and opened the email. The funeral had been booked in for the following Wednesday, noon at the local church, one-thirty at the crematorium. Thank you, but she didn't need or want financial help. Nothing else had been added, other than the bare details, and he knew he would be going.

There were two reasons – the first was, whether he liked it or not, Ella had been his daughter. The second reason was that two of the children they were trying to find were now dead, but that left another four. They would probably be at that funeral, and if he turned on the charm with Cissie, she would give him all their names.

He threw the phone onto the passenger seat and clicked on his indicator. The phone pinged again, and he pulled on the handbrake.

Carl.

Kenny stared at the screen, then opened the message from someone he had presumed to be a dead man.

Wife dead. Son in hospital. Did Grausohn order it? No more names. He's not killing anybody else I know.

Carl had done some serious thinking. He knew Megan had died because of Grausohn, and that he'd probably done it as a warning to him to pull his finger out and hand over all the kids' names. He put his bag in the boot and set off to spend a couple of nights in a nearby hotel. He needed to be out of the way 'til Daryl came out of hospital, and he thought he might ring Kenny that night, even though Kenny preferred texting.

He pulled into the Travelodge car park, glanced around him to make sure nobody else was arriving at the same time and headed for reception. His room was adequate, and he drifted off to sleep while watching some inane travel show. He didn't ring Kenny. He could have done, because Kenny wasn't asleep.

Kenny was worried. The plan had been for Carl Clarkson to die. Not his wife, not his son. He'd become too unreliable to live, and if the police picked him up, it could put them all in danger.

It seemed he hadn't even been in the fucking car. This wasn't the way Kenny worked; if somebody had to die, they died. Substitutes didn't die. And now, he'd probably have to tell the boss about the cock-up, because by tomorrow, Grausohn would be screaming at him to get Carl in, to find out who the kids were and exactly what they knew about his consignment.

He tossed and turned for most of the night, and Billy, as awake as his partner, would know there was something bad going on inside Kenny's head. Something really bad.

Eventually, Kenny gave in and left the bedroom to head downstairs for a drink. He poured a whisky, then poured a second one as he sensed Billy coming up behind him.

'Is it the little girl?' Billy asked.

'It's all sorts of stuff,' Kenny said. Billy was tolerant of most things connected with Kenny's job, but the last few days might be a step too far.

They moved to the table and sipped at their drinks. Billy remained quiet, waiting for Kenny to speak.

'I've killed three people this week,' he said, after some minutes of silence.

'Only three?' Billy asked with a smile, clearly thinking Kenny was being theoretical rather than truthful.

'Billy… it wasn't a joke.'

Kenny watched Billy's face change.

'You're serious?'

Kenny nodded. 'The first one I didn't really kill, but I was there.'

'Oh, that's good to know,' Billy responded with more than a touch of sarcasm.

'I was in the car,' Kenny tried to explain. 'Tommy was driving. The kid came straight for us on her scooter, and he couldn't stop in time.'

'The little girl? That was you? But she's the one who's…'

'My daughter? Yes, I know. I can't get her face out of my head. She hit the windscreen, that's what killed her, I'm sure. We drove away and left her, Billy. We drove away. And then, we had to go and tell the boss, because we were supposed to be snatching her, so she could tell us where the drugs had gone. Grausohn is convinced the kids who found the body in the woods know more than they're letting on.'

Billy stared at him. 'I don't believe I'm hearing this. You intended handing over this little girl to that thug? What do you think he would have done to her to get the information?'

'Don't,' Kenny groaned. 'Why do you think I can't sleep? I can't let him get his hands on any of the other kids. But that's not all. I had to get rid of Tommy. I knew Tommy was out of favour – he'd made too many cock-ups lately. As soon as he told the boss he'd been driving, Grausohn told me to terminate him. And then, he pushed and pushed to get Carl Clarkson, one of the other hangers-on, to come up with the names of the kids.'

Billy's tone was flat. 'You've killed Carl Clarkson as well?'

'No, I've fucking killed his wife and put his lad in hospital. I took it upon myself to cause an accident to Carl, put him out of the picture, but he wasn't in the car. I want out, Billy, but if I say that, I'll be next.'

Billy was quiet, taking in everything pouring from Kenny's lips. 'I'm going back to bed,' he said. 'You take the spare room. I need to think. And try not to kill me and make it four.'

He headed for the stairs, and Kenny's head dropped, supported by his hands. He couldn't lose Billy, he couldn't.

Cissie and Sally, accompanied by Mark and Dom, walked up the hill to Cissie's home. She had decided it was time to be there. She wanted to feel Ella around her, experience her presence. John had insisted the boys go with them, so that Sally wouldn't be walking back unaccompanied. Freya had said with a grin that she would stay home and guard her dad. John was grateful that she could laugh about it; he couldn't.

As they neared Darwin Close, Cissie's pace increased. She was almost running by the time they reached the front door.

The steps and front of the house were covered in bouquets of flowers. Cissie stared at them and knelt to read the labels. Most of them were from children from Ella's school, but some were from strangers who wanted to express their sympathy in the only way they could. Sally, Mark and Dom read the labels as well, and eventually, Dom took hold of his mother's hand.

'Can we bring some flowers for Ella, Mum?'

'Of course we can. We'll get some tomorrow and come and check that Cissie is okay.'

Dom nodded. That was good. It would perhaps let Ella know they were all missing her.

They cleared a path up to the door, and the four of them went inside. Cissie immediately switched on the kettle, made the boys a cold drink each and went around closing the curtains.

'It won't be dark for at least three hours.' Sally smiled.

'The curtains will stay closed now until after the funeral. It's the way it is, the way it should be. It's how I was taught by my mum.'

Sally nodded. 'Whatever you feel comfortable with, Cissie. Are you sure you'll be okay on your own? We're only a phone call away, if you need anything.'

'I'll be fine.' Her tone of voice said otherwise. 'You've been so good to me, Sally. I can't thank you enough.' The kettle clicked off, and Cissie poured the boiling water into the teapot.

She reached up and took the biscuits down from the cupboard and put some on a plate. Carrying them across to the table, playing the perfect hostess, she set everything down, told them to help themselves and then burst into tears.

Sally stood and moved to take her in her arms. 'Hush,' she said. 'You're doing so well.'

'Ella would have loved having you all around for tea and biscuits. She thought the world of your family, Sally.' Cissie dabbed at her eyes, trying to stem the torrent that threatened to flow. 'How am I supposed to carry on without her?'

'I don't know, but you're being so brave. Come and sit down and have this drink, and let's talk about Ella. Let's always keep her alive for you, for all of us.'

Dom and Mark sat quietly, not sure how to handle the strange situation. This was the first time they'd been in this house without Ella, and it felt wrong. They sipped at their drinks, and Dom tentatively reached across for a biscuit.

'Can't imagine not seeing Ella again, can you?' he whispered to his brother.

Mark shook his head. 'Shh, Ella's mum can hear you,' he whispered back.

Cissie turned to them, tears still glittering on her cheeks. 'Talk about her all you want, boys. It won't upset me any more than I am already, and we need to talk about her.'

Cissie and Sally re-took their seats at the table. Cissie was the first to speak. 'Know what my favourite memory is? It's her climbing the stairs every night, collecting Mr Grumps from the second stair up, before heading for her bedroom. Now, let's take it in turns to tell of a favourite memory of Ella, until she's lodged in our hearts for always.'

15

Daryl was released into the care of his father the following day. He was surprised to be taken to the Travelodge instead of home, and even more surprised to find his father had been thoughtful enough to bring him some clothes, as well as his own. The old selfish Carl wouldn't have done that.

The hospital had insisted that Daryl still needed rest, so they sat in the room, watching daytime television, both sleeping on and off.

By seven o'clock, Daryl was bored. 'Did you bring any books, Dad?'

'Books? No. Why?'

'I don't want to watch TV. Could do with a book.'

'There's a garage across the car park. Think you can manage to walk across there?'

Daryl shook his head. 'No, my knee's hurting. Is it time for some more painkillers?'

'Shit!' Carl had been given explicit instructions for medication times, and a quick glance at his watch showed he was an hour late. 'Sorry, son, I'll get you some now. And then, I'll go find you a book. Any sort?'

He popped two tablets from the blister pack and handed them to Daryl. 'You got enough water?'

Daryl nodded. 'I'm fine. Bit hungry, though.'

'I'll bring us something. And a book, if they sell them.'

Daryl held up a thumb, too busy trying to swallow the giant-sized tablets to talk.

Fifteen minutes later, Carl was back and earning multiple brownie points. The garage had boasted a veritable library of books, and the woman behind the counter had advised him to take a Rick Riordan book for a smart eleven-year-old. She'd handed Carl the first in the series and said they stocked the rest when his lad had read that one. He hoped Daryl was a slow reader; when did books become that expensive?

Carl also gathered some snacks together. He needed to lay low, not be taking them out for meals, although he did recognise that at some point, he would have to sort out funeral arrangements for Megan. Their teenage love had died a death a long time ago, but she was Daryl's mother, and the truth was, he would miss her anyway, even if they had drifted apart.

Daryl made himself as comfortable as he could on the bed, opened the book and was instantly lost. He finally fell asleep, a combination of the long day, and the drugs, and Carl removed the open book that was laid on his son's chest. He tore a piece of the newspaper and used it as a bookmark, then read the back of the book.

He turned it over and looked at the cover, then turned to the first page. He hadn't read a book since the enforced reading of *Of Mice and Men* at school.

Three hours later, he checked on Daryl, pulled the covers up around his shoulders and switched off the light. He was on page eighty-four, not the fastest reader in the world, but Daryl was much further into the book, so he wouldn't have long to wait before he could read again. And he would have to go and get Daryl the second one…

Maybe there was hope for the two of them.

Carl's head hit the pillow, and he was dropping off to sleep when his phone pinged.

Where the fuck are you?

He smiled. *Up yours, Kenny,* he thought. *I'm with my lad.*

Kenny was angry. He'd had a full day of Grausohn blethering on about those kids, he'd had Fraser with that smirk on his face, and he didn't know where the hell bloody Carl Clarkson was. The hospital wouldn't tell him anything, despite his reassurance that he was Daryl's uncle, and Billy was only speaking in monosyllables.

He was back to sharing a bed with Billy, but the conversation was lacking. He'd fired off the text to Clarkson after brushing his teeth and then hoped he wouldn't respond. It would only irritate Billy even further; he'd class it as bringing work into bed with them.

He tossed and turned for half an hour, then gave in and sat on the edge of the bed.

'Cup of tea?' Billy asked.

Kenny turned his head and looked at him. 'I'll do it. Anything in yours?'

'Milk. We need clear heads.'

Kenny went downstairs, returning a few minutes later with two drinks.

Billy was sitting up in bed with his glasses on and looking serious. 'What are our options?'

Kenny felt a sense of relief that Billy used the word "our." 'I don't know. If I walk away, I'll be looking over my shoulder for the rest of my life. I'll also be putting you in danger, because they'll see you as my weak link. Losing you, Billy, would kill me.'

'Then, there's only one answer. Grausohn has to go. And soon. No more children can die or even be hurt because of him. So, we need to think.'

'That might be the answer,' Kenny smiled. 'But it's a massive problem. There's always somebody there, and now he's got this new bloke, Fraser, he'll be there all the time. He very rarely goes out, and he's always well protected when he does.'

'You're thinking like a gangster, Kenny.'

'I am a gangster.'

'Stop thinking like one. When I say he has to die, you immediately think by the knife, or the bullet. There are other ways.'

Kenny waited. It was surreal, sitting at the side of his lover in bed, discussing how to murder his boss. But he had nothing but respect for Billy; he was clever. And he gave a lot of thought to everything before acting on anything.

'He lives in a penthouse suite, right?'

'Yes, stunning place. It has its own elevator, four bedrooms, one of which he is in most of the time 'cos he's set it up as an office, a lounge that's massive, with windows that open out onto a balcony, and a kitchen.'

'How does he eat? Does he have food sent in, or does he cook himself?'

Kenny laughed at the idea of Grausohn with a pinny on, standing at the cooker. 'No, he has a housekeeper, a German woman called Gerda. One of the bedrooms is hers, and she prepares all his food. He likes German food better than English, he says.'

'Okay, so there's two possibilities right there. The first is poison, and the second is the balcony. Are you ever in the lounge with him?'

'Only if something big goes off at night, and I need to contact him. He finishes in the office when he has his evening meal.'

'Could you get him drunk?'

'Maybe. I've only seen him drunk once, and that was when we had a meeting with him, Tommy and me, to discuss building up the troops. Bringing more people in to expand the network. Strangely, he's a happy drunk. In that damned office, you never even see him smile, but when he's drunk, he lets down his guard.'

'And he's likely to go out on the balcony?'

'Definitely. He makes us go out there to smoke, won't have smoking in the lounge. It can be bloody freezing in the winter.'

'It's not the winter. We need to do it now, so it looks natural you being out there. You got anybody you can trust to help you, who could be there? Not this Fraser bloke, obviously. It needs to be somebody who'd benefit from Grausohn being dead.'

'Carl Clarkson.'

'What?'

'Yeah. If Grausohn lives, Carl will die. He might think he can hide away, but it's only because I haven't bothered looking yet.

He's the key to these kids that Grausohn's after. His own lad, Daryl, is in the gang of them, and Carl knows who all the others are. He's seen what happened when we tried to snatch Ella, and he's not giving us any other names. This could be our way in.'

'Talk me through it.'

'Okay.' Kenny thought for a few seconds. 'This will have to take place fairly late so that Fraser's gone for the night, and so has Gerda. She goes out most nights, cinema or bingo or something. If I ring Grausohn and tell him I've got Carl, who's managed to track down most of the names, he'll say come around. He might not trust Carl, but he trusts me. I've got rid of Tommy for him, and he knows we were long time mates.'

'So far so good,' Billy said. 'But you're relying on him asking you to go up to the penthouse.'

'He will. I'll use the password. When we use that, he knows it's urgent.'

'And that is?'

'*Verstehen*. Using it means we need to see him immediately. If he's got somebody there he can't get rid of, he says, "*nicht verstehen,*" and we wait for a text telling us when he's free.'

'It's like being in a kid's gang.'

'He's no kid, Billy. Everything he does is carefully thought through. He leaves nothing to chance. Fraser hasn't proved himself yet, and Tommy's gone. That only leaves me he can trust. He's put the password system in place 'cos it was necessary. Don't underestimate him. He's a killer and doesn't think twice about it. He'll not order Carl's death until he's got the names out of him, but then he will. It will be fine for Carl to give him some names, because we'll chuck Grausohn over the balcony. He'll play out the game, you see. He'll even pay Carl for the information, but he'll have already decided to tip me the wink to finish him off.'

Deep inside, Billy was horrified. He knew Kenny walked a very narrow line, but he'd not realise it was this bad.

'So, all you have to do is convince Carl you're genuine. Are you? Will you let Carl go after it's finished, or will he follow his boss over that balcony?'

Kenny heaved a deep sigh. 'Ella's death has finished me, Billy. I want out, and Grausohn's death will be my last one. His business here is tied up so tightly, I don't think there's anyone to take it over. Whoever he was in cahoots with over this stash that's gone missing might try, but I'll be well out of it by then. This can work, if I can persuade Carl Clarkson to play along. And before you make any comments, this is definitely not a game. Tomorrow, I'm going to find him and Daryl. I've to put some things right with the lad, but I've to convince Carl this will work.'

Billy felt he was seeing a new person; he'd known from very early on in their relationship exactly what Kenny did for a living, knew why they could afford such a large home and the top of the range cars they enjoyed, but he'd never seen him like this before. One little girl had softened him; made him not like himself. His daughter.

Daryl couldn't stop the tears. He wished he could remember more about the man in that car, wished he could tell DI Roberts who it was, so that he could be sent to the electric chair for killing his mum. Except he didn't think they did electric chairs in this country.

He tried to turn over, but the pain in his shoulder made him scream out.

'Daryl? You okay?' Carl sat up and looked over at the other bed. 'You need anything?' He clicked on the bedhead light and saw his son's face, streaked with tears. He got out of bed and sat by Daryl. 'Can I do anything? You need more medication?'

'Get my mum back,' Daryl sobbed. 'I want my mum.'

'Shit, Dazza, I can't do that.' Carl felt helpless. He tried to put his arm around Daryl's shoulders, but it was obvious it hurt too much.

Carl poured some milk into the tooth glass, popped two tablets out of the pack and handed them to his son. 'Take these. They'll help the pain, and they'll help you sleep as well.'

'Can we go home tomorrow?' Daryl's tear-filled voice was pleading with him.

'Okay,' he said reluctantly. Carl had known they couldn't stay here indefinitely, but he'd have to make the house secure. He didn't want any of Grausohn's thugs getting in.

'We'll check out after breakfast.' Daryl gave a watery smile and took the tablets.

Ten minutes later, he was asleep, but his dad was awake. Carl's life was falling apart, and he had no idea what to do about it.

They checked out of the Travelodge and, fifteen minutes later, pulled onto the drive. Carl made Daryl wait in the car while he checked out the house; he was soon satisfied that nothing had been disturbed, and he helped Daryl out of the car and into the lounge.

Daryl sat down with a sigh of relief.

'I'll get the sun loungers, and then, you can sit out for a bit. That okay?'

Daryl nodded and wondered why his dad was being so caring. He'd spent eleven years trying to avoid contact with his son, and now, suddenly, it had all changed.

Carl helped him into the garden, after seeing how Daryl winced when he put weight on his knee. After a quick glance through the fridge, Carl realised they needed to get some food in, but knew he couldn't take Daryl and definitely couldn't leave him in the house.

He rang Aileen and explained the situation; within half an hour, she was pulling up outside. He handed her a wad of money and a list, then swiftly kissed her cheek as she left the house.

Carl sat with Daryl in the garden, chatting properly to his son, something he couldn't ever remember doing before. They talked about Sheffield Wednesday, about Daryl's friends, who he said he really wanted to see, and about Megan.

Neither of them could see a way through the next few weeks, not without Megan there. For so long, it had been Daryl and his mum, and now, there was nothing except a tentative relationship with a father Daryl was unsure about, and a rocky relationship with a son Carl was nervous about.

After nearly an hour of learning how to live together, Carl stood. He ruffled Daryl's hair. 'That sounds like Aileen bringing us food.'

Daryl grinned. 'Thank goodness. Can you cook?'

'Of course, cheeky blighter.' Carl heard the knock on the door and went to help Aileen in with the groceries.

They piled them onto the kitchen table, and Carl started to empty the bags.

'Not yet,' Aileen said quietly. 'Come upstairs.'

Carl looked startled. 'Daryl's in the back garden!'

'Not for sex, numpty. Come into your front bedroom with me.'

He followed her upstairs, puzzled by her attitude.

She pulled the curtain fully open. 'Look,' she said. 'See that car? There's a bloke in it that I'm sure I know, and I think it's to do with Vinnie. He's watching this house. Do you know him?'

Carl edged his way forward and stared down to the road. 'Shit. It's Kenny Lancaster. Vinnie was involved with him?'

'I think so. So, you do know him?'

Carl nodded. 'I do, and it ends now. He knows I've lost Megan, and I've got Daryl injured. Can you wait with Daryl while I go and sort this?'

'Sure. I thought I'd cook the pair of you a meal. That okay?'

'It's fine, but I'll be taking the sharpest knife with me.' His tone was grim.

He ran downstairs and into the kitchen, leaving Aileen in the bedroom. She stared out of the window, her eyes never leaving the man Carl had said was Kenny Lancaster. Was he the one who'd ordered the kill on her Vinnie?

She heard the front door slam and saw Carl dash across the road towards the car. She couldn't watch. Carl was an angry man; heaven knows what would ensue out on that road. She turned away from the window and went downstairs to join Daryl.

Daryl looked up, shielding his eyes from the sun. 'Hi, Mrs Walmsley. Dad said you'd gone shopping for us.'

'Already done, Daryl. I need to know what you like and what you don't like. I'm cooking a meal for you and your dad for tonight.'

'Jelly,' Daryl said.

'Is that it?'

'And ice cream.'

'What about real food? Like vegetables, and such stuff.' She was trying to keep her face straight.

He shook his head. 'Nah, don't like them.'

'Did your mum make you eat them?'

He shrugged. 'Well…'

'Right,' and this time, Aileen couldn't stop the smile, 'this is what's going to happen. I've picked up some pork chops, which we're going to have with carrots, cabbage and mashed potato. How does that sound?'

'Cabbage?'

'Cabbage.'

'Can we have jelly after?'

'Not today, it takes too long to set. I'll make one, though, and you can have it tomorrow. Deal?'

'Deal.' Daryl gave in gracefully. This one was like his mum; it didn't seem as if he was going to get away with anything with Mrs Walmsley, any more than he could with his mum.

'I'll make the jelly now,' Aileen said, and turned to enter the kitchen. She'd won that round, now to get him to eat the cabbage.

16

Carl walked up to the open window of the car and leaned in, his hand on the knife in his pocket. 'Looking for me, Kenny?'

Kenny nodded. 'I am. Get in.' He pointed to the passenger seat.

'Do I look stupid?'

'No, I'm sure you're not. I'm here to talk to you. You got half an hour or so?'

Carl didn't know how to respond. He knew Kenny killed without thinking twice about it; he'd guessed the man was involved in Ella's death, and he knew for a fact he'd been part of Johanna's disappearance. He hesitated, and Kenny waited.

'We don't drive off? We stay here?' Carl said, wondering if he really was stupid after all.

'We can go in your house, if it makes you feel any better, but I think Vinnie's mother is in there, and I'm pretty sure Daryl will be. It would be better if they didn't hear what I need to say.'

Carl walked slowly around the car bonnet and opened the passenger door. 'Five minutes,' he said.

'It might take longer,' Kenny said, and Carl could hear the stress in his voice. He'd always seen Kenny as a super-confident, do anything to anyone kind of guy, but his tone now suggested a change.

Carl sat in the passenger seat, his hand automatically going to the seatbelt.

'We're not going anywhere,' Kenny said. 'I'm telling you, we're here to talk. First of all, how's your lad?'

'Leave him out of it. I don't want that bastard knowing anything about him. He doesn't know owt about the bloody consignment. He's eleven years old, for crying out loud.'

'I was asking because I wanted to know,' Kenny responded. 'Believe me, Grausohn won't be told anything. And I don't want to know who the rest of the kids are.'

'Grausohn does. And Daryl's doing okay. Still in pain, but he's alive.' Carl gave the information grudgingly.

'I know. Let me ask you a question, Carl. Do you want out?'

'I am out.'

'No, you're not. You walk away from Grausohn, and he won't rest until you're dead. Nobody leaves his organisation. As soon as they're in, they already know too much to ever be allowed to leave. So, you're not out, not yet. But we can help each other with this.'

Carl felt his mind go blank. He didn't think he was hearing this properly. It seemed that the great right-hand man of Grausohn didn't want to be in that position any longer. Carl stared out of the side window, waiting for Kenny to expand on his words.

'Go on,' he encouraged.

'I want out as well,' Kenny said. 'But it's even harder for me. You, he would kill, me – he would kill me painfully. The only way we can get out is by him dying.'

'Whoa!' Carl put his hand on the car door handle. 'I'm no murderer, Kenny. Don't bring me into this.'

'You want to see Daryl strung up by his arms, having the soles of his feet burnt with a blow torch?'

Carl took his hand off the door handle.

'The fact that Daryl is a child won't make any difference to Grausohn. He hates kids anyway. And if it's not Daryl he eventually snatches, it will be one of the other kids. You ready to listen now?'

Carl nodded. He felt sick.

'Okay. This isn't thought through fully, so feel free to add your own ideas. Have you ever been in the lounge in the penthouse?'

'Once. He asked me to go and look for his mobile phone.'

'Can you remember the layout? Large room, raised area at one end with a dining table, and patio doors leading off it, onto a small balcony.'

'Didn't take a lot of notice, but I remember the raised area.' Carl's brow furrowed as he tried to picture what Kenny was describing.

'Right, the first thing you need to know is there's a new man, Fraser. He's taken over from Tommy.'

'Tommy? Why, what's happened to Tommy?'

Kenny extended two fingers and pointed to his heart.

'Shit. But Tommy was his main man…'

'Exactly. I'm currently the main man, but I reckon Fraser's got plans. He had to get out of London, and he's arrived here. The system has always been we finish sometime between five and seven for the day, then we have alternate weeks on call should anything be needed during the night. There's usually at least two nights in the week when I have to go back to see the boss. And there have been times when I've come across something, so I call him and tell him I need to see him. He gets rid of anybody he may be with, and I go up to the penthouse. We usually end up having a drink and a chat, then I go home.'

'Am I going to like where this is going?'

'You'll be safe. I'll have your back.' Kenny looked at him and knew Carl was hoping he could believe him.

Kenny paused for a moment, as if trying to get his thoughts in order. 'The plan is that I ring Grausohn and tell him you've come to me with the list of the names. I'll say it's taken a while to track them all down, especially after the death of that young lass, Ella.' He stopped once more, allowing the mention of his daughter to wash over him.

'I'm not giving him the list.'

'I want you to hand over a list that will look feasible. Make up the names from the initials and put in fictitious addresses. He has to believe it for maybe half an hour, and you could come out of it ten thousand pounds richer. Once the business end is out of the way, and he has what he wants with that list, he'll offer us a drink.

Be prepared to talk about anything German. He talks a lot about Auschwitz. Then, he'll offer us a cigar, and we always go out onto the balcony to smoke it. He won't have smoking in the lounge.'

Carl stared at Kenny. 'We're going to chuck him over the balcony?'

'We are. And the second he's gone, we have to go. We don't want to be bumping into Gerda on her way back from bingo, or wherever she's been.'

Carl felt sick. He was a bit player, earning insignificant amounts of money, enough to keep things ticking over nicely. It seemed he was stepping up a notch.

'What if Gerda is there?' Carl heard the stress in his own voice.

'She won't be. She goes out every night. She once told me he insisted she go out, because the evenings were kept for the shadier of his dealings, and he didn't want her hearing anything. She's at bingo most nights, got a feller there, so I understand. We don't need to worry about Gerda. And as it will be my week on call, we don't need to worry about Fraser Blake, either.'

'And when did you think we might do this?'

'I'm on call from next Sunday to the following Saturday. Shall we say Thursday? We can fine tune things during the week, make sure we have everything down perfectly.'

'I dunno, mate. I've got the kid to think about now. We're not getting rid of the body, are we? It's gonna be splattered all over the ground. The police will probably be there within five minutes.'

'We'll have alibis. They'll not tie us to it.'

'CCTV?'

'The cameras are dummies. Not one of them works. Grausohn likes all his minions to think they're for real, but his belief is that if the law got hold of CCTV recordings, it would be a bad thing for his business. And he's fuckin' right about that. If that camera in the lift had been genuine when Tommy took out Johanna…'

'You're certain none of them work?'

'Definitely. Don't think this Fraser bloke knows it yet, though. I'd been there a year before I found out. Grausohn will only tell people on a need-to-know basis, and only when they've proved loyalty.'

'All I need is an alibi?'

'Yeah, and I think you've probably got one in your house.'

'Daryl? Not an earthly, I'm not dragging him into it.' Carl shook his head angrily.

'I don't mean Daryl. That was Vinnie Walmsley's mother I saw going in, wasn't it?'

Carl grinned. 'Yeah, and she spotted you, mate.'

'I wasn't hiding, Carl. I was here to talk to you. I have information for you to give her – she'll be your alibi, but you'll have to tell her the truth about why you need one. You tell her Johanna Fleischer, Grausohn's bird, killed her Vinnie. She did it on Grausohn's orders. You'll get your alibi.'

'Shit. Is that true?'

'Johanna killed him because the package that we're all running around like headless chickens trying to find wasn't where Vinnie had hidden it. Grausohn was miffed that she killed him, which was why he had her taken out, because it meant he couldn't work on Vinnie to find out what had really happened to it. Now, I don't think for one minute that Vinnie knew anything, but that wouldn't have stopped Grausohn cutting off his balls or burning his feet to cinders. You must tell Aileen Walmsley all of this. She'll work with you on that alibi. And if the police question Daryl, he'll back you up that when he went to bed, you and Aileen were in the house and planning on watching a video. The alibi, of course, might not be necessary. There's no reason the police would suspect the pair of us, not if we get out of there via the basement. We'll go straight down to the bottom level once we've chucked him over, then send the lift back up. I'll make sure we're in a car with false plates, and we'll have black hoodies. We'll put them on before we set off, over our suits.'

'Christ, Kenny, you've thought this one through all right.' Carl was staring through the windscreen, his mind racing.

'Carl, why would they suspect us? He's got twenty or so people working for him, running clubs, the casino, the drugs… any one of them could have held a grudge. We need the alibi in case we're routinely questioned. Can you hack it?'

'If it means I'm out of it, I can hack it. You got your alibi sorted, then?'

'My partner… he'll cover for me. He's only found out over the last couple of days what Grausohn's been up to, and although he had to think it through, he's onside now. He's a careful man, we can trust him. And I think, once you've told Aileen about Vinnie's death, we'll be able to trust her as well.'

Carl stared at Kenny. 'He?'

'Yeah, he. His name is Billy Hanson, we've been together four years, and I'd like you and Aileen to come over next Tuesday night for a meal and a chat, finalise plans. We'll have to work round me being on call if Grausohn rings for anything. But I need you to work on Aileen first.'

'Shit, Kenny… you sure about all of this?'

'Carl, if we don't do it, he's gonna go for those kids. I've lived with most things he's done, but I can't stomach torturing little kids. And me and Billy want a quieter life.'

'Some bastard ran my wife off the road and killed her, so I need out like you've never known. I've got Daryl to sort, to bring up. Can't do time, that's a fact. So, I'm in. I'll talk to Aileen tonight, once Daryl's in bed. He's still in a lot of pain, and the painkillers knock him out, so he'll not hear what we're talking about.'

Kenny reached into his inside pocket, and Carl stiffened, his hand automatically going towards the knife in his pocket.

Kenny grinned. 'Carl, we're on the same side. Here.' He handed him a mobile phone. 'It's new. I've got one as well. Our numbers are programmed. Don't ring me on your phone, use this one. We'll throw them away when the job's done.'

Carl nodded and took the phone with the hand that had gone for the knife. 'Right. I'd better go in before Aileen comes out with a baseball bat or something. She'll have been watching us all this time, but it's been a long time, and she can be a bit tetchy.' Carl laughed. 'Text me about next Tuesday, and we can deal with details.'

He reached and opened the passenger door. This time, Kenny let him. 'Take care, Carl,' he said. 'And I'm sorry about your wife and lad, look after him.'

Carl nodded, checked the road and crossed back to his house. To his surprise, he felt buoyant, excited even. This life he'd somehow managed to fall into was starting to change.

Aileen was coming down the stairs as he opened the front door. She wasn't smiling. 'What the...?'

He touched his lips with his fingers and shook his head. 'Not now,' he whispered.

She stared at him, as if trying to decide what to do, then stomped off into the kitchen. 'I'm doing us a meal,' she snarled.

He smiled at her. 'And after we've eaten, when Daryl's in bed, we're going to talk. I'll tell you everything that's gone off.'

He continued through the kitchen and into the back garden. He could tell from Daryl's eyes that he had been crying.

'You okay?' he asked, knowing it was a stupid thing to say.

Daryl shook his head. 'No. I want my mum. It's not fair that she's dead. Can I have the others come up? Maybe tomorrow? They'll make me feel better.'

'Course you can, mate. Want the phone so you can give them a ring?'

Daryl nodded and brushed a stray tear from his cheek. He needed to tell the other five – no, four – about how brave his mum had been, saving his life and losing hers. He had to tell them. Had to.

He made the phone calls, and they promised to visit the following day, subject to availability of parents. It appeared that they couldn't go anywhere unaccompanied, not until things had been resolved.

Carl reappeared bearing medication, and Daryl took the tablets. His shoulder was hurting, but with his leg raised on the sun lounger, his knee didn't feel quite so bad. He suspected that as soon as he tried to put weight on it, the pain would return; for now, it was manageable. He needed to be able to walk without pain.

Ella's funeral was only a few days away, and he was going, with or without parental accompaniment.

Again, the tears leaked from his eyes, this time for his friend. He would miss her; she had been the stability in the group. Crazy ideas thought up by the others were squashed by Ella's logic, and he knew they would miss her forever.

Aileen popped her head through the door and smiled at the young lad. 'Daryl, you want to stay out there and have your meal on a lap tray, or do you want to sit at the table with us?'

'I'll come in,' he said. 'Eat at the table with you two. Might watch a DVD or something, later.'

'Read a book?' she countered.

'Yeah. In my backpack, there's the second Rick Riordan. I've not finished it. Dad's got my first one, somewhere. He started reading it in the hotel.'

'Your dad?' She looked surprised. 'Reading?'

Daryl laughed. He liked this woman. 'I know. I've never seen him read before, not a book anyway. I finished book one, and he picked it up. Can you find me my backpack, please?'

She helped him into the kitchen, and his knee hurt as much as he guessed it would once he put his weight on it. 'Bloody knee,' he grumbled.

'Hey, no swearing at your age,' she said, and brought him a small stool to put underneath his foot. It would save him bending his knee.

He watched her as she continued with the meal, and then, his dad came downstairs, showered and changed.

'You going out, Dad?' he asked, his voice trembling.

'No. I just wanted to change into shorts, jeans are a bit warm.'

'Daryl wants his backpack,' Aileen intervened. 'His book's in it. Is it upstairs?'

'I'll get it,' Carl said. 'I think it's in the hallway.'

Daryl shook his head. Who was this stranger masquerading as his father? Maybe there was hope that the two of them could share a life. Once more, tears sprang to Daryl's eyes. His mum. That was who he wanted for his childhood years, and some evil car driver had sorted out that issue.

Aileen plated up the food, and Carl, after depositing the backpack on the floor by Daryl, cut his son's pork chop into bite-sized pieces.

'That okay?' he asked and showed Daryl the plate.

'It's fine, thanks, Dad.' Daryl picked up his fork. It was like being a baby all over again, having to have his food cut up. The sooner he got his shoulder and his knee back in full working order, the better.

By seven o'clock, Daryl gave in. He needed to sleep; the tablets might be helping the pain, but they knocked him out.

'Come on.' His dad smiled. 'Let's get you up to bed and off to sleep. Hopefully by tomorrow, when your mates come, it won't be feeling quite so bad.'

Aileen kissed Daryl's forehead. 'Sweet dreams. Shout if you need anything.' She looked straight at Carl. 'We'll hear you. Your dad and I will be down here in the lounge, talking.'

17

Aileen listened to Carl. He passed on all the information that Kenny had relayed concerning Vinnie's death, and she said very little. He talked for what seemed hours but was, in truth, about half an hour.

He explained Kenny's plan to get rid of Grausohn and, in view of his lack of family, probably his whole operation. She still said very little.

He continued to talk, going into as much detail as he could remember from the discussion in the car, until, in the end, he forced her to speak. 'So, tell me what you think.'

'I think it's probably the truth.'

'You do? Do we go ahead with this crazy idea, then?'

'I think we need to talk, the four of us, around a table, before saying yea or nay. If it's yea, that's good, I can live with it. If it's nay, that's good also, because I will kill him. Maybe not in the same way, but he'll wish he'd taken an easier route, like falling from a balcony.' Her tone was icy. He flinched as he realised she meant it.

'We'll go to Kenny's on Tuesday, then?'

'Can we get somebody in to look after Daryl? We can't leave him.'

Carl thought for a moment. 'I'll sort it. He won't be on his own.'

Joe Walker, Sammy's older brother, walked down to the Brownlows' home, chatting to his sibling about a variety of subjects that covered football, girls, Xbox, and crisps.

Sammy didn't respond; he let Joe talk. He'd too much on his mind to want a conversation.

Mark, Dom, and Freya were all waiting, ready for the trek up the hill to Daryl's home. Freya held on to Joe's hand all the way until they reached the path leading to the Clarkson's front door.

Carl had been watching for their arrival, and he ushered them in and through to the back garden.

Daryl was on his sun lounger once more, feeling much better than the previous day. His knee wasn't as painful with weight on it, and he felt he'd found the right position for his arm and shoulder to be in to rest more comfortably.

At first, the others were a little reticent; they didn't know what to say to him about his mother, his own injuries, his father. None of them, including Daryl, had liked Carl. He had shown himself to be obnoxious and a bully at the police station, but he seemed different now.

He made them all a drink and opened a couple of packets of biscuits. 'Enjoy yourselves,' he said, and smiled at the five of them. 'Daryl, give me a shout if you need the toilet, or if you want any more food and drink. I'll be in the lounge.'

'Okay, thanks, Dad.' Daryl watched his father disappear, then whispered to Dom. 'Close the kitchen door.'

Dom did so, then moved back to the circle they had created with garden chairs.

'We've things to talk about,' Daryl said.

Everyone responded silently, with thumbs up.

'We have to talk really quietly. I've had lots of time to think, and although I don't know how, I think all this bad stuff that's happened is because of that powder in the Wendy house.'

'Ella told us to hand it in,' Freya said. 'If we'd done that, she might still be with us.'

'No, Freya, she wouldn't. If we hand it in, it goes to the police. It's not the police who've killed Ella and my mum and hurt me. It's somebody bad.' Daryl emphasised the point by banging his good hand down on the arm of his chair.

'Then, why don't we hand it into the bad people?' Freya said, using logic instead of clear thinking.

'We don't know who they are,' Daryl explained patiently. 'And there's something else I wanted to talk about. We're not the Gang of Six anymore. I think we should change our name to Ella's Gang. What do you think?'

There was no hesitation. Five thumbs were raised immediately.

'That's good, then.' Daryl paused, and moved his shoulder a little. He winced and carried on. 'We've now got another problem in that we can't do anything with the powder, other than hand it into the police. We're not allowed out without somebody older with us. We can't bury it where Vinnie buried it, we can't stick it in the Shire Brook, and I don't feel safe leaving it where it is. So, what do we do?'

Mark looked at Daryl and sensed a change in leadership. Daryl seemed to have grown up and assumed the role of leader. In that moment, Mark stepped down.

Nobody answered Daryl's question. They couldn't.

'I think our biggest problem,' Mark eventually said, 'is that we can't get out any more. I know your knee and shoulder will get better, Daryl, and you'll be able to move, but we still can't meet up. We've been threatened by our parents. No skiving off, no going beyond our four walls without one of them going with us… I tell you, it's rubbish. And it's all because we dug up that powder.'

Daryl sighed. 'But we're not coming up with answers. What if we told one of our parents?'

'Are you crazy?' Dom laughed. 'If we told our parents we'd got a stash of drugs in Freya's Wendy house, we'd be grounded 'til we were twenty.'

'I've got an idea,' Sammy said, his voice low. 'Who's going to Ella's funeral?'

They all nodded.

'Right, so our parents will be taking us. This is going to be down to you two, Mark and Dom, I reckon. You need to bring that package with you in a backpack, like we've carried it before.'

He paused, and they all waited. 'We'll have a little more freedom at the church, because there'll be lots of adults around and our parents won't be quite so worried about us. Surely we can stash it behind a gravestone or something? Or under a bush?'

Sammy shrugged. 'That's it, that's all I can come up with. I don't care anymore about what happens to it after that. I want it away from us, and not our problem.'

'What if we're seen?' Freya's forehead creased with worry.

'We need to disguise it, so it doesn't stand out as white powder.' Mark turned his head towards his brother. 'Dom, if we wrapped it in a Sainsbury's carrier bag, it wouldn't be obvious what it was, would it?'

'It's still a big package to hide, whether it's white or orange,' Dom pondered. 'I think we need to give this some thought. Getting rid at the funeral is the best idea we've had, but we can't turn up there without a bit more of a plan. Tomorrow's Sunday, so we need a volunteer to go with Mum to church… Freya.'

'What?' The little girl looked indignant. 'Why me?'

'Because you're young enough to end up in Sunday School, and they're bound to take all the little kids outside. They usually do in the summer. Mark and I are too old for Sunday School,' Dom explained, and Freya glared at him.

Mark joined in. 'We need you to have a good scout round the churchyard. Mum said this morning the service is at the church before going on to the crem. I don't think we'll be allowed to go to that part, so our only hope is the churchyard.'

'What's the crem?' Freya turned her eyes towards her brothers.

They looked at each other, and Daryl spoke. 'It's where they will take Ella after the church service. It's the last little bit of the funeral.'

He hoped she wouldn't ask for any further details. He didn't want her having nightmares. 'So, you'll go with Mum?'

'I suppose so,' Freya sighed, feeling well and truly stitched up. 'We go through part of the churchyard when we come out of church to walk round to the church hall. Even if they don't bring us out after that, I'll see what I can find at the beginning.'

'Good girl,' Mark said, and winked at Dom.

They could discuss nothing further until Freya reported her findings, so they moved on to Daryl's adventures over the past few days.

By lunchtime, it was clear that Daryl was falling asleep, so Carl walked the Brownlows and Sammy back home, leaving Aileen to help Daryl upstairs for a nap after taking his medication.

Sitting on the sofa in the quiet house, Carl took hold of Aileen's hand. 'Thank you for all you've done over the past couple of days. You've been a star.'

'No problem. Daryl's a lovely lad. Shame he had you for a dad, really.'

'Thanks. I am trying, you know. I've not been allowed to have much to do with him. He was always Megan's lad. I'm having to learn how to be a dad.'

'Have you contacted this Kenny, then?' she asked abruptly, changing the subject.

'Yes, I texted him, and we're going to his home about six for a meal. He says if Grausohn does call him in for anything, it's generally after nine anyway.'

'Doesn't Grausohn ever go out?'

'Very rarely, according to Kenny. I've never seen him anywhere outside of his office.'

'It could work, this ridiculous plan,' Aileen grudgingly admitted. 'But what you really need is something to make it look as though he committed suicide, rather than being pushed over the side. Is he a big man, by the way?'

Carl gave a short bark of laughter. 'I would say twenty stone, or thereabouts. It's a good job Kenny's got muscles like Goliath. It'll certainly take both of us to get him over.'

She nodded. 'I've got several questions, but I'll make a list and ask them when we get to this meal. Have you met his partner?'

'Not yet. Didn't even know of his existence 'til yesterday. I had no idea he preferred men. He always comes across as quite macho. Each to their own.'

'You were right,' he continued as he fondled her breast.

She smiled and relaxed.

'Will you stay tonight?' He'd been quite disappointed when she had insisted on going home the previous night.

She sat up straighter. 'Nope, I'm going home. I'll walk up in the morning, make us all a full English, if you like.'

'I'd prefer if you stayed.'

'Probably, but I'm still going home. I like my own company, Carl. And Daryl's lost his mum. He's devastated. He'll not want another woman on the horizon before she's even been buried.'

'And are you? On the horizon?'

Aileen laughed. 'Not bloody likely. I've my own house, my books, my telly when I'm waiting for my next book – what would I want a man for? No, don't look in this direction, matey, it ain't going to happen. I don't mind the odd bit of sex, but only when I want to, not when you want to. Understood?'

'You're a hard woman, Aileen Walmsley…'

'Understood?' she repeated.

'Understood.'

They sat in silence, then Aileen stood. 'I'm going to get off before it goes dark. I'll be back about nine in the morning, and I'll do breakfast. Ring me if you need me, but only if you fall down the stairs, or the house is on fire. Emergencies only, Carl.'

She kissed him long and hard on the lips, pressed her breasts against his chest, then turned and walked out of the door.

She was still chuckling as she walked down the street and up her own path.

She closed the front door behind her and leaned against it. It felt empty without Vinnie, quiet and empty. She'd tidied and cleaned, and it had remained tidy and clean. She wanted empty cans on the kitchen table, dishes everywhere, empty pizza boxes. She wanted Vinnie home again.

Sunday morning started a little grey, but by nine, the sun had come out, and the world, as Aileen knew it, was waking up.

Daryl and Carl were in the kitchen, Daryl at the table reading his book and Carl making his second cup of tea of the morning.

'Morning, you two.' She smiled. 'Daryl, any better?'

'I can walk round the table without having to hold on.'

'And your shoulder?'

If it hadn't been so painful, he would have shrugged. 'It's okay. Still hurts,' was all he said.

'Full English?'

'Do you mind if I have a bacon sandwich? It's easier to eat than having to use a knife and fork.'

'No problem.' She leant over and kissed his forehead. 'Carl? Full English?'

'Please. I'll make drinks.'

They worked quietly, and Daryl became immersed in his book. It was as Aileen handed him the bacon sandwich that he heard the church bells. Church. Freya would be there now, sourcing somewhere for them to dump the bag of drugs.

He wondered if this was the right thing to do; he knew it was much too late to hand them into Roberts. They'd be in so much trouble if they did that, and not only from the police – they all had parents. It was so hard being a kid.

'Can all the children who are attending Sunday School please go with Doreen and Jennifer? They're waiting at the back of the church for you.' There was a shuffling of feet, clattering as books were knocked to the floor, and around six or seven children, including a reluctant Freya, made their way to the two women who would be telling them about the Good Samaritan within five minutes.

Freya held back and watched as the two women led the children across the front of the church and around the side, before heading into the hall. She looked around her; she could see really old gravestones, some at odd angles, most of them dirty with years of Yorkshire air ingrained into them, and she could see five or six large old ones, reared up at the side of the wall that surrounded the churchyard. She thought it quite strange that people would be buried under a wall.

She took a quick look around, saw there was no one to watch her and headed for the gravestones. Because the stones were leaning, there was a gap at the back of them; she knew she had found their dumping ground. She ran into the church hall, and Doreen regarded her with something approaching shock.

'Did we forget you?' she asked.

Freya laughed. 'No, I had to stop to take off my shoe. It had a stone in it. It's fine now.'

'You should have said. One of us would have helped you. Anyway, never mind. Sit at the table with the others. We're going to talk about the Good Samaritan today.'

Freya sat at the table and immediately switched off, choosing to stare out of the window instead. She listened to Jennifer's voice, flat, emotionless.

'Freya!'

Freya jumped and knew she looked guilty.

'What are you staring at through that window?'

'It's that gravestone, Jennifer. It's leaning. It looks as if it's going to fall over.' Freya inwardly congratulated herself on coming up with a feasible answer.

Jennifer moved to the window. 'Freya, I don't think it's going to fall today. It's probably one of the stones down for removal.'

'Removal?' Suddenly Freya felt uneasy.

Jennifer laughed. 'Don't worry, I didn't mean removal altogether. When stones lean dangerously, they must be taken to the side and reared up against the wall, for safety. Like those over there.' She pointed to the gravestones Freya had already visited, and the little girl breathed a sigh of relief. So, people weren't buried under the wall. It was a way of keeping the headstones in the churchyard, without the headstones falling and killing people.

Freya turned to Jennifer with a smile, said 'sorry' and listened for the rest of the lesson.

Sunday afternoon was spent in the garden for the Brownlow twins and their sister. She had with her a drawing pad and a pencil. She sketched the plan of the churchyard as closely as she could remember it and showed it to Mark and Dom.

'That's where the old headstones are, leaning against that wall. They've all got a gap behind them, but three of them are kind of on top of one another, so that might be the safest spot.'

'And they're close to the church hall?' Dom was staring at the drawing.

'Not too close. I think we'll be okay.'

'Okay. We need to get our fingerprints off the plastic Tuesday afternoon and get it wrapped in a carrier bag. We could do with a darker colour than the bright orange, though. You've done well, Freya.' Dom handed the drawing to his brother. 'We might get away with this.'

'Okay,' Freya said. 'You two bullied me into doing this, into going to church with Mum. Payback.'

She handed them two drawings of the Good Samaritan. 'Jennifer at church wants these coloured in for next Sunday morning. I told her I'd take your copies in, at the same time as mine.'

They stared at the pictures with something like horror written across their faces. 'You didn't…'

'Oh, I did. Don't tangle with a Brownlow girl, ever. Especially not this Brownlow girl. Mum's taking them into Jennifer, so get colouring.'

She walked away from them, trying to hold in the laughter. *One up to us, Ella,* she thought. *One up to us.*

18

The meal, cooked entirely by Billy, was delicious. They had started with a simple pâté salad and small crispbreads, and that had led on to steak, with new potatoes and vegetables. The pièce de résistance was the most delicious apple pie and cream Aileen had ever tasted.

She raised her glass of wine in appreciation of the meal and said a simple thank you.

'You're very welcome, Aileen,' Billy said. 'I'll put on some coffee, and we can take it out onto the patio and have a chat. Kenny, take our guests through and don't forget your phone in case he rings.'

Kenny took them through to the patio, and the three of them sat quietly, enjoying the perfume from the nearby rose garden, while waiting for Billy to join them.

Carl tried to start the conversation, but Billy waved his hand at him. 'Enjoy some coffee first, Carl, before we talk of death.'

It almost seemed civilised. They sipped from their bone china coffee cups, and then, eventually, Kenny spoke. 'Okay, now we have to talk. I am assuming you have both thought things through.'

Aileen and Carl looked at each other.

'We have,' Carl said, 'and we're in.'

Kenny looked closely at Aileen. 'You'll alibi Carl?'

She nodded. 'Fully. If I could, I would kill him myself. You must realise that. Vinnie was my only child, my world. Because of this evil… thing… I've lost him.'

'Then, I suggest we change the evening to Friday, instead of Thursday. Gerda, his housekeeper, always goes to bingo on a Friday, because there is a massive jackpot on that night. She stays later than normal. Carl, you will need to come up with a list of the kids' names for him, and some addresses from round here, so that he believes they are genuine. Names you can invent, but make sure the addresses will stand up to scrutiny.'

Carl nodded.

'I'll ring him around eight on Friday night – that would be quite normal for me. I'll tell him you've finally managed to get the names, and can we pop up with them, so we can get organised for snatching one of the kids. I'll build you up to him – say it's taken so long because nobody was saying anything about the kids. That way, you might get the payment he promised for the information. It's no good thinking we can help ourselves after we've chucked him over, because whatever is in there, is in his safe, and we have to leave immediately, almost before he's hit the deck outside.'

Again, Carl nodded. He knew how much thought had gone into this plan, and whatever Kenny said was fine with him. He wasn't looking forward to the actual deed of hoisting the huge man over that balcony; he was no killer, merely a small-time crook. And he was also a little concerned that even between them they would struggle to lift him, especially as he would be fighting back.

They enjoyed refills of the coffee, Kenny answered a couple of minor points that had occurred to Aileen, and at nine o'clock, they headed home.

Liam had stayed in with Daryl, who was now in very little pain. His knee was fine; the bruising was spectacular, but the pain had all but disappeared. Only a careless movement caused it to remind him it was still in recovery. His arm was in a sling, supporting the damaged shoulder, and he was sleeping on his good side, but in general, he was pain free, simply irritated by only having one arm in full working order.

Liam said goodnight, adding that Daryl had been in bed quarter of an hour and telling Aileen that if she needed anything before Monday, the day of Vinnie's funeral, to ring him. She smiled briefly, kissed him on the cheek with a whispered thank you and watched as he walked down the road, heading for home.

'Nice lad,' Carl said.

'Mmm. He booked tonight off work, so he could stay with Daryl. He works nights at Asda, stacking shelves. Him and Vinnie have been best mates since they were about four years old. It's hit him hard.' Aileen felt her eyes prickle with tears. 'You want a cup of tea?'

'No, let's have something stronger. Round the evening off properly. Whisky?'

'Only a small one. That wine was lovely, but it was strong.'

'Then stay the night, and you won't have to worry about wobbling home.'

'Ever the opportunist.' She smiled. 'Okay, I will. I'll need to be up early, though, to get ready for Ella's funeral. I bet that's why Daryl took himself off to bed.'

Carl handed her the drink, slightly larger than the requested small one, and they settled on the sofa. They talked through the plan details once more, and both agreed it had to work; if it didn't, Grausohn wouldn't stop until they were all dead.

By ten o'clock, they were asleep. Daryl was still reading, wishing it was Thursday, and Wednesday would be out of the way.

'Sir?' PC Craig Smythe spoke into his phone, feeling uneasy. He'd never had a phone call at home from DI Roberts before.

'You got a darkish suit, lad?'

'Yes, sir, navy blue.'

'Good. Wear it tomorrow. We're going to a funeral. Sorry it's short notice. I was supposed to be taking Dan Eden, but his wife's gone into labour.'

Craig smiled. 'I can promise that won't happen here, sir. Is it the Ella Johnston funeral?'

'It is. Eyes and ears open. Strange things can happen at funerals.'

'Very good, sir.'

'Night, lad.'

'Night, sir.'

Craig stared at the phone for a moment. The last time he'd worn a suit had been for his police interview. He hoped to God the trousers would still fasten. The jacket he could leave open…

Aileen was home by ten; she had seen to the three of them having a good breakfast, because she didn't know when they would eat again. The church service was at midday, with the cremation at half past one. It would be mid-afternoon before they reached the Yellow Lion, where Cissie had arranged for the wake to be held.

She changed into a dark skirt and pink top, as requested by Cissie. She wanted her little girl's send-off to be a sea of pink. She had arranged to pick up Carl and Daryl in her car around eleven-thirty, in the hope that she could get parked somewhere close by the church.

She looked at herself in the mirror, worried by the image that stared back at her. She had lost the… glow? The life force? Whatever she had had, it was no longer there. Over the next week or so, she had three funerals, one of whom was her own son. She remembered the afternoon of the day before Vinnie had died, when she had been laughing because she had showed him up in front of Liam. How she wished she could have that afternoon back again. This time, she would do the washing, make him a cup of tea. Tell him how much she loved him.

She watched the clock tick the time slowly away, and just before eleven-thirty, she locked up and drove to Carl and Daryl's house. She noticed there was still a slight limp to Daryl's walk, despite his protestations that he was much better, hardly in any pain at all.

She dropped the two of them outside the church, figuring it would be better for Daryl, then drove around the corner to park the car. By the time she'd walked back around, Daryl was standing with the Brownlow kids, and Sammy. Their parents were huddled together in a group, talking and looking downcast about the situation they now found themselves in.

The children moved over to the headstones reared up against the wall. Mark dropped the backpack down by the first headstone and unzipped it quickly. He pulled out two books, then the hefty package wrapped up in a dark green carrier bag. Sammy followed Mark's actions and pulled down his shirt sleeve, so that it encased his hand, and took it from him while the others stood in a line, forming a barrier between them and the distant adults. It was the best they could do, and Sammy pushed it as fast as he could into the cavity formed behind the middle headstone. Mark stood and held out the two books towards Daryl, who tried not to look surprised.

'Sorry, Daryl, but you have to take this bag now. I thought Mum might kick off about me taking a backpack to the funeral, so to stop her, I told her you'd asked me if you could borrow a couple of books, 'cos you're bored with sitting around. That's why I put two books in.'

'Brilliant thinking, Mark,' Daryl said, 'especially as it's true. I can't put it on my back, though, I'll carry it.'

They heard a cry of 'kids,' and they turned towards the adults. They were beckoning so they guessed Ella had arrived.

They navigated the various graves and headed towards their parents. And Daryl froze. The bag dropped from his hand, and Freya turned, sensing something was wrong.

'Daryl? You hurting?'

He couldn't speak at first.

Freya picked up the bag and tugged on his hand. 'Come on, they're waiting for us.'

He blinked and looked around seeking out his dad. He took the bag from Freya, thanked her and limped as fast as he could to where Carl and Aileen were waiting for him.

'Dad…' There were tears in Daryl's eyes.

'I know, son. She was your friend. You're going to cry. Don't worry.'

'That's not it.' Now, the tears were really flowing. 'That man over there, by that big white angel grave, he's the one who was driving the car that killed my mum.'

Carl spun around, searching for the angel. It was easily seen, especially with Kenny Lancaster at the side of it.

'Are you sure?' But he knew Daryl was right. Now, it made sense. Kenny was here because he'd killed Ella, and Carl suspected he had been next on the list so that he couldn't give out any more names. Megan had paid the price for him not being in that car.

'Can you keep quiet about it?' he whispered. 'I promise I'll deal with it, but not here. Today is for Ella.'

Daryl nodded, and Aileen looked on, a perplexed expression on her face. Something was wrong. She reached forward and handed Daryl a tissue.

'Dry your eyes, sweetheart. And when we get inside, sit between us. We're here to look after you.'

They moved as the small white coffin reached the church doors. Cissie was calm, upright and dressed in a pink dress. She showed no grief, and she carried a pink rose and Mr Grumps.

As they processed down the aisle, Carl was aware of Kenny some way behind them, and he thought it was best that way. He wouldn't be tempted to say or do anything by being near him.

The service began, and Cissie fell apart. Her sobs filled the church, and she stood and took Mr Grumps and the rose towards the coffin. She placed them on top and laid her head on the lid.

Sally moved forward and stood with her, then led her gently back to her seat, remaining with her and leaving John to cope with the wide-eyed disbelief of their own three children.

So many children crying; almost every child from Ella and Freya's class was there, and it seemed to be beyond their comprehension that they would never see their friend again; so much sound, so much distress.

It seemed to be a wave of pink that followed the white coffin out of the church and back to the hearse. Sally stayed with Cissie, limpet-like; she knew her friend was on the point of collapse, and it wasn't going to happen, not on her shift. Several people tried to speak to Cissie, but with glazed eyes and no real comprehension of what was happening, they received nothing in return.

The five members of Ella's Gang watched as the hearse began its journey to the crematorium; none of them spoke. Mark and Dom held on to Freya's hands as if they never wanted to let her go. She was one month older than Ella had been. It could have been their little sister in that coffin.

Daryl looked around trying to spot the man he had recognised but could no longer see him. He must have been one of the first out of the church, and now, he had disappeared. The sense of relief he had felt at finally getting rid of the package of drugs had been washed away by seeing the man. Still, his dad had said he would deal with it – he had to trust that it would happen.

They drifted away, some to their homes and some to the Yellow Lion. Daryl saw his father speaking with DI Roberts and wondered if his dad was telling him about his son's recognition of the man. He thought his dad might deal with it himself. Sometimes, you didn't need the police to sort things out.

Aileen brought the car around to the church, and Daryl limped across to get in, helped by his dad. 'You okay, sweetheart?' she asked. 'I've got your medication in my bag, if you want some when we get to the pub.'

He nodded. 'Thanks, Aileen, I will. I'm a bit achy all over.'

Nobody spoke for the rest of the short journey, and they went into the pub and quickly found a seat, together with the Brownlows and Janey Walker. The children all sat together and were provided with lemonades.

They needed to talk, but in the noisy environment of the Yellow Lion, it was impossible.

Only a few people had accompanied Cissie to the crematorium, and she was back in their midst within the hour. She looked drained, and Sally made her sit with them; she felt she needed to be with her, to offer what comfort she could on such a horrific day.

Mourners started to leave around four o'clock, and by half past five, the staff were cleaning away the detritus left. Sally took Cissie back with them, asking Janey to drop off the twins on her way home.

By six o'clock, all of Ella's Gang were in their own homes, trying desperately to come to terms with their first funeral, and the finality of losing Ella.

Daryl needed to speak to Carl, and when Aileen said she was going home, he felt relieved. Carl walked her to the door, kissed her and watched as she walked to her car.

'Take care,' he called, and she waved a hand in acknowledgement through the open car window.

He turned around, and Daryl was standing immediately behind him. 'Nearly knocked you over there, pal,' he said with a smile. 'You want something?'

'I want to know who that man is. The one who killed Mum. Why was he at Ella's funeral?'

'I have no idea, but I don't want you worrying. It will be sorted. And don't go saying anything to DI Roberts if he calls 'round.'

Daryl stared at his father. 'What you gonna do?'

'I've told you, I'll sort it. Now, you want to watch the telly, or are you going to bed?'

Daryl's face showed his disgust. 'I'll go to bed. I've got some new books from Mark and Dom.'

He left the room, feeling overwhelmed by anger. His dad clearly hadn't changed; it was all an act, this caring for him. He didn't care at all.

Roberts was at his desk, going through every report, every scrap of paper that had filtered through with regard to the Vinnie Walmsley murder. Nothing new hit him; every tiny lead – and they were tiny – had been followed up, and still, they didn't know who the woman was. Or where she was.

He heard the door open, and Craig Smythe stood framed by the jamb. He had loosened his tie off a little, now that he was going home.

'Heading home now, boss, unless you need me for anything else.'

'Come in a minute, will you. I'll not keep you long.'

Craig closed the door and sat down opposite Roberts. 'Sir?'

'You okay after today?'

Craig shrugged. 'If the truth is what you're after, no, I'm not okay. It's the first child's funeral I've ever been to, and I don't want to go to another one. The mother…'

'I know,' Roberts replied. 'She was a mess. She's a lovely woman, and it was just her and her daughter, so she's lost everything. There's no dad to the little girl, to Ella.'

'And the size of that coffin, so tiny. And all those kids…'

'They came from her class at school. God knows how the school will deal with it when they go back in a couple of weeks.'

'I saw that her friends from that little gang they had were there. He's still limping, the lad from the crash at Dinnington.'

'Yeah, nice kids. And, of course, he's got his mother's funeral coming up. This shouldn't be happening to any kid, it's too much. Okay, Craig, wanted your thoughts. Try not to dwell on it, it might be your first, but it won't be your last.'

Craig Smythe stood. 'Thank you, sir. Back in uniform tomorrow. The trousers fit me better than these do.'

'Best get you out patrolling on the push bikes, then,' Roberts joked. 'See you in the morning.'

'Goodnight, sir. There's one thing about that funeral that struck me as being a bit strange – that feller that we stopped in the woods, the one with the little white dog. He was there.'

19

Kenny saw the police car pull up outside and stubbed out his cigarette. Eight o'clock seemed a bit early in the morning for a routine police visit, and he wondered what the hell they wanted.

'Billy,' he said quietly, 'there's a squad car outside. Do you want to disappear?'

'I'll go take a shower, a long one. Shout if you need me.'

Kenny went to the front door, opening it as Roberts knocked.

'Mr Lancaster? DI Roberts, and, as you probably remember, this is PC Smythe.' Roberts showed his warrant card. 'Can we come in for a minute, please, sir?'

Kenny opened the door wide. 'Of course. What can I do for you, Detective Inspector?'

He led them into the lounge and indicated that they should sit down.

Roberts spoke first. 'It's about a funeral you attended, yesterday, Mr Lancaster.'

'Yes, what of it?' Kenny's mind was racing.

'Did you know the deceased?'

'Sort of. I found out last week that she was my daughter. Prior to that, I had assumed, wrongly it seems, that her mother had had an abortion. When Cecily Johnston told me she was pregnant, I said I wasn't ready for children, and she said she wasn't either. We weren't even that close at the time, and we simply split up. I never heard from her again. Then, last week, she contacted my sister, the woman whose dog I take for walks, to get her to pass a message onto me. When we were together, Cissie and I, I had lived with Katie, my sister. She remembered her and found her through Facebook.'

He paused for a moment, as if gathering his thoughts. 'Katie gave Cissie my email address. Would you like to see those communications, DI Roberts?' He stood and walked over to pick up his phone. He logged on to his emails.

Roberts joined him, watching as he clicked on one that said Cecily Ann. Kenny walked away, his stomach churning. He could have done without this.

Roberts read through them. It was clear Lancaster was telling the truth.

'Then, indeed, I am deeply sorry for your loss, Mr Lancaster. Can I ask you to forward those to my email address, please? Just for our files, and we won't bother you any further.' He handed his card to Kenny, and Craig Smythe stood.

A minute later, they were back in the squad car and heading back to the south east of the city.

'Must have been a bit of a shock for him,' Roberts said, staring out of the passenger window. 'First time he hears he has a daughter, and he finds out it's because she's dead.'

'You don't think it's a bit suspicious, then, sir?'

'He didn't invent those emails, Craig. He'd no advance warning we were about to turn up on his doorstep.'

'It's not that. It's the fact that he's there. Why was he in that tiny strip of woodland? He doesn't live anywhere near here. He said he was on his way to Rother Valley, when his date rang to cancel, so he took the dog there. But that bit of woodland isn't on the way to Rother Valley. It's not really on the way to anywhere. Everything that's happening seems sort of interconnected. Gives me goosebumps.'

'Promise me you won't put goosebumps in any report, PC Smythe,' Roberts said drily. 'It's not really official police language.'

Roberts hesitated. 'But you're right. Vinnie Walmsley dies, and this Lancaster feller turns up in the woods. Ella Johnston dies, and he turns up at the funeral. Wonder if he'll turn up at Megan

Clarkson's funeral? Or Vinnie Walmsley's? Let's go back and see what we can find out about him. I'll stake my pension on him being on some database or other that's in our system. Don't put the suit away. We've two more funerals to go to.'

Cissie Johnston wanted to close her eyes and never open them again. She had insisted on going home after an hour at the Brownlow's; it was too hard seeing Freya running around fully recovered, knowing that Ella had died because she wanted to make sure her friend wasn't too ill.

Cissie didn't explain her reasons for wanting to go home, not the real reasons, anyway. She simply said it was time to open the curtains.

John walked up with her and checked everything was okay, then waited outside until he heard the lock click on the front door. Satisfied that she was as safe as possible, he headed back home to his own three children. He was dreading their imminent return to school life; they would be away from their protection.

Thursday morning in the Clarkson household was a quiet one. The funeral of the previous day had left its mark. Carl had reassured Daryl that he would sort out what he called "the situation with the man." He preferred not to use his name, preferred not to reveal he knew him; he didn't want Daryl saying anything to Roberts.

He didn't want Kenny to know that Daryl had identified him; it was important that Kenny thought they were allies.

Carl's mind wandered a little when he saw the strappy top Aileen was wearing, but he dragged his thoughts back to his current problems.

She gave him a brief kiss and asked how Daryl was.

'He's okay. He's watching some movie or other in the lounge. Bit quiet, but he's bound to be. Come in the kitchen. I need to talk to you away from Daryl's ears. I spent most of last night trying to come up with a plan, but it means I need your help.'

'Good God, Carl, I'm already giving you an alibi. What more can you want?'

'If I can persuade Kenny and Billy to come here for a meal tonight, to say thank you for Tuesday night and to go over the plans for tomorrow, will you be able to do it? I might manage chips and egg, but I don't think that'll impress them.'

Aileen laughed. 'Sure. But why? We went over it in detail the other night. You can't have forgotten in two days.'

'I don't want to tell you the reason yet, but it's important.'

She stared at him; she could see the strain on his face. 'That's good enough for me. Of course I'll do it. Text them and check they're free. About six? Then, if Kenny's called in, at least he'll have eaten.'

Carl pulled her close and hugged her. 'Thank you,' he whispered, and kissed the top of her head. 'Now, I need to get Daryl out of the house – I don't want him meeting up with Kenny and Billy. That side of my life is over after tomorrow night.'

'You could pay for Liam to take him to the cinema – and a McDonald's, of course.'

'He's not working?'

'No, he's got some time off. He's got Vinnie and Megan's funerals next week, so he thought it better to book a two-week break. He's a good lad.'

'You think he'll do that?'

'Give me five minutes, and we'll know. You contact Kenny and Billy, make sure they can come first. If they can't come, then it's pointless asking Liam.'

'They've got to come,' Carl muttered.

He texted Kenny on the new phone, and it seemed only seconds before a reply came through.

Thanks. About six? Stop worrying, it'll be fine.

With Liam agreeing to take Daryl out, Carl breathed easier. He handed Aileen some money and gave her instructions to get something spectacular. He wanted Billy and Kenny mellow.

While she was out, he washed the whisky glasses until they sparkled, took out Megan's finest crockery and polished her best cutlery. He also polished a small silver tray until it gleamed, then stood the whisky glasses on it, with his most expensive malt standing proudly in the centre. None of the glasses had so much as a single fingerprint on them. He had made sure of that.

The table looked beautiful, and Kenny and Billy arrived on time. Aileen welcomed them with a smile and led them through to the lounge. She told them the meal was almost ready, because she wanted them to have relaxed slightly after eating, if Grausohn chose that night to call Kenny in.

After eating in the sparklingly clean dining room, they headed out to the patio, where Carl switched on the heater. The temperature had dropped slightly, making them all aware that the long, hot summer was drawing ever faster towards autumn. He carried out the tray set with the whisky decanter and the glasses; they gleamed in the late evening sun.

'Malt?' Carl asked.

Billy responded with a smile and a 'please,' but Kenny shook his head. 'Best not,' he said. 'If Grausohn rings… and I've already had that very fine wine.'

'Then can I tempt you with something else?'

'Got any tonic water?'

Carl nodded. 'Only tonic water? Or something to go with it?'

'No, a tonic water will do, thanks, Carl.'

Carl breathed a sigh of relief as he returned into the house to get the requested drink.

He poured it into the glass and stood the bottle on the table. 'Help yourself,' he said, and sat down. Aileen had poured one for Billy and one for Carl, and he sipped at it gratefully. For a moment, he had thought that his plans would go awry.

They quickly went through the details for the following night, and just as they were thinking Kenny wouldn't be going out, his phone rang.

'Boss?'

There was a brief pause while Kenny listened to Grausohn, and then, he said, 'Ten minutes,' before disconnecting the call.

'I'm sorry, we have to leave you. Thank you, Aileen, Carl, it's been smashing. We'll celebrate properly once tomorrow is over.'

Kenny and Billy stood, and both placed their glasses back on the tray. They headed through the house and out of the front door.

Aileen leaned against it. 'Thank goodness that's over,' she said shakily. 'I was starting to worry that Daryl might get back before they'd left. Did you get what you needed?'

Carl nodded. 'Definitely.' His tone was grim. 'Roll on tomorrow night.'

'Come in, Kenny.' Grausohn looked up as he heard the knock on the door.

'Boss,' Kenny acknowledged, as he entered the office. 'Problem?'

'Carl Clarkson.'

'What's he done?' Kenny felt a flicker of unease.

'Nothing. And, Kenny, that's my point. Where is the list of these kids he promised?'

Kenny smiled. 'You should have it by tomorrow. He's been thorough with this one. Two of the kids are out of the picture – one's dead, and one's hospitalised. He knows who the other four are, and he's got two addresses to sort. We've got to be careful, boss. Can't make any mistakes with these.'

'When will I get this information?' Grausohn's eyes were piercing.

'Tomorrow, at some point.'

'Okay, here's the deal, Kenny. I want him here at eight tomorrow evening.' His German accent was getting ever more guttural, the angrier he got. 'No pissing about, Kenny. You bring him, with that list complete. And the day after, I want one of those kids here.'

'Yes, boss, no problem. Eight o'clock it is.' Kenny couldn't believe his luck. It was as if Grausohn had read their script. It was only later that he realised it was a perfectly normal arrangement for Grausohn to make; anybody who was in trouble dreaded the eight o'clock appointment. And it always meant nobody else would be there; no witnesses to orders issued.

'Is there anything else you need tonight?'

'Yes, my fucking consignment. I've smoothed things out for the rest, but I still need that back. You've not heard anything?'

'No, boss, and I've got people out there asking questions. Not a sniff of it. Somebody's stashed it away, and they're waiting.'

'These kids know something. And one of them will talk.'

Kenny nodded. 'You'll get it, I'm sure.' He wasn't talking about the drugs.

'Come and have a drink with me, Kenny, and tell me what you think about this Fraser.' He stood and walked through to his lounge. 'Whisky?'

'A small one, thanks, already had wine with my meal.'

Grausohn nodded. 'Good man. Reliable Kenny. You're the only one I trust around here. Can't get my head around this Fraser. I brought him here as a favour, but he doesn't know me like you do, Kenny.'

'He'll be okay,' Kenny said. 'He needs to settle in. It's not easy coming from London to Yorkshire, you know. It'll take him a while to work things out.'

'Aye, there's nowt so queer as folks,' Grausohn said, the Yorkshire phrase with a German accent sounding… strange.

'What?' Kenny laughed, taking a sip of his whisky.

'Tommy taught me that. I miss Tommy, but he was becoming a liability.'

Just like me, Kenny thought. Tommy had seen what a thug Grausohn was, and now, he had. The only difference was that Tommy had done nothing about it; he was going to stop it, to shut down this whole caboodle, if he could. Maybe Fraser would take it over, bring his pals up from London, but whatever happened, he would be out of it.

He and Billy had their place in Crete, and that would be their immediate stop, but then, they would decide what to do. He'd always fancied Hawaii…

Grausohn interrupted his thoughts. 'Cigar, Kenny?'

They stood out on the balcony, staring across the city. The sun was setting, and darkness was approaching fast. Kenny studied the layout carefully and knew that it would be fairly simple to tip him over. They would need to lift the huge man by one leg each and leave the rest to gravity. But they wouldn't get a second chance – it had to be first time, and over.

'Somewhere out there, Kenny, is my package.' Grausohn sounded almost contemplative. 'I want it back. It belongs to me. And I know those kids are the answer.'

'By tomorrow night, we'll know who they are. Carl's done a good job on this. He had to be careful asking the questions. It's kids, and people are a bit too quick to scream paedophile these days. But he's almost there. He's earned the money.'

'Yes, I know.' Grausohn sounded strained. 'I feel it's taken him so long…'

'And if the police had learned he was asking questions about kids and their addresses? No, it was never going to be quick, this job. And he's almost there with the answers. Keep him on side, boss, he's a good worker. And at least we know him, not like this Fraser bloke.'

'You're right. If he has all their names and addresses, there'll be a hefty bonus. Think he's likely to be able to step up to the top table at some point? Think we can trust him?'

'I'm sure we can. I've kept in close touch with him while he's been doing this job for you – and don't forget his wife's died, so he's had that to deal with as well. He's okay, is Carl. I think we can bring him in properly. Up to you, boss.'

They carried on smoking, both deep in thought. Different thoughts. Kenny was trying to work out exactly where his boss would land when they tipped him over, and Grausohn, Kenny assumed, was wondering where his package was.

By ten o'clock, Kenny had said goodnight and was heading back to the ground floor in the private lift. The car park was on the opposite side of the building to the balcony of Grausohn's flat, so at least Grausohn wouldn't land on his bonnet. There was, however, a small matter of CCTV cameras pointing down to the car park; this was an exclusive block of flats with expensive cars in the car park, and he had to get around that. They had to park elsewhere, which would add to their getaway time. And they had to escape via the basement, scene of the wheelie bin disposal of Johanna.

He put the car into gear and drove out of the car park. He turned right instead of his usual left and drove slowly, looking for the ideal spot. He made a note of a probable one and hoped it would be available the next night, then drove home, feeling jittery and needing a hug from Billy.

Carl wrapped the glass that had contained tonic water in kitchen towel. He had chosen small glasses deliberately, not because it was his most expensive malt whisky, but because he needed to fit it into the inside pocket of his suit, without it being obvious. He would also put the fictional list for Grausohn into the same pocket, so if Kenny said anything about the bulge, he would be able to say what was in there.

Aileen came up behind him and put her arms around him. 'That was a good night. I'm not sure what you're playing at, but I like them, Kenny and Billy. Want me to stay tonight?'

He turned around to face her. 'I do,' he said, and kissed her.

They heard the front door open, and Liam and Daryl walked in. Daryl's limp was hardly noticeable, although the sling was still in place, supporting his shoulder.

Liam was carrying a half full bucket of popcorn, and he put it on the kitchen table. 'Good film,' he said, and high-fived Daryl, who grinned.

'We've seen a couple of other trailers that looked good, Dad, so next time you want me out of the way, we'll go to the cinema again. Okay?'

20

Friday morning started overcast, but by ten, the sun had come out, and blinds were adjusted at windows. Roberts walked out of his own room and into the bustle of the main office. He glanced around; everybody seemed to be busy, and he decided he wouldn't start interrupting them now, they were obviously updating reports, researching potential leads… and he was doing nothing except thinking.

He walked over to the whiteboard and stared at it. Vinnie Walmsley, a young lad now dead, connected with drugs, although nothing proved; Ella Johnston, a nine-year-old child knocked down in a hit and run; Megan Clarkson, killed in a road traffic accident that was no accident, and Daryl Clarkson, injured because of that RTA. What linked them? Three different cars with false number plates, Kenneth Lancaster at various scenes…

He stood for a while staring at the pictures and notes, arrows drawn with tentative connections and links.

Craig Smythe walked across to him and handed him a piece of paper. 'He's on our system, sir. Kenneth Lancaster. Years ago, he was arrested for stealing a car, got a suspended, then a year later, he was locked up for three months for aggravated burglary. But that was all in the past. He was only nineteen when he went to prison. It obviously sorted him, because there's been nothing since. Not a sniff. Over twenty years clean.'

'Don't you mean over twenty years of not being caught?'

'Yes, sir, I do. I think he's in this little lot,' he indicated the whiteboard with a sweep of his hand, 'right up to his armpits.'

'So, how do we prove it?' Roberts mused, his eyes once again back on the whiteboard. 'Thank you for this, Craig.'

'No problem, sir. What next?'

'Let's go and see how young Daryl is getting on. In fact, let's call at the Brownlow house and the Walker house. We'll see if the kids have anything else to say, because there's something niggling…'

'Squad car, or you want it low key?'

'We'll take a squad car, if there's one available, I think, Craig. Makes it a bit more official.'

The Brownlow children were in the back garden, feeling out of sorts. What had started out to be a brilliant summer was rapidly fading away into a miserable autumn.

Freya was missing Ella; they had been best friends for four years, and suddenly, the friendship had been ripped apart. Freya sat watching her brothers as they played one-a-side football, knowing that they must be feeling like her. She pulled out her whistle from under her T-shirt and blew her own call sign. Both the boys turned around, looked at each other then walked over to their sister.

'Freya? What's up?'

Her eyes were full of tears. 'I miss Ella, and Sammy and Daryl. I'm sick of colouring, that's not what I want to do. But we can't go anywhere, can we?'

Mark and Dom looked helplessly at each other. They pulled out their own whistles, twins acting in unison, and blew their own call signs.

'We feel the same, Freya. We needed to blow our whistles as well. And I bet it's the same with Daryl and Sammy.' Mark plonked the football on the garden table, and they sat down.

'What do we do?' Dom asked, clearly unsure how to handle a tearful sister who was normally the strongest of the three of them.

Freya stood and swept her hand across the table top. The pencil crayons scattered across the garden, along with the colouring book and the football.

'Freya!' Sally's horrified shout echoed across the garden, and Freya looked up, trying to brush away her tears, to see DI Roberts, a policeman in uniform, and her mum standing in the kitchen doorway.

Freya took one look and ran for the Wendy house. Dom and Mark stared, unsure whether to follow her or let their mother deal with it.

Sally moved purposefully across the garden, and the two police officers came to sit at the table with the boys.

'She's missing Ella,' Dom said.

Roberts nodded. 'I can imagine. They were in the same class, weren't they?'

Dom nodded. 'Been best mates for a long time.'

'Then, lads, she's going to need a lot of support. You're all still in the same school when you go back next week?'

'No,' Mark said. 'We're going into year seven. Freya is two years behind us.'

'That's a shame. You think it's hard for her now, but it'll be worse at school when she doesn't have Ella by her side.'

The boys nodded, watching their mother kneeling on the grass with her head inside the Wendy house.

After a couple of minutes, Sally stood and walked back to the others. 'She's upset, and she's going to stay in there for a bit. Can I get you a drink?'

'We'll have water, if that's okay, Mrs Brownlow.'

She nodded. 'Boys, you want anything?'

They settled on orange juice, then waited with a touch of fear going on inside their heads.

Sally brought out the tray, and they all helped themselves. She carried one across to the Wendy house and handed it in through the window.

Freya remained inside her bolthole.

'What did you want to see us about?' Sally asked. She felt a little tetchy towards them; she had enough on her hands, trying to bring some normality back into her family.

'Just a chat, really. See how everyone is, if you've heard anything in the estate gossip, that sort of thing. I can see Freya is out of sorts.'

'She's a little girl, never experienced death before. What did you expect? She's also very scared, which is down to us, in part. John has turned this house into a fortress. We take the kids everywhere; we can't leave them for a moment. They can't play anymore, not as they did before, and it's heart-breaking to watch them be so quiet. Do you know we had a nickname for Freya? It was feral Freya. Does she look feral now, or does she look like a scared little girl?'

'I understand what you're saying. But you have to continue like that, keeping them close by and safe, until we catch whoever killed Vinnie Walmsley, Ella Johnston and Megan Clarkson.'

Sally's eyes opened wide. 'What do you mean? Do you think the same person killed them all? But why? What on earth had Ella, or Megan for that matter, done to deserve to die?'

Roberts watched as Sally's hand trembled. Calming down time. 'No, Sally, that's not what I'm saying. I do think there is something connecting all three deaths, but as yet, we've not found that connection. And it's not necessarily the same person who killed them all. We've come here today to talk to the children again, to see if time has brought anything to the forefront of their minds. We're clutching at straws, I know, but sometimes, it happens like that. A person suddenly remembers something that didn't seem important first time around. We do this with every major case, believe me. We're not specifically targeting anyone, just chatting. We're going to see Sammy and Daryl later.'

Sally nodded as she listened to his words. She had felt fractured inside by seeing Freya's distress, and Roberts' explanation had calmed her mind a little.

'I don't think you'll get anything out of Freya, but talk to the boys. Mark, Dom, have you anything you can tell DI Roberts?'

Again, the twin connection was obvious as they looked at each other as if making up their minds if they should speak.

Mark spoke first. 'I don't think we've anything new to say. All we did was find a body. There was nobody else there, just us, the six of us. I remember Freya being sick, because she was so upset, and when we'd sorted her out, we came to tell you. After that, you took over. There really was nothing else.'

Roberts nodded. 'And which twin are you?' He made a quick notation in his notebook, more to make Mark think he'd said something significant than anything else, then turned to his brother.

'Sorry, I'm Mark.'

Roberts turned to the other boy. 'Dom?'

'Exactly the same. It was as Mark has said, I can't think of anything else. We saw the body, we stayed with him 'til you came, and that's it.' And then, Dom changed. 'You leave Freya alone. She can't tell you anything more than we can, but she's in a state over Ella.' He was angry, and it showed.

'I'll leave Freya in her little house, I promise,' Roberts said quietly. He was beginning to realise that even if these kids did know something, they certainly weren't going to reveal it, and it wasn't through fear. It was through togetherness, and that wouldn't be broken.

They finished their drinks and stood to leave. Roberts thanked them all, shouted bye to Freya, and Sally escorted them through the kitchen and towards the front door. 'I would have sent you down the side of the house,' she laughed, 'but it's all locked up. Nobody's getting to our kids.'

'You think that's a possibility?' Roberts was quick to jump on her words.

'Yes, I do. Ella has gone, Daryl is injured. It doesn't take a genius to recognise they were targets, does it. We're living on our nerves, John and I, and trying not to let the kids see it. I know they're fed up of playing in the garden all the time, but I can't take the risk. I'm going to contact Janey Walker and Carl Clarkson to see if the other two can come down here for the day tomorrow. I can watch them all, and I know they're missing each other. They have a brilliant friendship, and I won't let the evil scum who have caused all this be the winners.'

'I don't know if this helps ease your mind a little, Sally,' Roberts said, 'but we've stepped up patrols in this area. Like you, I'm worried that the children are being targeted. You'll see a lot more squad cars, so have a little faith in us. Oh, and tell Dom and Mark I knew they were having me on, I can tell which boy is which.'

Sally laughed. 'I wasn't going to correct them. They can be who they want to be, their choice. And you did stress how informal it was…'

Carl Clarkson didn't look too impressed when Roberts arrived, but he led him through to the back garden where Daryl was reading.

'Good book?' he asked and sat down by Daryl's side.

'It is. It's the fourth Rick Riordan. Dad keeps saying I'll bankrupt him.'

'Go to the library.'

Daryl laughed. 'Not likely. I'd have to take them back when I've read them. These are keepers. I want the whole set, so Dad keeps going on Amazon and grumbling. Funny how he's reading them as well, though.'

'You okay with your dad, now?'

There was a hesitancy in Daryl's words. 'I think so. He doesn't seem like the same person he was when Mum was here.'

'That's because he's had to step up, Daryl. Some dads come to it later in life. That's probably the case with your dad, because he saw how close you and your mum became. Perhaps he felt a bit left out. Was he?'

Daryl nodded. 'I suppose so. He never seemed to be around when we had to do anything. Always with that boss of his.'

'Boss?'

'Dunno who it is. He calls him the boss.'

'Do me a favour, Daryl, don't tell your dad you've mentioned his boss to me; he might not like it, and I don't want him falling out with you because you've told me. Okay?'

Daryl nodded. They went on to discuss finding Vinnie's body, and again, Roberts came up against the wall that surrounded the children. They all said the same, and no more.

Five minutes later, Roberts and Smythe were with Janey Walker, and Sammy was excitedly telling them that he was going to the Brownlow's house the following day. Sammy also repeated, virtually word for word, everything the others had said, and finally, Roberts and Smythe headed back to the station.

'Tight little bunch of kids, aren't they? Craig said.

'Certainly are. And I still think there's something that will come out one day. Maybe that was something, the thing that Daryl said about his dad always being with the boss. I thought Megan worked, and Carl was out of work. Strange. Worth looking into?'

'Leave it with me,' Craig said. 'I'll see what I can find. It might take a while, he's a canny feller.'

Roberts collected a coffee and headed back to his office. He needed some quiet thinking time. He saw Smythe go straight to his computer, but he didn't expect results. It was such a throwaway line from Daryl – his dad was always with the boss. It was probably something as simple as Carl having a job on the side that he didn't want anybody knowing about, certainly not the people who paid him his benefits every week.

Roberts sipped at his coffee, his mind going back over the afternoon. The whole saga had clearly affected all of the children, and he knew he wouldn't be chasing them again. Whether they knew something or not, he would have to solve this one without their help.

He finished his coffee and aimed it at the basket. The cup missed it, so he stood with a groan and went around his desk to pick it up. The phone rang.

'DI Roberts.'

'Yes, sir. It's PC Marks, on reception. I have ERF on the phone for you. They have a body.'

Roberts' mind went into overdrive. ERF? A lorry? A body in a lorry? 'Put them through.'

'Good afternoon, DI Roberts. My name is Michael Danbury, and I'm a supervisor at ERF, that's the Energy Recovery Facility, off the Parkway.'

'Yes, Mr Danbury, I know it. What can I do for you?' Roberts grinned. So, it wasn't a lorry with a body in it. How wrong could anybody be?

'We have a body, sir, on our conveyor belt in the sorting room.'

Roberts sat up. 'Lock the room down, get all the staff out and give them a cup of sweet tea; we'll be with you in ten to fifteen minutes. Don't let anybody touch that body.'

'Nobody wants to, I can assure you,' Danbury said drily.

Roberts headed for the main office. 'Brian, Heather, Craig, with me. We've got another dead one. At ERF, off the Parkway.'

'ERF?' queried Craig.

'Energy Recovery Facility,' DS Brian Balding said.

'Smart arse,' Heather muttered.

They took a squad car and, with the lights and sirens activated, reached the facility in seven minutes.

Michael Danbury met them at the door and ushered them in. The room was empty, the conveyor belts stopped. He led them over to the end belt, and Roberts heard Heather Shaw gasp. Women always recognised a designer dress.

The black and white dress, now looking extremely grubby but instantly recognisable, was covering a body that had already begun to decompose.

'Forensics are on the way,' Roberts said. 'This room will be closed for a while. Sorry if that causes problems, but we'll let you know as soon as we're clear.'

Michael Danbury shrugged. 'I'm sending everybody on this shift home. This is a twenty-four-hour facility, so maybe we can pick up with the next shift. I'll stay. If you need any help with knowing the system, I can give you details. I can also mash tea.'

The four police officers viewed the body from as many angles as they could, without touching it, and then retreated to a safe distance when the forensic team arrived.

Michael made them drinks, and they sat at a table, discussing what was obvious and what wasn't so clear.

'She's got no knickers on,' Heather said. On the conveyor belt, the dress had hiked up almost to the victim's waist. 'A designer dress, and no knickers.'

'And?' Brian Balding queried.

'I don't know,' Heather conceded. 'It seems odd. We need to check rubbish in the same area, find her knickers. They'll be white.'

'How the hell do you know that?' Craig said.

'She's a classy looking lady. You can tell she was beautiful, even at this stage of decomposition. If she'd worn any coloured knickers, they would have shown through on the white sections of the dress. If she wears white ones, they don't show through on the white, and definitely not on the black. Simple, isn't it, when you're a genius?'

'Right,' Roberts said. 'As soon as forensics have finished, we need to get into the stuff on that conveyor belt. If the knickers are there, and despite Heather's brilliant summing up they might not be, there might also be some rubbish, letters or something, that will tell us the location of the bin that she was dumped into. It's going to be a long night, so if you need to let anybody at home know, do it now.'

Phones were taken out of pockets, messages were sent, and replies were received.

Even Michael Danbury joined in the activity; he hadn't had anything as exciting as this for a long time. It did briefly occur to him that if the body had been put in black plastic bin bags, it might have escaped their notice, but it was clearly this woman's lucky day.

21

Carl felt jittery. Time was fast approaching when he and Kenny would be leaving for Grausohn's penthouse. He checked through the list of names and addresses for the kids and knew it looked feasible. Grausohn would be dead anyway, before he could act on any of it.

The glass fitted comfortably in Carl's pocket, unwashed and wrapped in kitchen roll. He would have to be more than careful when he removed the paper. No part of his hand must touch the sparkling crystal. He had promised Daryl he would take care of things; he was doing exactly that.

Aileen walked with him to the door. She leaned against him for a moment. 'You can still back out of this, you know,' she whispered. 'You don't have to do it.'

'I do. I have to get Daryl away from all of this, start to be a proper dad.'

'And me?'

'We'll discuss us when I'm safely home, and Grausohn is dead. While he's alive, there can be no me and you, or me and anybody. If we don't kill him tonight, he'll come for me. And probably Daryl. I don't doubt Kenny will come out of it smelling of roses, but I won't. I'm handing over a list of fictitious names and addresses. That's why I can't back out.'

Aileen nodded. 'I'll be waiting. And if you're not back by ten, I'll also be panicking. Take care, Carl.' She kissed him, and he headed down the path towards his car.

His hands trembled all the way to Kenny's house. Carl wanted to be sick, and he kept touching the pocket with the glass in it. He liked Kenny; he didn't like the fact that Kenny had killed Megan, said nothing and had tried to kill Daryl. Without the bravery of his mother, Daryl would be dead now. Kenny had to pay.

Carl arrived with time to spare, and Kenny invited him in. 'You need a drink?' he asked.

Carl shook his head. 'No, I'm good thanks. Just want to do it and get out of there.'

'We're coming out of the basement. There's no CCTV round there. Then, it's a quick jog to my car, and we're clear.'

'You make it sound so easy…'

Kenny laughed. 'Tell me that when we're trying to lift that big bugger over the balcony. Remember, Carl, when this is done, we're free. If somebody muscles in and takes it over, they're not getting our services 'cos we won't be here. Right, to get back to lifting him, we can tackle it one of two ways. Either knock him out first or go for his knees to lift him.'

'Knock him out? We going in carrying a baseball bat, then?'

'He's got one, keeps it under his desk. If we knock him out, he becomes a dead weight; if we stand either side of him at the balcony, we grab his knees and chuck him over. We're big lads, Carl, we should be able to lift him. But if he's unconscious…'

'You're right. We've got to go for chucking him over while he's conscious.'

'For definite?' Kenny asked.

'For definite. Come on, let's go and get it done.'

Billy followed them to the door, concern etched into his features. 'Take care, you two. There's a lot riding on this.'

They nodded, neither wanting to speak. Full concentration was needed from this point on.

Kenny parked his car a few yards from the original place he had decided would be safe. They got out and walked towards the basement entrance, nerves gone, determination taking over.

'I've not been down here before,' Carl said.

'Count yourself lucky,' was Kenny's dry rejoinder.

The lift arrived, and the men stepped in. It was one minute to eight.

At eight o'clock, they entered Grausohn's office.

'Evening, boss,' Kenny said cheerfully. 'Told you he was doing a good job. Full names and addresses. Tomorrow, we can probably have one of the kids here.'

'Evening, Kenny, Clarkson.' He held out his hand. 'The list?'

Carl took the envelope out of his inside pocket, lifted the flap and carefully pulled it out by using his fingernails. He wanted no fingerprints on it. He handed it over.

Grausohn looked at it for a while, then lifted his head. 'We go for the girl. She'll be easier to break. These are accurate addresses, Carl?'

'They are, boss. Took some getting though.'

Grausohn opened his drawer and handed Carl an envelope. 'There's five thousand in there. There'll be more, if we get the information we want out of any of these kids on this list. Okay?'

Carl took the envelope and slipped it into his pocket, making sure the glass was once again disguised. 'Thanks, boss.'

'Now,' Grausohn said, 'drinks?'

Kenny nodded. 'That would be good'

'Carl?'

'Whisky for me too. Thanks, boss.'

Grausohn poured the drinks and handed them to the two men. Carl took a small sip. He wanted no alcohol in his system that night.

Grausohn came out from behind the desk, carrying his glass, and rolled his bulk around the room, heading for the lounge. 'Do you smoke, Carl?'

'I do.'

'Cigars are on the coffee table. We'll smoke out on the balcony.' Grausohn placed his glass on the coffee table and took a cigar out of the box. Both Kenny and Carl helped themselves to a cigar and placed their drinks at the opposite end of the coffee table. There had to be no confusion as to which drink was Grausohn's and which was theirs.

'There's a lovely sunset tonight,' Grausohn said, leaning against the wrought iron railing. He felt hands around his knees, and his huge body rose. His cigar fell over the edge, as he scrambled for some sort of purchase on the railing, but to no avail. His huge belly rested on the rail, and the two killers heaved him over.

They stuffed their cigars in their pockets, poured the whisky down the sink and quickly washed the glasses, careful not to add fingerprints while drying them.

'You go and hold the lift open,' Carl said, 'and I'll put these glasses away.'

Kenny ran for the door, and Carl took out the glass he had brought from home from his pocket. He carefully removed the kitchen roll and placed the glass on the coffee table at the side of Grausohn's. A quick glance around showed him all was good, and he legged it for the lift. Kenny was standing with his back to the edge of the door, holding it open.

It descended to the basement at speed, and they ran.

Two minutes later, they were accelerating away, heading for Kenny's home.

The team was busy sorting through rubbish at the facility when the call came through of a jumper from the exclusive flats.

'Brian, ring the station and get two PCs in here to help you. I'm taking the others with me. We've a death at Cardale Apartments.'

'Suspicious?'

'With our luck at the moment, probably. Balcony fall.'

Roberts took Heather and Craig with him and set off to visit the grand apartment block where you needed real money just to ring a doorbell, never mind live there. As a result of this exclusivity, there was a lot of activity, and Roberts walked up to the forensic team who had only been away from the ERF for an hour.

'You lot out trawling for customers, or something,' he joked.

And then, he saw the body. It was a huge man, massive in every area.

'Do we have a name?'

'According to his wallet contents, he is called Nicolas Grausohn. Mean anything to you?' Ray Sandler asked.

Roberts shook his head. 'Not at the moment. Anything suspicious about it?'

'I'll know more when I get him back in the lab. Thank God for trolleys on wheels, or I'd be doing the autopsy right here.' Ray lifted one of Grausohn's arms and looked at his nails. 'No sign of a fight, but how do you fall off a balcony by accident? Especially when you're this size. At first glance, I'd say he took his own life, but we'll see.'

Roberts was searching through the contents of the wallet. 'He lives in the penthouse, then?'

'Yes, I understand it has its own private lift. He's no keys on him, so don't know how you'll get in.'

'Right, come on you two,' Roberts said to Craig and Heather. 'Let's go and see what we can find out. Let's find this bloody lift for a start.'

The foyer was massive, with two lifts to service the lower flats, and one lift in the corner for servicing the penthouse. They went in it, and it rose at some speed. It stopped on the penthouse level, with hardly a sound or a movement, and they left it to walk on one of the thickest carpets Heather had ever seen.

'Pure bloody luxury,' she whispered.

Craig pointed to a door, the only visible one. 'How we going to get in that without a key?'

'If it's locked, we'll send for a locksmith.'

He handed out gloves and shoe coverings to Craig and Heather, then put on his own.

The door handle was round, made of brass so shiny, it cast a reflected glow, and sleekly smooth as it turned, resulting in the door swinging silently towards the interior of the penthouse.

'Unlocked,' Roberts murmured. 'Why? A visitor?'

The room they had entered was a large hallway; they crossed it and went into what appeared to be an office.

'Heather, check the desk. See if there's anything… unusual on it.' She moved around to where the chair was, a heavy leather contraption built to take extra weight, and sat down. She saw the baseball bat immediately and pulled it out to show Roberts.

'Well prepared,' she said, and placed it back in the same place. There was very little on the desk, and it didn't take her long to rule out anything that would help with the investigation, except for maybe a list of names and addresses, with all the addresses being in the locality of their own police station. All four of the drawers were locked.

She felt around on the underside of the desk top and found a small hook, with keys hanging from it. The third one fit the drawers, and she looked in the top one. It contained several brown envelopes, three with five thousand in each, two with ten thousand in, and one with twenty thousand in. She wondered what the recipient of the twenty thousand envelope had to do to get that amount. The other drawers contained ledgers, journals, all sorts of books with handwriting in. She stacked them up; they had to go to the station, where they could be inspected properly. She put the list of names inside an evidence bag and left it on top of the books, then used her mobile phone to take a picture of it.

Roberts and Craig went through the rest of the flat. Roberts bagged up the empty glass from the coffee table, then carefully sealed the glass containing the whisky inside another bag. He placed them both back on the coffee table, ready for when forensics could come in and do their work. The patio doors leading to the balcony were wide open, and both of them moved outside. A chair was on its side, the other chair neatly placed by the small patio table.

'So, Mr Grausohn, did you stand on this chair and then jump? Or were you helped over the balcony by someone who obligingly put this chair here, thinking to fool us?'

Roberts' phone rang, and he saw Ray Sandler's name on the screen. 'Ray?'

'We're going to try to move the body. Are you ready for the lads up there? I'm assuming you got in, as you haven't come back down.'

'Yes, send them up. The door was unlocked. I've bagged up two glasses. One is empty, the other has a liquid in it. I thought we should maybe verify what it is, in case anything's been added that might make our victim believe he could fly.'

'Will do. I need to head back, but Colin, my second-in-command, will be in charge up there. Liaise with him, if you need anything. And try not to find me any more bodies. I've got a proper backlog.'

Roberts smiled as he disconnected.

Within a couple of minutes, Ray Sanders' colleague Colin arrived, carrying equipment that must have taken up most of the lift space. Roberts showed him the two glasses, and the overturned chair, and Colin instructed one of his team to start taking photographs of everything.

It was in the middle of all this mayhem that Gerda arrived home, well satisfied with the two hundred and fifty pounds bingo win. She was stopped in the foyer, prevented from using the lift to take her to her home.

'But I bloody live there!' she screamed. 'And what has happened to Mr Grausohn?'

A female PC attempted to calm her down but to no avail. She was incandescent that she was being prevented from returning to the penthouse and didn't believe them when they said he had jumped from the balcony.

'My Mr Grausohn would not jump. Why would he? He didn't need to die. No, you must look closer at this, somebody has killed him.' The more adamant she became, the stronger her German accent grew.

Roberts and his team appeared in the foyer to see Gerda pushing the PC to one side. 'Oy!' he shouted. 'What are you doing?'

Gerda turned to him, tears evident in her eyes. 'She won't let me go home, and she says my Mr Grausohn is dead.'

'Please, come and sit over here.' He led her to a settee, and they sat together.

'Now, tell me your name.' He took out his notebook.

'I am Gerda Bauer, Mr Grausohn's housekeeper.'

'And you've been out?'

'Yes, I go to bingo most nights. Mr Grausohn likes me to go out. He sometimes has business to conduct in the evening.'

'Had Mr Grausohn been depressed recently?'

She gave a small laugh. 'No. He was annoyed about something, but depressed? No.'

'Do you have somewhere you can stay tonight? You won't be able to get back into the penthouse until we're finished in there.'

'Yes, I have a friend…'

'Then, please call them and make the arrangements. I will need to speak to you tomorrow, so I'd like your telephone number and friend's address please.'

She took out her mobile phone, navigated it and read out the number it showed on the screen as being hers.

He smiled. 'You don't know your number?'

'No. Why should I? I hardly ever use the phone, and I never ring myself.'

'Then, can you use it now and ring your friend? I can have someone take you, or we can call a cab.'

She looked at him, her face like thunder. 'I will ring,' she said. She dictated her friend's address reluctantly.

It appeared that the woman would collect her, and ten minutes later, Gerda had gone, clutching a piece of paper with an appointment time for the following day for her to visit the station to give a statement. She had forgotten about her bingo win.

He was watching her leave when his mobile phone rang. It was Brian, and Roberts hoped his sergeant was now at home. It had been a long day for all of them.

'Brian? You finished?'

'We have, Dave. We found them, the knickers. White ones. Heather was right about that. But we found something else in the locality of the body. A couple of letters, still showing an address. Only junk mail, but it shows where this rubbish came from. Didn't you say you were attending a suicide at Cardale Apartments?'

'Don't tell me that's the address. Everything over the last few bloody weeks seems conjoined. I'll follow that address up tomorrow, then. It does look like he jumped, but there's something going on in this penthouse. It'll bear a closer inspection, I think. We'll seal it off tonight and come back tomorrow. Forensics are just finishing. Now, get off home, if you think you've got everything you can. Is Mr Danbury still there?'

He laughed. 'Yes, he says it's one of the best evenings he's had. There's never been so much activity in the ERF before. And he's kept us supplied with tea.'

'Then make sure you thank him; we might need to go back,' Roberts said with a laugh. 'You and whoever else is there finish up. You get off home and send the others to the station. I'm assuming they're night shift?'

'They are. Good lads. We got a lot done. I'm bagging stuff up that we've pulled out and bringing it to the station with me. There's not a lot, but I've put the knickers in an evidence bag.'

'Thanks, Brian.' Roberts disconnected.

They loaded the journals removed from the drawer into the car, and Heather hung on to the evidence bag containing the list of names and addresses. She glanced through it, taking advantage of not having to drive. She knew all of the addresses mentioned and decided the following morning would be her time to do a little desk work. She'd follow up on the information.

Roberts drove back to the station, sent Craig and Heather home, then carried the books and the list of addresses up to his own office. He smiled as he remembered Heather's insistence that she wanted to check the addresses. She was a good copper.

He sat down for a moment, then rang his wife. 'Tell me you love me,' he said.

'I love you,' Erica Roberts responded, 'very much. Bad day?'

'Awful day. Two deaths, frightened kids, over-tired officers working too many bloody hours…'

'Come home,' Erica said. 'I'll make you feel better.'

And she did.

22

Kenny and Carl didn't speak on the journey back to Kenny's home. They took as many back streets as possible, and as they pulled onto the drive, Billy opened the door for them.

He raised his eyebrows in query, and Kenny nodded.

'Done.'

Billy handed them both a whisky, and Carl downed it in one, then coughed as the fiery liquid hit the back of his throat.

'I needed that,' he said. 'I can't believe what we've done.'

'It had to happen,' Billy said slowly. 'He was a truly evil man. We couldn't let him get to any of those children.'

'I know you're right,' Carl said, 'but, remember, I've never played up there with the big boys. I've collected debts for him, delivered a few packets, nothing major. Suddenly, I'm a killer, and I've killed the boss. Doesn't get any bigger.'

'The first time you kill is the hardest, but after that…' Kenny spoke slowly. 'We're out of it now, Carl. Stay out of it. Look after your lad and Aileen and forget all this.'

'I'm heading home. I've been away over an hour. I need to be in that house as soon as possible.' He shook both their hands and left them having a second drink.

His drive home was nerve-wracking. It would only take a small accident, a flash of a speed camera, and his alibi would be gone. He drove carefully, while his mind was screaming "put your foot down."

Aileen cried as he entered the room. 'Oh my God, you're home,' she said, and walked into his arms.

'Hey, stop crying. It went well.'

'He's…?'

Carl nodded, kissing the top of her head. 'He is. I don't really want to talk about it, but he's gone. I have to leave here, though. As soon as word gets around that Grausohn is dead, somebody will muscle in, and I don't want my name bandied about. And I'll have to go quickly. Next week.'

He felt her stiffen. 'I'll miss you. I'll miss Daryl. And what about Daryl's friends?'

Carl lifted her face to his. 'Then, come with me. Think about it. We'll be going by the end of next week, I've got to move fast. Don't mention anything to Daryl, yet. Promise me you'll think about it.'

'We've got two funerals next week…' Her voice faltered as she spoke.

'That's Monday and Tuesday. We can have left all this behind by Thursday. Start again. It's why tonight happened.'

'Give me time,' Aileen said. 'It's a massive thing for me.'

She pushed him away and walked through to the kitchen. Her cup of tea was still on the table, and she drank deeply, her thoughts chaotic. How many times had she vowed no more permanent men? It seemed a pretty permanent statement to move away with a man, start a new life.

She heard him go upstairs, heard Daryl's door open and then gently close as he checked on his son, and she laid her head on her arms.

She didn't like decisions. Decisions were hard work. She usually put them off for as long as possible, but that wasn't going to happen here.

So much to think about; she knew Daryl would be devastated to leave his friends. If she went with Carl and Daryl, she maybe could help soften that blow for the boy, but was that a good enough reason to uproot herself from Sheffield and move away? And what if it all went pear-shaped in the future, and the police came for Carl? He had committed murder, alibi or no alibi.

And how did she feel about Carl? Although she'd known him from a distance for quite a long time, she'd only had close contact with him for a couple of weeks. Did she feel she could trust him? She'd once trusted another man, Vinnie's dad, and look how that had progressed. Backwards.

She heard Carl come into the kitchen. 'Where would we go? I mean, supposing I said I'd go with you. I need some answers first.'

'Okay,' he said. 'I'm going to tell you something now that nobody else knows. Not Daryl, not Kenny, not even Megan when she was here.'

She waited, knowing this face was his trustworthy one.

'I did a big collection job for the boss some time ago. He paid me well. I bought a mobile home, with the intention of it being an escape if ever I needed one. It's in Lincolnshire, on a lakeside site. I fish, so it was perfect for me. You have to remember, I was shut out from my family. Since Megan died, this is the closest I've ever been to Daryl, and I've had a lot to learn. She knew what I did and didn't want Daryl to have anything to do with me. She was happy with the money I gave her, but not happy with me. So, that's where me and Daryl will be going, and I'd really like it if you came with us. In a year or so, if things are quiet, I'll put this place up for sale, and we can go wherever we want, then. No commitment ever, Aileen, you can walk away whenever you want. I know you're scared.'

'Fucking petrified. Do you know what Vinnie's dad did to me? Never had more than a one-night stand since. And now, you're here, and that lovely lad of yours. That man beat me up so badly because I refused to have an abortion that he put me in hospital for a month. Vinnie was born during that month because my body couldn't keep him inside me any longer, and he was two pounds three ounces; tiny, tiny baby. But he survived, and I survived. Couldn't have any more children, but I lived through all the pain, the nightmares, wondering if my baby would live. So, you see why I have to think everything through.'

Carl pulled her to her feet and hugged her. 'Take as much time as you need. Daryl and I will be going next Thursday, because I think we have to. I can't put him in danger. If you don't feel you can come with us then, you can come whenever you feel ready. Honestly, Aileen, there's no pressure at all. Hang on to your home as a bolthole, sell it – it really doesn't matter. We've enough money to live on until we need to make decisions.'

Roberts woke early. He needed answers, lots of them, and they all involved results from pathology. He had to start hounding people; too many had died, and he knew they were connected.

He was in his office by seven, checking on what had been logged in already, trying to find out what he could justifiably demand, given the short timescale from the previous afternoon and evening.

He needed identification of the woman – no bag had been found, just the very skimpy white panties. By finding her body, he hoped that something would show up as transference between her and Vinnie Walmsley. She clearly had dirt on her knees after following Vinnie into the woods, so unless she had showered before being killed, that should still be discoverable. Roberts knew she had killed him, but proving it was another matter; he couldn't write it off as solved on a gut feeling.

Ray Sandler rang him at eight o'clock. 'Can you come down here?'

'You've got something?'

'On Grausohn. I need you to see something.'

Inwardly, he groaned. Grausohn had to be suicide, the toppled chair indicative of a leap into the unknown, the momentum of the forward falling body pushing the furniture over. And suicide wasn't his priority in a case riddled with murders.

'Okay. Five minutes.'

The body, stripped of its clothes, was huge; a massive whale-like structure lying on the table. There was significant damage to the head, and he tried to avoid looking at that. Maybe that damage was what was concerning Sandler – had he suffered head trauma before going over that balcony?

He was surprised when Sandler moved towards Grausohn's legs. They were already placed in stirrups, and Sandler hoisted them up so that they could see the underside easier.

'Look here,' he said. 'There were clearly visible bruises on each leg, and Sandler placed his own hands on one leg, indicating what the bruises represented.

'Two hands, around each leg above the back of the knee. That's four hands in total, Dave, and that means two men helped him over that balcony. Sorry, pal, this isn't a suicide. It's murder.'

Add it to the fucking list, Roberts thought angrily.

He stared at the bruising and knew Ray Sandler was right. The hand marks were obvious.

Roberts sighed, feeling frustrated. He'd like to solve at least one murder, before having another thrown at him.

Sandler was lowering the stirrups and removing the legs so that Grausohn was once again flat on the table.

'And all this damage to the head?'

'I've looked at it carefully. It's consistent with a fall – in other words, he wasn't attacked while he was on the balcony, I think he was there with somebody he knew. Of one thing I am sure, one person, unless he was called Iron Man, could not have lifted him over that balcony. It would definitely take a minimum of two.'

'Thanks, Ray. There were two glasses on that coffee table. Hopefully, we'll get something from them.'

'They're in the lab, liquid being checked, and glasses fingerprinted. You'll know if we've any print matches within the hour, the liquid within two hours. We're pulling out all the stops on this, Dave. I'm moving on to our lady. I've already fingerprinted her, so you may know pretty quickly who she is.'

'Concentrate on her knees, will you, Ray. Last time she was caught on CCTV, this lady had soil on her knees and legs, and as she's still wearing the same dress, I'm hoping she didn't wash it off before she was killed. And the soil should match the sample from the Walmsley scene.'

'Will do,' Ray said, and wheeled Grausohn's trolley back to the fridge. 'I'll give you a ring when I've finished the next one.'

'Thanks.' Dave Roberts left the room before Ray pulled out the body; she was decomposing, and the smell wasn't Roberts' favourite. He knew Ray would still have her on the table when he next came down, and once a day was enough.

As Roberts headed back up to his office, Heather waved him over. 'These addresses, sir. They don't make sense. The addresses are genuine, but nobody with these names live there.'

'All five of them?'

'Yes, sir.'

'Let me look.' She handed him the copy of the list, and he quickly read down it. Five names. Five.

He moved to his office, still holding the list, and placed it flat on his desk; David Williams, Max Williams, Fay Jones, Dylan Cartwright and Scott Layton. Four male names, one female name. Five names in total. A gang of five.

His gang of five. His children he was trying desperately to protect, from somebody who had managed to kill one and injure another.

Why the name changes? He had no doubt that this list represented the remaining kids, but why?

He called in Heather and handed the list back to her. 'It's fictitious,' he said.

'I'd gathered that,' she laughed. 'Nothing matched.'

'Okay, let's suppose these aren't adults on this list. Now, does that suggest anything?'

She looked at the list once again, although Roberts guessed she already knew it by heart. 'Five kids,' she muttered. 'Oh my God! Five kids! Our kids!'

'I can assure you, Heather, I have had no children with you,' he said with a smile, 'but I know what you mean. Our kids who found Vinnie Walmsley's body, our five kids. I have no idea of the significance of this, not yet, anyway, but I'm sure we're on the right track. The Christian names on the list have the same initials as our five.'

He sat down at his desk and hit the space bar on his keyboard. The computer sprang into life. He typed in his password and saw he had mail.

Results were starting to come in, and fingerprints had been found on both glasses. The one with liquid in it, which proved to be whisky with nothing added, bore the fingerprints of the deceased. The other glass bore a set of fingerprints traced to Kenneth Lancaster.

'Yes!' Roberts punched the air. 'I knew that bastard was involved in all of this.'

He repeated the results to Heather, and she said, 'I wonder if they'll find his fingerprints on this as well,' indicating the list of names and addresses.

'The original's been sent down, so the results could be here now. In itself, it's a document that doesn't mean anything, everything on it is false, but fingerprints will tell us a lot.'

He opened up a second email to find that the black and white dressed female lying on a table in the morgue was a lady called Johanna Fleischer and known to German police as well as English forces. Prostitution and drugs had brought her into contact with both police forces, hence her fingerprints being on file.

Three Germans, Roberts mused. Grausohn, Johanna Fleischer and Gerda Bauer. And Johanna's body had been found mixed in with refuse from the Cardale Apartments, so who had killed her? Grausohn?

Or did Grausohn employ others to do the dirty work? His gross size would preclude him from actually committing such acts; he wouldn't have the agility required. Fleischer had looked to be an extremely fit lady, so unless a bullet had killed her, he didn't think Grausohn was in the frame for the job, maybe just the instructions.

A third email confirmed there were no fingerprints anywhere on the list of names, other than Grausohn's.

Roberts picked up the phone and rang through to the morgue.

'Dave, I was going to ring you. You might want to pop down.'

'On my way.'

He stopped outside the doors of the autopsy suite and put a smear of Vicks under his nose. Even after that precaution, he could sense the smell as he walked through the doors.

'Ray? You have something?'

'I do. She had sex, either pre-mortem, or post-mortem. Very close to the time of death, anyway; we've been able to harvest a significant sample of seminal fluid. It's been sent for DNA analysis. We found traces of saliva on her breasts, and that's also been sent for analysis. Off the record, I'm inclined to think the sex was post-mortem, because whoever killed her tried to get rid of her undergarments. If the sex had been before she died, she would have put them back on. There was no seminal fluid on the white undergarments. We can link those panties to her, because there was a small discharge stain. It's also gone for testing, to provide you with that confirmation. And I did find soil on her knees, so that's gone off to be compared to the soil we took from the Vinnie Walmsley scene.'

'She was called Johanna, Johanna Fleischer.'

'I'll tag her properly, then. I've not checked my emails yet.'

'We've also got fingerprint results on the glasses. The empty glass had prints from a person of interest, Kenneth Lancaster. The liquid in the other glass was whisky, nothing added.'

'Are things any clearer?'

'Not really. We know that it took two people to push Grausohn over, but we've only got one person's fingerprints. Who else was there? Maybe the person who had sex with Johanna? I need that result urgently, Ray. I don't want to pick up Lancaster, until we know who the partner is. I don't want this second man doing a runner. I want them at the same time.'

And he wanted them both in a line-up, with young Daryl viewing the faces.

It was several hours before they had results from the semen. Thomas Raines. And the soil on Fleischer's knees matched exactly the soil taken from the Walmsley crime scene. Suddenly, science was giving them answers.

'What the fuck? Craig! I need to know everything about a Thomas Raines. He must be on file, because they've got his DNA.' Roberts passed over the handwritten name. 'That's how it's spelt. Quick as you can, lad.'

Thomas Raines? That name hadn't come up once, until then.

Within five minutes, Craig had returned bearing printouts of his searches, and it appeared that Thomas "Tommy" Raines lived locally, not far from the penthouse recently inhabited by the late Nicolas Grausohn.

His file confirmed he had been held at her Majesty's pleasure in Armley jail, for assault and aggravated burglary, serving twelve months of an eighteen-month sentence, back in 2002.

'Right, Craig, you're with me. Let's go and get this chap, bring him in and ask him a few questions.'

Fran Raines saw the police car pull up, and she watched with almost an air of detachment. Since Kenny had told her about Tommy, she'd not felt well, almost as if she wasn't in this world. He'd brought lots of money for her, but all she wanted was her Tommy, or at least his body, so that she could say goodbye properly.

Perhaps that was what the police were there for – to tell her that Tommy had been washed up on Dover Beach. She didn't stand but watched them walk up her path. She waited for the knock, then the open letterbox; Thomas Raines was the name shouted.

At that point, she stood. Why would they be shouting his name if they had found his body? It didn't make sense.

Craig, looking through the letterbox, saw her walk out of the lounge door and down the hallway. 'A woman's coming to the door, sir,' he said quietly.

The door opened a few inches and then stopped. The chain was on.

'Yes?' she said, and Dave Roberts stepped forward, holding out his warrant card for her to inspect.

'DI Roberts, ma'am. We'd like to speak to Thomas Raines, please.'

23

Fran hesitated for a moment, then closed the door slightly and removed the chain. 'I don't understand,' she said.

'Are you Mrs Raines?' Roberts asked.

'I am, but my husband is dead. He said he would clear it with the police.'

'Who did?'

'Kenny. Kenny Lancaster.'

'Clear what with us?'

'Tommy. He's dead, but there's no body because he was pushed... fell off a ferry coming back from France. I thought you'd come to tell me he'd washed up in Dover.'

Craig Smythe looked bemused, and Roberts asked him to find the kitchen and make them a cup of tea.

'Right, Mrs Raines, let's start at the beginning. When did your husband disappear?'

'A couple of weeks ago, maybe three. I didn't know he'd disappeared until Kenny came to tell me. I didn't even know he'd gone to France, but that was nowt unusual. He was always going off somewhere for that boss of his.'

'Who was his boss, Mrs Raines?' Roberts held his breath.

'That German bloke. Nicolas summat. Can't remember. And call me Fran, please.'

'Thank you, Fran. And what did Kenny tell you?'

Her hesitation was clear. 'He said... he said that the Dover gang had taken against my Tommy being on their patch, and one of them had pushed him overboard. He gave me an envelope with some money in it and said it was to help us get back on our feet.'

'How much was in the envelope, Fran?'

'Twenty thousand. I've not touched it, though. I'm okay for now. Tommy saved some money. And I keep finding envelopes with money when I clear his things. It's not nice chucking his stuff out, or taking it to the charity shop, but I do check the pockets.'

She took a handkerchief from her jeans and dabbed at her eyes. 'I miss him. He was a lovely man.'

Craig brought the drinks through, and Roberts stood. 'Can you excuse me for a minute, Mrs Raines? I need to make a phone call. Craig will keep you company while I'm gone.'

She nodded and watched as he walked through her kitchen and out the back door.

'Brian? Take Heather, Dan and George, and perhaps one of the others that you can trust to do the job properly, and head over to Grausohn's place. I want it taken apart. I need everything back in the office, and I want it sealed off. It's a crime scene, nobody there but authorised personnel. And I want somebody on duty until further notice outside the door. Okay?'

'Okay, Dave. I'm on it now.'

Roberts disconnected and headed back in to continue interviewing Fran Raines. 'Fran, have you got rid of all your husband's things?'

She shook her head. 'No, I've not touched his suits. There's about twenty of them, loads of pockets to go through. His T-shirts and his shirts have gone. I've chucked all his boxers and socks, and I've not done his shoes.'

'Then, I have to tell you, Fran, that I'll be taking them with me. I'll give you a receipt for everything that we take, and eventually, they will all be returned to you. If you can show Craig where they are all kept…'

She stood, looking flustered. 'Come on, then,' she snapped.

Craig looked at his cup of tea, then followed her from the room. Roberts contacted the station and asked for a van to be sent, along with evidence bags and large boxes.

Once organised, he stood and walked around the room, inspecting photographs and waiting for the return of Fran and Craig. Eventually, they both staggered downstairs with their arms weighed down by suits; expensive, designer suits.

'There's a van coming to collect everything. They'll collate it all and give you a receipt.'

She nodded. 'Have I done something wrong?'

'No, but I don't understand why you didn't come to us when Kenny told you this story of your husband being thrown overboard. It's a death, Fran. It should have been investigated, and will be now, of course. Please don't contact anyone. We don't want charges of perverting the course of justice, do we?'

He saw the look of fear cross her face, and she shook her head. 'I've not heard anything from anybody since Kenny turned up that day, and I don't suppose I will.'

A large van pulled up outside, and Craig let the two officers into the house. They quickly bagged and tagged everything, then handed over a receipt.

Roberts and Craig left Fran, who had been joined by her son, and both of them felt concerned by her fragile state. She hadn't seemed to understand that a person had to be reported missing if they had suddenly disappeared. Roberts suspected maybe Tommy Raines had controlled her to the extent that she no longer thought for herself; Roberts comforted himself with the thought that she had the rest of her life to recover.

'Let's call at Cardale Apartments before we head back.'

'Okay, sir. You have the key?'

'No, we've got a team in, looking for anything and everything. Whatever's happened in this case, I reckon it originated in that penthouse.'

Ten minutes later, they were showing warrant cards and ducking under crime scene tape before travelling up in the penthouse lift. The door was open, and boxes were stacked outside in the small lift foyer.

Heather was standing at the desk, her hand across her mouth, her eyes wide open, and… Roberts didn't know what it was, maybe sickened.

'Heather?'

'You have to see this, sir.' Her voice was almost a whisper. 'If this is Grausohn's bedtime reading… I found it in the bottom drawer of his bedside cabinet. It was hidden inside a very neatly folded pair of pyjamas.'

It was a small photograph album, the kind normally favoured by grandparents for showing off photos of their grandchildren. This was not the work of a doting grandfather.

Roberts slipped on his gloves and took the album from her.

The first picture was of a man with a rope tied around his wrists and hanging from a hook in the ceiling. He was clearly dead; he couldn't have lost that amount of blood and lived. Roberts stared at it for some time, but he couldn't give him a name. The second picture was of a man tied to a chair, and it looked as though it was the same location – a garage. There were tools hanging on the wall in the background, and the same tools were in both photographs.

Roberts closed the book with a snap. 'I'll take this back with me. With the facial recognition programme we have, I bet we can trace quite a few of these.'

'Wait,' Heather said. 'I went all the way through the book. It's sickening, but you need to look at the end.'

Roberts re-opened the book and flipped quickly through to the end. It was a picture of a little girl lying in the road. 'Ella Johnston,' he breathed. 'What sick bastard would take this picture?'

'Somebody who needed to prove to the boss that this had happened? I can't see that huge fat man doing his own dirty work. If you look at the picture before Ella's, you'll see it's a grave in some woods. He would have had to walk to get to it, I'm guessing, and I reckon carrying all that blubber, he'd have struggled to even walk to his bedroom at night. No, I think he has others who terminate people, but he needs proof, so he can drool over it.'

He flicked back to the picture before Ella's, to see if it resembled the woods at the side of the station, but he didn't recognise it. He did recognise the body in the grave though.

'Well, well,' he said. 'He was pushed overboard from a ferry, was he?' He handed the book to Craig Smythe. The picture showed Tommy Raines in a grave, covered in blood. 'That, PC Smythe, is our Tommy. Does he look as though he's swimming in the channel?'

'How do you know it's him, sir?' Craig was peering closely at the picture.

'While you and Mrs Raines were upstairs sorting through this poor bloke's clothes, I was nosing around downstairs. There are several pictures of him in the lounge, and this is definitely him. No doubt at all. We need to find where this wooded area is and go dig him up. Then, Mrs Raines can have the closure she said she wanted. Heather, when we get back I want you to circulate this photo to all our stations in and around Sheffield. Ask them if anybody can enlighten us with the location.'

'Yes, sir.'

'Right, has anything else earth-shattering showed up?'

'Yes, lists of people, with phone numbers. No addresses. And loads of journal type books, covering transactions. Lots of cash amounts listed. It's going to take an expert to decipher this lot.'

'We'll send it through to fraud. They're the best people to tackle it. Anything else?'

'There's a safe,' Brian called from the lounge. 'Can't get in it, so I've sent for somebody.'

'Is it a legal somebody, Brian?' Roberts called back.

'Yep, we've locked Harry 'Safecracker' Cooper up for the duration, haven't we?'

'Unless he's picked t'lock on his cell,' somebody else wisecracked.

Roberts grinned and moved into the bedroom. He could see that Heather was still upset by the photo album, so he indicated to her to follow him. 'Have you checked the clothes?'

'Only a brief glance so far. We're going to be here for ages, sir. His suits are enormous, and he had dozens of them.'

'Did you look through the whole album?' he asked quietly.

She nodded.

'Did you recognise anybody else?'

'Yes. The black and white dress woman. I'm sorry, I can only remember her first name, Johanna.'

'It's unravelling for the whole set-up, isn't it? Grausohn going off that balcony has virtually given us all the answers, because we really had very little before that happened. Just guesses and supposition. Is there a mobile phone anywhere?'

'Not found one yet, but I bet there's one somewhere. Those pictures in that album aren't proper photos, they're prints on ordinary A4 printer paper. He could hardly take them into Boots and have them printed, could he? I reckon he's bluetoothed them from his phone to his printer.'

'Right, keep looking. I'm taking this album back with me, I'm going to go through it properly and see if I recognise anyone.'

He raised his voice so that everyone could hear. 'Listen up. No working after five o'clock. We can come back tomorrow and finish off. There'll be two uniforms on duty outside all night, so we'll be secure.'

He heard a chorus of 'thanks, guv' and headed for the lift, taking Craig with him.

'Back to the station, Craig, in a bit. Let's get some expert help on these pictures. Tomorrow afternoon, we'll have a briefing, but for now, let's go get Kenneth Lancaster. Let's go scare the shit out of the murdering bastard. He'll regret taking the photo of that little lass for the rest of his life.'

Billy took a cup of tea and a glass of water into the back garden and watched as Kenny deadheaded the roses. His love of roses seemed so at odds with the way he lived his life.

'Drinks,' Billy called, and Kenny walked across to him.

'Thanks. I'll give the garden a good hosing tonight, this soil is baked solid.'

'We go Monday,' Billy said quietly. 'I got us into first class, and once we've arrived in Crete, nobody will be able to find us. You heard from Carl?'

Kenny shook his head. 'Not today. But I don't need to, it's done now. I don't really want him to know when we're going, or anything. He was good to work with, though. I felt he had my back, and it was a lot easier lifting Grausohn than I thought it was going to be. We'd better start packing then?'

'As soon as possible. We can't take too much, but we get quite a lot of weight allowance going first class. I'll nip up to the loft, sort out the biggest suitcases.'

Billy headed upstairs, let down the ladder and headed up into the disorganised roof space. He heard the doorbell and hoped Kenny had too. Footsteps echoed on the hallway parquet floor, and he nodded. He didn't need to get down out of the loft just yet.

He didn't hear the door open, and he couldn't hear Kenny's words, but he did hear the deeper tones of DI Roberts. He crept quietly back to the loft hatch and eavesdropped on what was happening.

Billy was transfixed. He thought he heard Roberts say something about Kenny accompanying them to the station. Then, he heard Kenny say, somewhat louder, 'Why?'

Roberts then said something about Grausohn, and Billy froze. Again, he could hear Kenny's raised voice. 'I'll go upstairs and get a cardigan,' he said, and Billy moved away from the hatch.

Kenny walked upstairs, accompanied by Craig Smythe and pressed the button for the loft ladder to raise, and the hatch to close.

'I had intended getting down a suitcase,' he said drily to the young constable.

'Leaving the country, sir?' Craig asked, trying to hide the smirk.

'No, I was planning on heading to Wales for a few days. Doesn't matter. I can go tomorrow.'

He went into the bedroom, took a cardigan out of the wardrobe and headed back downstairs, Craig no more than a few feet away from him. It was much too warm for the cardigan, but he'd had to use some excuse to get upstairs and put the ladder away; he didn't want Billy involved yet. If the alibi was needed, fair enough. If it wasn't, he had to keep Billy out of it.

Kenny got in the car and looked back at the house. Thought transmission would have been a good skill to have, but he didn't have it. Still he tried. *Stay out of sight, Billy, 'til I need you.*

Billy waited ten minutes, then cautiously pressed the button in the loft. He watched the hatch silently rise, and then, the ladder dropped to the landing floor. Shakily, he climbed down, went to their bedroom window and peered around the curtain. No police car in sight.

Once again, the loft ladder disappeared, and Billy went downstairs. He drank a full glass of water and sat at the kitchen table wondering what to do. They simply hadn't discussed this eventuality.

Kenny had assured him they had left no trace of themselves in Grausohn's place; Carl had sorted the whisky glasses, they had brought the cigars back with them. They had touched nothing on the balcony, even leaving the chair that had been accidentally knocked over. CCTV wasn't an issue, either, so how had the police linked him to that night?

Carl. He had to tell Carl. Maybe the police had already picked him up, but if they hadn't, Billy would have valuable time to decide what to do.

And then, he had to go through the house, get everything out that could possibly be of use to the police, and into their lock-up.

He picked up his phone and rang Carl. It seemed ages before he answered, and Billy was scared. It seemed they had already picked up suspect number two.

'Hello, Billy.'

Billy breathed a sigh of relief. 'Carl? You okay?'

'Yeah…' Carl's guarded reply told Billy what he wanted to know.

'The police haven't been in touch?'

There was a long, drawn-out silence.

'What about?'

'I'm not a hundred percent sure, because I was up in the loft when they arrived, but they took Kenny to the station, and I think I heard Roberts say it was relating to Nicolas Grausohn.'

'Shit. Will he keep his mouth shut?'

'Of course he will. I was concerned they'd found something in that apartment to implicate both of you.'

'But we cleaned everything up, avoided touching anything… unless it's something from when Kenny was there officially. Wonder if they've picked Fraser up? His fingerprints have to be in there as well, I guess.'

'You're right, of course. I'm glad I rang you. I feel a bit better now. That's what it must be. Right, I'm going to move his laptop, iPad and stuff, and his phone, if he's not taken it, and there's some paperwork here… I'll get it all out of the way, in case they decide to do a search.'

'You got somewhere safe to stash it?'

'Yes, we've got a lock-up. Not sure what's in it, but the key is on Kenny's car keys.'

'Good luck, Billy. Let me know how he gets on and ask him to ring me when he gets back.'

'He will come back, won't he?' Billy felt drained.

'Sure he will,' Carl said, smiling.

Billy disconnected and systematically went through every room, removing two phones, a laptop, an iPad, a significant amount of paperwork.

When he felt the house was clear of anything even remotely incriminating, he placed it all in the boot of his car and drove to the lock-up.

Billy hadn't been there since they had signed the lease for it.

The chair bolted to the floor, the hook hanging from the ceiling, the blood sprayed everywhere, the blood encrusted tools hanging from the walls, they hadn't been there on that long-ago day.

His eyes roamed around, and he took everything into his brain. This was the work of the man he had planned to spend the rest of his life loving. He wiped his brow, stood the laptop and other paraphernalia prominently on the chair and pulled down the door. He didn't lock it; he would ring the police with the address when he reached Crete.

Twenty minutes later, he was back home, praying that the phone would ring; he needed to hear Harding, Kenny's brief, say that Kenny had been charged.

24

The Brownlow garden had come alive with the sound of children playing. The remaining five members of Ella's Gang had met up and simply talked for the first hour. Sally then produced food and drinks, and afterwards, they set up the croquet. The elephant in the garden was Ella, and everybody wanted to talk about her, but nobody dared.

Sally, standing at the kitchen window, watched them playing and saw the sorrow. She wished she'd had a group of friends as close as these seemed to be, when she was a child. It would have made all the difference to her childhood; hers had been a lonely existence created by a domineering father who hadn't let her breathe without asking permission.

But it was obvious how much they missed Ella. They had gone into a huddle over by the church wall, at the funeral, and their parents had left them alone, knowing they were grieving in their own way. They were far too young to have to deal with these sorts of feelings.

To make matters so much worse, they couldn't go anywhere without an adult. They were all due back at school in eight days' time, and even then, unless Roberts turned up with an answer to everything, they couldn't let them do anything on their own.

And Daryl, no longer limping but still favouring his shoulder slightly, had to face another funeral the next day. Sally sighed. She was going to Megan's funeral, while John was going to look after the children. Daryl didn't have that option. And from the way Daryl had spoken earlier, it seemed that his dad and Aileen had become very close, so it was equally possible he would have to face yet another funeral on Tuesday, when Vinnie Walmsley was buried.

She gave a huge sigh and delved into the freezer to find pizzas for lunch for the kids. The too-quiet kids.

Kenny was sitting in the interview room, his mind racing. What the fuck could Roberts possibly have? If they'd found his fingerprints on the desk, that was perfectly feasible; he worked for Grausohn. He'd helped Carl wash their glasses, and Carl had placed them back in a cupboard with other glasses. No fingerprints there. They had left Grausohn's glass on the coffee table, but only Grausohn had touched that.

Kenny was tapping his foot angrily on the floor when the door opened. Neil Harding, his solicitor, walked in, placed his briefcase on the table and shook Kenny's hand. 'Been a naughty lad, Kenny?' Harding asked with a smile.

'Not as far as I know, Neil. But I haven't actually seen anybody to find out what they think I've done.'

'They think you murdered your boss, plus a few others.'

'What?'

'So they say. Let's get it sorted and get you out of here.'

'Billy called you?'

'He did. Very worried, didn't know what was happening. Said something about being up in the loft when DI Roberts arrived, so couldn't really hear anything.'

'I put the loft ladder away, so they wouldn't know he was there. I needed him to be my cavalry, not taken in for questioning purely because he's my partner.'

'Okay, down to business. What have they got?'

'Nothing. If they've got fingerprints or DNA placing me in the penthouse, then that's fine, I work there. If there was anything dodgy going on, then Tommy Raines is the man to ask. He did some dirty work, and some clean. I stuck to clean.'

Neil nodded and made some notes on his pad. 'Okay, well, they shouldn't be long, and we'll find out what this really all about. I suppose you've got an alibi for Friday night?'

'Of course. I stayed in with Billy.'

Again, Neil nodded and made a notation.

'This is getting boring,' Kenny said.

They looked up as the door opened, and a uniformed officer came into the room. 'You won't be interviewed until tomorrow, Mr Lancaster. Have you finished your talk with your solicitor?'

Kenny looked startled. 'I can go home?'

'No, sir,' the uniform said, 'I'm to escort you to a cell for the night. You will be interviewed tomorrow morning. We'll notify Mr Harding an hour before your interview, to give him time to get here.'

Harding nodded. 'Try to get some sleep, Kenny. I'll see you in the morning, move some appointments around.'

Suddenly, to Kenny, it had stopped being boring. Now, it was scary.

Heather had hardly slept. They hadn't left the Grausohn place until after six, despite Roberts' instructions to finish at five. They'd opted to carry on and finish the search, so they didn't have to go there next day, but Heather had felt unsettled, unhappy, un-bloody-everything. Her eyes feeling full of grit. She arrived at work at just after six, determined to sort out the album.

By ten o'clock, results were promising. Of the eleven photographs in the book showing assorted deaths, they had tracked down nine of the identities. Heather felt she never wanted to see a dead body again; it had been a harrowing job. Their success in identifying the nine had been a combination of recognition by police officers, and the facial recognition programme. The two unidentified bodies appeared to be very young men, maybe late teens, and who had clearly been tortured.

Their missing persons list showed sixteen males who were in the age group, but it would take time to tie any of those with the two in the photographs, both pictured hanging from a hook by a rope around their wrists. They could hardly go to see parents of the missing youths with these photographs and ask if they could identify their son.

She looked at the list of names and sighed. From their appearances, most of them were under thirty. What an utter waste of life, and she had no doubt that when they informed parents or wives, there would be a lot of distress and angst flying around.

Johanna Fleischer
Tommy Raines
Ella Johnston
Andy Brough
Peter McCormack
Pete Stanton
Ernie Lightfingers (only known by nickname)
Alan Jenson
Ray Fenton

She looked up as Roberts approached her desk. 'It's ready, sir. We're still working on the last two names. The photograph of Tommy Raines' burial site has been emailed to every station within a fifty-mile radius of Sheffield, with a request that they contact me if anyone recognises anything.'

'Thanks, Heather. If you get that information, and I realise it's a bit of a long shot, pull me out of the interview.'

'Will do, sir. You going in now?'

'No, having a sandwich and a coffee first. Let the bugger wait. Has somebody sent for his brief yet?'

'I'll do it,' she said. 'What time shall I tell him you'll be ready?'

Roberts looked at his watch. 'Let's say around one o'clock. Lancaster will be well pissed off by then.'

She handed him the list. 'We're still working on Ernie Lightfingers' real name, sir. Should have it shortly. Nat March recognised him, but couldn't remember his real name. It will be on file somewhere.'

'It's Paramore. Ernie Paramore.' He picked up the album. 'Nat was right. It certainly is him. I've come across him a few times, but nothing seems to stick. Chatty bloke who could talk himself out of everything. Didn't manage it this time, though.'

He slipped the album inside his folder. 'I'm taking this with me into the interview room. I think he'll break when I show him the photo of his daughter. He may not have known her, but he cared enough to go to her funeral.'

He headed to his own office for the promised sandwich and coffee and opened the folder. He had the list of identified bodies, now with Lightfingers crossed out, and Paramore inserted, he had the album, he had the fingerprint results taken from the glass and, by now, he should have a very annoyed Kenny Lancaster, who was likely to let his temper get the better of him.

His phone rang, and he listened to the caller, then smiled. He was still smiling when he walked back into the main office.

'Brian, take Dan and George and go to Lancaster's house. We've got the warrant, pick it up on your way out, along with his house keys. Check everything, no stone left unturned, okay? I'm sending a recovery vehicle to bring his car in, see what blood we've got in that little beauty. If you find anything significant that I need for this interview, I want you to ring Heather. She'll keep me informed. Craig, you're with me. We'll be going downstairs in about an hour, okay?'

'Yes, sir. I'll grab some lunch now. I reckon this might be a long afternoon.'

'I reckon so, as well, Craig.' Roberts thought the young officer was shaping up well; nothing seemed to faze him, and he thought when this case was over, he might very well be having a chat with him, bringing him on to the team properly, instead of being seconded to help wherever he was needed.

'Sir?'

'Yes, Heather.'

'Mr Harding didn't sound very happy, said he'll be here at one and would appreciate the interview starting on time. He apparently changed his appointments for this morning to this afternoon. His actual words were, "he's buggered me about enough."'

Roberts smiled. 'Craig, we'll go down around half past one. Never did like solicitors.'

Billy saw the looming shape of the recovery truck appear outside but didn't think too much of it, until it became clear which car was being taken. He had heard nothing from Kenny and merely a text message from Neil Harding informing him the interview had been postponed until the morning.

He went outside. 'What are you doing?'

'And you are?' the uniformed officer asked.

'I live here.'

'And is this your car, sir?'

'No, it's my partner's car. Kenneth Lancaster.'

'And your name, sir?'

'William Hanson. You can't take his car! He's done nothing wrong!'

'Then I'm sure, if he really has done nothing wrong, the car will be returned in the same condition as it is now. This is the documentation giving us permission to take it.'

PC Yardley was enjoying himself. The man was obviously aggrieved that the car was being taken. How would he react in five minutes when the search team turned up?

The car was loaded onto the truck, and Yardley handed Billy a receipt. 'It will be at the police compound. We'll let you know when you can collect it.'

He thought Billy was going to explode. He was laughing inwardly as he climbed into his police car and used his radio. 'DS Balding, are you on your way?'

There was a crackle, and then Balding's voice came through. 'I am. Who's this?'

'PC Yardley, sir. Thought I'd better inform you that there is somebody already at the address you're about to search. He's a William Hanson, says he's Lancaster's partner. I'm still outside, but about to follow the recovery vehicle.'

'Thank you, PC Yardley. We're about a minute from you, so he's not had time to spirit anything away. We knew nothing about the premises being occupied. You go, we'll take over now.'

Billy stood at the window watching the truck indicate to pull out, followed by the police car, only to be zapped with the arrival of two more police cars.

'DS Balding, DC Eden and PC Marks,' Brian Balding said, offering his warrant card for inspection. 'And this is a warrant to search the premises and remove anything we feel we need to take.'

They entered en masse past Billy, and he said nothing. He was currently beyond speech; he felt numb. So much blood...

'Okay, this is what's going to happen, Mr Hanson. My two officers are going upstairs to search. Do you have access to the loft via a ladder? I will remain downstairs to search.'

Billy nodded. 'Underneath the light switch on the upstairs landing, there is a push button. It lowers the loft ladder.'

'Thank you for your co-operation, sir. We'll create as little disturbance as possible.'

Dan and George headed upstairs, leaving Billy sitting on the sofa while Brian systematically went through every drawer, every cupboard, every possible place that could hold something incriminating.

Two hours later, they had a few bank statements and precious little else. Billy had denied they owned a laptop or any other computer. He produced his own mobile phone, which they took, but said he had no idea where Kenny's phone was. He assumed Kenny had it with him. DS Balding rang the number on Billy's phone attributed to Kenny, but there was no sound. It was difficult to hear it when it was ringing in a lock-up a mile away.

Kenny sat silently at the side of Neil Harding. He had expected his interview to start before eight o'clock, but they had simply left him in the holding cell, getting angrier by the second. Added to that were his worries about Billy. How would he be holding up?

When they'd met, Billy had had no idea of Kenny's criminal activities. They had been living together for two years before Billy asked him one night.

Kenny remembered the phrase with clarity. 'Kenny, does your job with this Grausohn involve you working outside the law?' And he had lied and said 'no.'

The door opened. Harding glanced at his watch and tutted. 'You're late, DI Roberts.'

'That time was an estimate, a bit like solicitor's bills,' Roberts responded smoothly, sitting down across from Lancaster. He put his file on the table and went through the routine of setting up the tape and naming the people present.

'Okay, Kenny. Let's see what we can get you to talk about, and you can listen to what we can talk about. We can start by saying something concerning fingerprints on a glass.'

'Really?' Kenny smiled.

'Uh huh. Now, we know you worked for Nicolas Grausohn, but can you tell me the last time you entered his office?'

Kenny hesitated, as if trying to think back, and be accurate for the nice police inspector. 'It was Thursday evening. He rang me about nine-ish, asked me to pop around and have a drink and a chat. He was my boss, so I did. We had a whisky and a cigar, I left about ten o'clock.'

'Thank you.' Roberts noticed Craig was starting to making notes, with question marks at odd intervals.

'When we entered the flat after Mr Grausohn's untimely fall from his balcony, we found two glasses on the coffee table, one held whisky, the other was empty. Did you drink all of yours, Kenny?'

'I don't know what you're talking about. I told you I was there on the Thursday night, not the night he jumped.'

Roberts stared at him for a moment. 'Now, we have two issues. One, he didn't jump, he was helped over that balcony, and two, the second glass that was on the coffee table had your fingerprints on it.'

'I've already told you, I was there the previous night. I had a whisky with him.' Kenny could feel sweat trickling down his back.

'We also have a statement from Gerda Bauer – you know Ms Bauer, I believe? – and she says unequivocally that the lounge was pristine when she left for the bingo. She states that it had to be like that, Grausohn insisted on it. Nothing was ever out of place, and everything had to be spotless.'

Kenny said nothing.

'Now, this leaves us with a puzzle. The glass that you drank out of on the Thursday night had obviously been washed up. If you didn't go there again after ten on the Thursday evening, how does a glass with your fingerprints appear on a coffee table at the side of Nicolas Grausohn's glass?'

'I have no idea. Maybe it was the whisky glass from the previous night, that Gerda had missed. Maybe Grausohn took it through to make sure it was washed. I don't know,' he said, a touch of temper showing in his voice.

'Kenny, it didn't have whisky in it. It had tonic water. Did you choose tonic water because you didn't want alcohol slowing things down?'

Harding leaned across and touched Kenny's arm. He whispered in his ear.

'No comment,' Kenny said.

'You know what, Kenny? I'd have put money on you saying that. Right, let's move on to other things, like Tommy Raines, Ella Johnston, Johanna Fleischer, Andy Brough and half a dozen others. Would that suit you better than talking about a glass of whisky that didn't contain whisky?'

25

There was a knock on the door. Heather looked in and nodded.

'Excuse me, gentlemen.' He made the first of several messages to the tape, saying he was leaving the room.

'Heather?'

'There's good news on the grave location, sir. Two people, both from Ecclesfield Police Station, are pretty sure they recognise it. One walks his dog and the other runs through those woods every day. They want to know if you want to get over there, or if you want them to begin to excavate the site. They've already been to have a look, or at least the runner has, and there is evidence of soil disturbance.'

'Right, I'll postpone this, and we'll get over to Ecclesfield. Can you tell them, Heather? And ask forensics to go as well. I'll take you with me.'

'Thank you, sir.'

He went back into the room, spoke to the tape and closed down the interview.

'We'll continue this tomorrow. Mr Harding, we will be starting at eight o'clock on the dot. I suggested you be here, your client will need you. Oh, by the way, Kenny, Billy hopes you're all right. We sent the search teams in this afternoon and brought your car in for forensic examination.'

Kenny blanched, then coughed. He tried to hide the dismay, unsuccessfully. He prayed Billy had cleared the house of technical stuff, but he prayed even harder that Billy had removed his gun from the special compartment Kenny had had fitted under the driving seat.

Craig followed Roberts out of the interview room. 'Sir?'

'Possible lead on Tommy Raines body, Craig. I'm taking you and Heather, we're going now. It's somewhere over at Ecclesfield.'

'You know Ecclesfield, sir?'

'Not really, I've always worked south and south-east of the city.'

'Then, I'll drive, shall I? I live that end.'

'Good lad. Go and find us a car, if there are any left. If not, we'll take mine, but take good care of it, Craig.'

Five minutes later, they were heading down the Parkway, towards the M1. Heather was in the backseat, clutching on to her mobile phone. She had asked for information from several different areas and told them all to contact her, whether by email, text or voice. She had no intentions of missing any.

When the Harry Potter theme pealed out from the back of the car, both the officers in the front creased.

'Heather Shaw,' she said, glaring at them.

There was silence while she listened to the message, and then, she thanked the caller and disconnected.

'They've found a gun, sir, in a specially made compartment in Kenny Lancaster's car.'

There was an exultant 'yes' from her boss, and she grinned. Suddenly, all the pieces were fitting together. It hadn't been obvious from the photo of Tommy Raines that he had been shot, but if she had to make an educated guess, she would say it had been a bullet and not a knife that had killed him. Maybe a bullet from the gun found in Lancaster's car.

They drove up The Common and turned into the police station car park. Within five minutes, they were in a van and being taken to the woods. Forensics had been there about two minutes and were preparing to dig. The second any human remains were found, they would erect a tent. It took about a minute to reveal a hand.

Kenny was taken to the interview room a few minutes before eight o'clock. Neil Harding was already there.

'You know anything about a body in Ecclesfield Woods?'

'What? No, I don't. How long are they going to keep me here?'

'Until they're done with you. And if they don't like what you say, it could be a long time.'

Kenny sat down, reeling from news of a body. Surely not. The hole had been deep enough…

Roberts walked in, followed this time by Heather Shaw. He placed his file on the desk and started the tape.

'Mr Lancaster, do you know where Ecclesfield Woods is?'

'I think so.'

'Good. That's a start. I know where it is also, because I've been there most of the bloody night, and at the moment, I'm feeling a little tetchy, as are all our forensic team, who worked overtime last night to get me the results of our investigations in the woods, so that I could tell them to you this morning.'

Kenny stared at him. He said nothing.

'Don't you want to ask me what those results are?'

'No. I haven't a clue what you're talking about.'

'Then, let me fill you in.' Roberts took out the album. He opened it and showed the picture of Tommy to both Kenny and Harding. 'For the benefit of the tape, I am showing a picture of Thomas Raines to Kenneth Lancaster. Kenny, do you know the identity of this person?'

'It's Tommy Raines.'

'Tommy Raines, who, like you, worked for Grausohn? That Tommy Raines?'

Kenny nodded.

'For the benefit of the tape, please, Kenny.'

'Yes,' he barked.

'You're saying you don't know how Tommy met his death. Tommy must have laid down in this grave and shot himself?'

'No comment.'

'I didn't really expect a comment on that, Kenny.'

Harding glanced at his client and looked as though he was about to speak; he thought better of it.

'Let me tell you what our forensic team have found, Kenny. First, they found a gun in your car. That little compartment you had built into the car under the driving seat was the perfect size for it. And the gun had only one set of prints on it. Yours.'

Kenny remained silent.

'And then, to make our evening complete, we found a body. We already knew Tommy was dead – remember pretty Johanna, with the sexy black and white dress? Killed by Tommy? Either before or after he killed her, and we do think it was after, he screwed her, Kenny. We found his semen inside her, and just to make things really awkward for Tommy, his DNA was on our database. Of course, when we went to pick him up, his wife told us you had been to see her, to tell her he had been thrown over the side of a cross-channel ferry. Whoever took this picture of Tommy in his grave, Kenny, really helped us. A couple of our colleagues at Ecclesfield police station know these woods very well, particularly that strangely shaped dead tree in the background.' Roberts rested his finger on the tree in question. 'Pinpointed the exact location.'

Kenny was visibly sweating.

'Anyway, we dug Tommy out of his grave last night, so that Mrs Raines can say goodbye properly. Guess what? He was killed by a single shot to the heart. With a bullet that came from a gun with only one set of prints on it.'

Harding finally spoke. 'I need to have a word with my client, DI Roberts.'

'Mr Harding, take as long as you need. As soon as you've finished, we will be charging Mr Lancaster with the murder of Thomas Raines, for starters. We have lots more dead people to look at, with a view to further charges. Dead people like this one.'

He flicked the picture of Tommy over, so that the next page was exposed, and showed it to Kenny and Harding.

Kenny looked away, refusing to look at the picture of Ella. 'Put it away,' he grated. 'Put it away.'

'Okay, Kenny, we'll talk about it later. To put your mind at rest, we know Johanna Fleischer, of the black and white dress, killed Vinnie Walmsley, so you don't have to worry about that one. There are another eleven pictures in this book; bit of a coincidence that he's not in it, young Vinnie. You're going down for a very long time, Kenny, probably for these eleven people, plus Nicolas Grausohn. If you, and whoever you persuaded to help you, hadn't chucked him over that balcony, we would still have been walking around scratching our heads. So, while you're talking to Mr Harding, you need to be thinking very carefully about giving us the name of your accomplice last Friday evening. Unless you've got four hands, you definitely had someone helping.'

Roberts stood, gathered up his paperwork and walked from the room, followed by Heather. Her eyes were shining.

'Way to go, boss, way to go!'

'Thank you, Heather,' he grinned. 'I enjoyed that.'

Billy stared at the telephone on the console table in the hall and willed it to stop ringing. He didn't want to talk to anybody, and he could see that it was Carl calling him.

It did stop but then began again almost immediately. He snatched it up and said, 'Carl, I said I would ring when I heard something.'

'Then you'd better ring Carl, right after this phone call, Billy.' Neil Harding spoke precisely and softly. 'I'm ringing to say they've charged Kenny with Tommy Raines' murder, and they're currently lining up the other dead bodies as we speak. He's asked me to tell you to get out of the way, go to Crete and lie low. I think by the end of the day, they'll have charged him with Nicolas Grausohn and Ella Johnston. He says he didn't kill Ella, Tommy was driving, but unfortunately, he took care of Tommy, so there's no way he can prove it. They're throwing everything at him, Billy; there's a sort of photo album of dead bodies, eleven in total. He's not admitting to anything, but I think they'll be able to link him to nine of them.'

'No…' Billy's grief was palpable. How could the gentle man he had loved be the monster Harding was describing?

'He also said will you ring Carl and tell him to get out of the way. The police know there was a second man involved for Grausohn's murder.' Harding was relentless. 'Oh, and he says he loves you.'

'I'm never going to see him again, am I?'

'Not if you're sensible, no. He'll never come out from this. Life is going to mean life.'

Billy said goodbye and replaced the receiver. A car horn sounded outside, and he looked around the room. It was clean and tidy, so he picked up his suitcase and his flight bag and headed out of the door. The driver climbed out and opened the boot, taking the case from him and lifting it in.

'Plenty of stuff in there, pal,' he said. 'Long holiday, is it?'

'Very long,' Billy said. 'Manchester Airport, Terminal One, please.'

He opened his flight bag, took out the two tickets they had planned on using that day, and sighed. He tore up one of the tickets and slipped it into the front pocket of the bag. He'd throw it in an airport bin, but he'd keep all the cash the search team had missed, hidden in the cleverly crafted steps of the loft ladder. And just before his flight was to leave, he would call Roberts with the address of the lock-up…

Roberts stared at the list of people his team were working to trace. Unless Kenny Lancaster came up with some details, he doubted that they would ever find the bodies. Most of the pictures had been taken in some sort of garage or lock-up; only Tommy Raines, Ella Johnston and Johanna Fleischer had been in obvious locations. There was no picture of Megan Clarkson; he wouldn't have been able to hang around long enough to take one.

He knew his team, and he knew they wouldn't give up. His mind was whirling, and he gave it free rein.

And then his thoughts exploded into action. 'Heather,' he called through his open office door, 'you got a minute?'

She appeared in the doorway. 'Sir?'

'Come with me, let's go and bring young Daryl in. Is Craig there?'

'Doing a coffee run. He'll be back in a minute.'

As if by magic, Craig waved a cardboard coffee cup at him around the door jamb. 'White, no sugar, boss.'

'Craig, just the man. I want you to get together five men who all vaguely resemble Kenny Lancaster, make sure they're wearing suits similar to his, and get them here in an hour. Dan will do for one of them; he's the right height, similar hair. Check with our list of locals who are happy to do line-ups and get them here. I'm bringing Daryl Clarkson in to see if he recognises anybody.'

'Right, sir.' Craig deposited his cup of coffee and disappeared.

'I'll get my bag,' Heather said. 'We taking a squad car, sir?'

'Yes, reckon young Daryl will like that.'

Aileen saw the car pull up outside and felt sick. She'd been feeling sick on and off since Friday night; in fact, every time she thought about Grausohn going over that balcony. Kenny's arrest had made her feel even more nervous, and now Roberts was outside the house in a police car.

She opened the door with a smile. 'Come in, DI Roberts.'

'Mrs Walmsley. Is Mr Clarkson in? And Daryl?'

She breathed a sigh of relief. They wouldn't be here to arrest Daryl.

'Yes, they're in the kitchen. Both reading, but with Carl, it's the sports section in the paper. Daryl's nose is in a book, thank goodness.' She knew she was babbling.

Roberts and Heather followed her through to the kitchen, and Carl looked up, his face drained of colour.

'Mr Clarkson, Daryl. Good morning. I've come to take you both down to the station. We need Daryl to watch a line-up for us.'

'What?' Carl frowned.

'You can come with him, Mr Clarkson, although in the past, parents have been known to make suggestions to their child, so we will ask you to sit outside the viewing room while Daryl is looking at the line-up. DC Shaw will be his appropriate adult for that short time. So, if you're ready?'

Daryl and Carl stood and walked to the door, a worried Aileen following them. She kissed them both as they left.

As expected, Daryl was impressed with riding in a police car. Heather demonstrated the blue flashing lights and gave a brief spurt of siren before pulling into the car park.

'We won't keep you hanging around,' Roberts said. 'I imagine the line-up is organised by now, but if not, I'm sure we can rustle up a coffee and a coke while we wait.'

They did have drinks; they had to wait for a volunteer for the line-up to get out of the barber's chair.

Roberts said nothing about the identity parade until they were in the room. Carl was left outside, sitting on possibly the most uncomfortable chair in the station.

'Okay, Daryl, I haven't said anything so far, because I was worried your dad would try to talk to you about it. I need you to be completely yourself, lad. You are now going to look at six men. If you see the man who was in that car that hit you and your mum, I need you to tell DC Shaw. Heather will be with you. Each man will hold a different number. Just say the relevant number, but you must be absolutely sure it is him, Daryl. Now, they don't know who is on this side of the glass, they can't see you, or hear you, although you can see them clearly. Don't say the number immediately, because halfway through they will be asked to turn sideways so that you see the sides of their faces. Take your time, and if you don't see the man, it doesn't matter.'

Daryl nodded. This was something to tell the others, they'd be well jealous. Heather touched him on the shoulder and turned him to face the glass. 'We're switching on the lights now.'

He remembered everything Roberts had told him; he took his time even though he recognised number two immediately. He walked the length of the one-way mirror, then walked back again.

'Ready?' Heather whispered. He nodded.

She moved to a speaker box and asked all the men to turn sideways. Again, Daryl went through the motions and was doubly convinced it was number two. His eyes on that awful day had seen this man half in profile, as he sat waiting in the car to let them out of the petrol station. But still, he took his time. He was enjoying himself.

'Seen enough?'

He nodded at Heather, and she switched off the light. She moved to the speaker box again and said, 'Thank you, gentlemen.'

'It was number two,' Daryl said firmly. 'Definitely, no doubt at all, number two. I saw him at Ella's funeral as well and told Dad, but he said not to say anything to anybody, he'd sort it.'

'Thank you, Daryl. You did a good job, there. I need you to sign a statement confirming it was number two, and then, I'll run you and your dad home.'

Kenny was taken to the interview room, instead of back to his cell. He asked for a drink of water and was given one. The bottle was almost empty by the time DI Roberts arrived.

He started the tape.

'Good morning, Mr Lancaster. Thank you for co-operating in the line-up.'

'Did I have a choice?'

'Yes, we could have used photographs, but a physical line-up is, by far, the best, both for you and the person viewing. You will not be pleased to know this, but you were picked out at that line-up by our witness to the murder of Megan Clarkson. There was no hesitation at any point. When we have finished, you will be taken and charged with Megan Clarkson's murder. Mounting up, aren't they, Kenny?'

'Fuck off, Roberts.'

'And Megan wasn't even on that list! What's the matter? Did you have to speed away too fast to be able to take a photo?'

Roberts could see the anger building in Kenny Lancaster. He wondered how much more he could push him before the explosion happened, and Kenny said something that would incriminate him even further.

And then, his face relaxed, and he smiled. 'No comment, DI Roberts. No comment.'

26

Kenny lay with his hands underneath his head, contemplating his future. It was looking bleak from any angle, and he was feeling really pissed off with Grausohn; he had always said to send the pictures to his phone, but then, they would be deleted. For a man who had steadfastly said no CCTV, it could be too incriminating. He had been spectacularly stupid in printing off the pictures.

And then, there was Billy. He hoped Harding had spoken to him, hoped Billy had had the sense to go to Crete, and then on to somewhere else where nobody knew him. Billy had done nothing wrong, but that wouldn't stop the police hassling him, if only because they were partners.

Kenny had listened to Roberts read the list of people they had managed to identify, and although most of them were down to Kenny, he was not going to carry the can for Johanna Fleischer and Ella Johnston. He was going down forever. It made little sense to plead not guilty; they had fingerprint evidence, gun evidence and probably DNA evidence when they started finding the bodies.

And it would save Cissie having to go to court and re-living the death of their daughter.

He didn't sleep much and, the next morning, asked to speak to DI Roberts. It was time to stop playing games.

When Roberts walked into the main office just after half past eleven, he was greeted with applause and cheers.

'Well done, sir,' Brian Balding said. 'Has he confessed to them all?'

'All except Johanna Fleischer and Ella Johnston. According to Lancaster, they were down to Tommy Raines. We have locations for the bodies, and the two young lads in the photos have now been identified. They were brothers, sixteen and eighteen years old. They're buried together. Once we've found them, we'll be going to see their parents. Their names are Darren and Stephen Summers. We've also had a phone call confirming the address of a lock-up used by Lancaster, and it's been used for God knows what torture. There's blood everywhere, and the forensic team are in there now, and will be for some time.'

'Has he said who helped him with Grausohn, sir?' Heather asked.

'He says nobody helped him. We know that's a lie, but he's saying nothing else on that subject. Grausohn gave him the kill instructions, so to be perfectly honest, I might have been tempted myself to give him a helping hand over that balcony. Right, drinks tonight in the Yellow Lion. Thank you. This case has been hard, and I appreciate everything you've all done. If we could only tie up the mystery of the missing package, my life would be complete,' he added, looking around at them all. 'Those drugs – and I'm sure it was drugs and not money – are still out there in our community, and they need tracking down. It seems several of our victims are already dead because of that package, and it's not from the drug itself.'

They once again clapped, and he returned to his own office, a smile on his face.

He made phone calls to Sally and John Brownlow, Janey Walker, Carl Clarkson and Cissie Johnston. Cissie was distraught; he tried to placate her, but all she could say was that Kenny was Ella's father, and she couldn't believe he played a part in her death.

Roberts knew they would feel much safer now, but they would never forget the beautiful little girl, with the light brown skin and eyes like deep brown pools of water.

Epilogue

Two months later

Freya sat on her own every lunch break after finishing her food. It had felt strange going back to school; she knew they had grown up during that summer of 2016. She didn't mix with her peers, and the teachers kept a close eye on her, aware she had become insular. Encouragement to join in playground games was met with a blank stare and politeness, as she said she was fine on her own.

She missed Ella. She had been the quiet one, but she had been the contrast to crazy Freya; and Freya was no longer crazy, simply unhappy.

Daryl had settled down to a life with his dad, and Aileen was becoming something of a permanent fixture in his life. He had fully recovered from his injuries, and his dad took him every week to place flowers on his mum's grave. They went as a threesome; Aileen took flowers for Vinnie, while Carl and Daryl told Megan all their news over the past week.

Sammy and Freya were still as close; he knew it was his job to protect her, to stop her getting too upset when suddenly something happened to remind her of Ella.

Mark and Dom watched over all of them. They had gone through something children shouldn't have to experience, and closeness was the answer. Whistles were still practised, Uno was still played, but the laughter had died along with their beautiful friend. Heartbreak had taken its place.

They had some discussions about building a new den for the next summer holidays, but by mutual agreement, they decided it wasn't a good idea. Secondary education was now a part of life for four of them, and they had to leave their childhood behind.

It was time to stop playing games. Ella's Gang had to move on.

The PCC meeting at the church was late starting, as usual. It had taken so long to make the teas and coffees, then hand out the relevant paperwork, that they didn't begin the agenda until half past seven. It was a large group of people, the youngest being sixty-two, the oldest eighty-three, and they all attended because they liked their vicar and would do anything to help him. And their church gave them a feeling of peace not felt anywhere else.

Beth, the vicar's wife, gave her husband's apologies. A parishioner was close to death, and he had had to go to his house. She didn't know if he would be back before the end of the meeting. She would chair it in his absence.

'Now, we have an issue that we need agreement on, although I know we've been waiting for this to start. This agreement tonight is simply to formalise it,' Beth began. 'Item one on the agenda is that Overend's, the builders, can start work on the churchyard next week.'

She paused for a moment to refer to her notes. 'They will start by re-siting the headstones that are laid against the churchyard wall, making good any other headstones that are starting to lean, and then move on to the final piece of work covered by the lottery grant, the churchyard wall.'

There was a brief round of applause from the PCC members, and when she asked for a vote, everyone held up their hands.

'It will be so good when we finally get all the rubbish out of our churchyard,' old Mrs Carmichael said, 'so good.'

THE END

Acknowledgements

I absolutely loved writing this book; the children played a bigger part in it than I had envisaged, and that is what made it so enjoyable. I hope you felt the same!

My thanks, as always, go to Bloodhound Books – to Betsy Freeman Reavley, Fred Freeman, Alexina Golding, Sumaira Wilson and Sarah Hardy, your rapid responses to any queries are so much appreciated.

Massive thanks go to Morgen Bailey, my editor, who saves my blushes by correcting any errors. A confession too – I have stolen your character name list idea, brilliant!

And I have a huge thank you to say to Tyrone Wilson, of Sheffield City Council, whose comprehensive knowledge of the Energy Recovery Facility in Sheffield helped me write that section of the book, with considerably more ease than if he hadn't helped! Thank you, Tyrone.

I needed help with knowledge of the Drugs School Education in Sheffield, and my gratitude goes to Alison Marshall-Wyse for all her assistance with this.

And Katie Wild, crazy friend of my crazy daughter, you're in this one!

Sheffield
January 2018

Also by Anita Waller

Psychological thrillers

Beautiful *August 2015*

Angel *May 2016*

34 Days *October 2016*

Strategy *August 2017*

Captor *February 2018*

Supernatural

Winterscroft *February 2017*

Lightning Source UK Ltd.
Milton Keynes UK
UKHW01f1024110518
322449UK00003B/61/P

9 781912 604296